Being Exposed Has Never Been More Deadly . . .

I shrieked like a B-movie starlet and bolted sideways, making for the door again. He lunged after me. I skidded to a halt at the end of my desk, teetered on one shoe, and dashed off in the other direction. He was close behind. I screamed again. His hand closed on my jacket. Fabric tore. Buttons popped. I turned in desperation. There was no hope now. He was twice my weight and strength, but there was nothing to do but fight, so I swung with all my might. My fist thudded against his ear like the swat of a swallow's wing. He caught my wrist with little effort and grinned into my face as he pushed me to the floor.

I was blubbering something incoherent, promises or threats or prayers. Who knows? Then suddenly, his grip gave a little. I scrambled backward, trying to gain my feet. He staggered, grabbed his chest with clawed hands, and dropped to his knees. I lurched toward the phone, jabbing at numbers with spastic fingers and yammering into the receiver.

He rolled his eyes up toward mine. I dropped the phone and stumbled against the wall. Then, like a melodramatic overactor, he fell to the floor, dead as a thumbtack.

Unzipped

Lois Greiman

A DELL BOOK

UNZIPPED
A Dell Book / June 2005

Published by Bantam Dell
A Division of Random House, Inc.
New York, New York

This is a work of fiction. Names, characters, places, and incidents
either are the product of the author's imagination or are used
fictitiously. Any resemblance to actual persons, living or dead,
events, or locales is entirely coincidental.

Dell is a registered trademark of Random House, Inc., and the
colophon is a trademark of Random House, Inc.

ISBN 0-440-24262-2

Printed in the United States of America
Published simultaneously in Canada

www.bantamdell.com

OPM   10   9   8   7   6   5   4   3   2   1

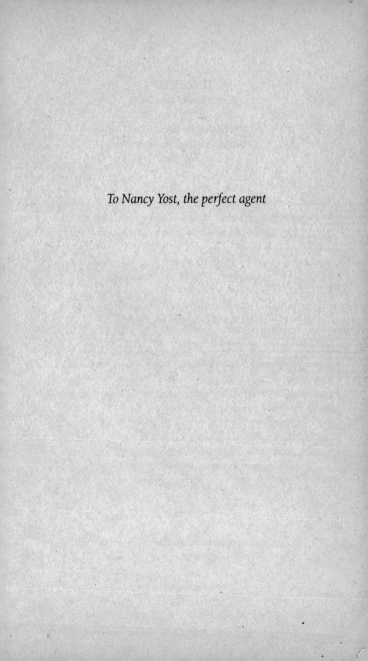

To Nancy Yost, the perfect agent

Acknowledgments

Special thanks to Mary L., psychologist extraordinaire, whose spunk and intelligence has inspired and enlightened me.

Unzipped

1

Some people are street-smart, some people are book-smart, but most people are just dumber than dirt.

> —Chrissy (Mac) McMullen,
> upon finding her boyfriend in
> the backseat of her Mazda
> with a majorette

MR. HOWARD LEPINSKI was an intelligent man. He was well educated, articulate, and precise. Unfortunately, he was about two aces short of a full deck.

"So what's your opinion?" he asked, peering at me through thick-lensed spectacles. He was a little man with a twitch, a mustache, and a strangely unquenchable need to discuss, in minute, droning detail, every decision that crossed his path.

I looked him full in the face. Dr. Candon, my psych professor, had once said he couldn't possibly overemphasize the importance of looking patients full in the face. It filled them with, and I quote here: "*... the soothing reassurance*

that they have your undivided attention, not unlike that of a
mother suckling her newborn." Perhaps I should consider the
possibility that Dr. Candon had a few issues of his own, I
thought.

"Ms. McMullen?"

"I'm sorry, Mr. Lepinski," I said, using my much-
practiced nurturing tone. It was as far as I was willing to
go on the suckling mother scenario. "I'm not certain I fully
comprehend your question." The truth was, I'd become a
smidgen distracted, but it was closing in on seven o'clock
and I hadn't eaten since noon when I'd had a carton of
cherry yogurt and a somewhat dehydrated orange. And if
we're going to be perfectly honest, I wouldn't call that *eating.* It was merely something I did to prevent my mouth
from committing suicide before dinnertime. On the other
hand, the roll of flab that had engulfed my midriff since
I'd kicked the nicotine habit...again...had become a
rather ponderous problem and now threatened to droop
over my waistband like rising bread dough—white, not
wheat.

In some ways my life had been simpler as a cocktail
waitress. True, delivering drinks to the town of Schaumburg's intoxicated populace had been hell on my bunions,
and the propositions sent my way were often punctuated
by belching of competition caliber, but at least in Chicago
I'd *had* propositions. L.A. men were of a different breed.
Which was what I had been hoping for, of course, but
still...

"The sandwiches," Mr. Lepinski repeated. There were, I
noticed, several droplets of sweat on his forehead. "Should
I take pastrami or ham to work?"

I considered his luncheon dilemma with all due sobri-ety, but feared my sagacious expression might have been ruined by my rumbling gut. "Perhaps," I said forcefully, doing my best to drown out the sounds of impending star-vation, "the question is not so much what you should take for lunch, but why you are so *concerned* about what you should take for lunch."

"What?" His mustache twitched like hamster whiskers, and he blinked at me, as if distracted from a run on his exercise wheel.

"I mean..." I steepled my fingers. I'd seen Kelsey Grammer do it on *Frasier* once and thought it looked pretty classy. Classy was good. Even now I regretted the less-than-classy splotch where I'd dropped cherry goop on my silk blouse. It was a burnt-umber color and matched the freshly refurbished hue of my hair. The blouse, that is, not the splotch. Elaine, my part-time secretary and full-time friend, had suggested trying club soda on the stain, but now I wondered if I couldn't just suck the stuff out of the fabric until I found something more substantial to sus-tain me. "Perhaps you should give some thought to why you're obsessing about sandwiches," I finished, nodding with ruminative intellect.

His twitching stopped abruptly, and his bird-bright eyes flickered toward the door and back as if he were consider-ing flying the coop. "I am not obsessing," he said. His lips were pursed, his tone stilted, and in that moment I doubted he would have been more insulted if I had sug-gested his mother had, in fact, belonged to another species. Touchy! Still, it wasn't good to offend one's clients, not when one is in my financial straits. But the man was paying a hefty sum for his Thursday evening sessions and spent most of his time discussing brown-bag options. It seemed a little strange to me, but who am I to say? I once knew a guy who used seventeen different toothbrushes every day of the week. Seventeen. I was never sure why, even though I knew him pretty well. Intimately even. Okay, truth is, I'd lived with him for eighteen months. He was as loopy as hell, but he had great dental hygiene, and if I've learned anything in my thirty-odd years, it's that sometimes a girl can't be too fussy.

"Perhaps obsessing is not the proper word," I said. "I only mean, surely you have more important things to worry about."

Lepinski shifted his gaze once more toward the door, then returned his full attention to me and said, "I don't," in a tone that challenged me to disagree.

So I did what any fledgling therapist worth her double-matted, mahogany-framed diploma would do. I fantasized about fudge mocha and gave him another maternal smile.

"And I take umbrage with your choice of words," he added. "I am not, nor have I ever been, obsessed."

I considered telling him the truth, that he was as wacky as a tennis racquet, but when I glanced at the clock on the wall I saw that his time was up.

"I'm sorry, Mr. Lepinski," I said and managed, just barely, to avoid ejecting from my chair like a maniacal jack turned loose from his box. Instead, I rose with dignified calm and extended my hand. Thanks to Monique the magical manicurist, it was magnificently well groomed except for that one damned nail that had popped loose on my frenetic flight to work a full twelve hours before. "I'll see you next week."

He scowled as if considering the possibility of canceling his standing appointments, but the thought of handling his sandwich crises alone must have been too daunting, because he slipped a noodly hand into mine and nodded. "Next week," he said, not meeting my gaze. "Say, you have a stain on your..." He motioned, limp-wristed, toward my chest.

I extracted my hand and tucked my blouse more firmly beneath its coordinated jacket. It wasn't as though I was self-conscious. After all, the man wore canary yellow socks with his rumpled tweed suit.

"What is it? Ketchup?"

"I beg your pardon?"

"On your shirt. Is it ketchup?" he asked.

"No," I said, and gave him a smile that was polite but dismissive. I'd had a good deal of practice with polite-but-dismissive working at The Warthog in Schaumburg, just around the corner and down the street from where I'd grown up. "Have a good evening, Mr. Lepinski."

His mustache twitched again as if he might catch a scent of the fascinating stain. "Barbecue sauce?"

"I hope you don't mind seeing yourself out. I'm afraid my secretary had to leave early tonight."

"Tomato juice?"

On my desk, there was a letter opener shaped like a sword and stuck into a fake stone. It was more ornamental than utilitarian, but I wondered now if it might not make an effective weapon. Surely I couldn't be condemned for defending myself from mind-imploding frustration in the wake of nicotine withdrawal.

"I'm afraid I have another client, Mr. Lepinski."

"You put a little Mexican soap on that, it'll come right out," he said, still staring at my chest. I'm not Dolly Parton, but I'm not Calista Flockhart either. Still, I doubted if Lepinski had even considered the possibility that there was flesh hidden somewhere inside my over-priced ensemble. The stain was all-consuming. "Unless it's grape jelly. It's not, is it?"

I found, to my surprise, that my fingers had closed around the letter opener. It felt good in my hand. I could see the headlines. *Hungry Psychologist Attacks Crazy Loon with Miniature Version of Excalibur.* Maybe they'd want to edit that a little. *Woman with Stained Blouse Assaults Wacko.*

"Or grape juice. Grape juice—"

I raised the letter opener.

"Hello."

I jumped. Lepinski twitched. We turned toward the door in breathless tandem.

"Sorry to interrupt." Andrew R. Bomstad leaned through the doorway and grinned shyly at me. It was a strangely in-nocuous expression for such a large man, especially con-sidering his past. He'd played tight end for the Lions until a groin injury had sidelined him from the glory of his gladia-tor days. Now he appeared on local commercials and owned stock in companies that probably netted him an hourly rate that was more than I made in a month. It was something of a mystery why he had chosen me as his therapist. But he had secrets he didn't want aired and maybe he thought I wouldn't have anyone of importance to tell, even if I broke my vow of confidentiality. "There's nobody at the receptionist desk. Didn't know if you'd heard me come in."

"No, I didn't," I said, returning his smile. True, Bomstad had his share of problems, but next to Lepinski, he glowed with sparkling normalcy. "Sorry to keep you waiting."

"No. No problem. Take your time. I'm probably early," he said and smiling apologetically, closed the door behind him.

"Well," I said, and abandoned the letter opener with some regret. "Good night then, Mr. Lepinski."

He blinked. "Was that the Bomber?"

"Pardon me?"

"That was Andy Bomstad, wasn't it?"

"I'm not really in a position to say," I replied, but I've got to admit, it did my heart good to have a client who was recognized for something other than peeing on his neighbor's lawn. "Give some consideration to what we talked about this week, will you?"

"What's he here for?"

I stepped around my desk and reached out to usher him toward the door. *Shoo now. Shoo, before I poke you in the eye with my thumb.* "A client's visits are confidential. You know that, Mr. Lepinski."

"Professional or private?"

Ushering wasn't working. I opened the door with polite authority and considered tossing him into the hallway like yesterday's laundry. I was pretty sure I outweighed him by a good ten pounds. Not that I'm fat. "Good night, Mr. Lepinski."

He seemed to be thinking about pestering me some more, but one glance at Bomstad's impressive presence must have changed his mind, because he closed his mouth with a snap and stepped briskly through the lobby and out into the night, yellow socks flashing like lighthouse beacons.

I turned my attention from the crumpled little man and looked with some relief at my next client. His jeans were pressed just so and his shoes were Italian.

"Tough day?" he asked, and gave me that smile that had once made a roommate of mine compare him to Tom Cruise. My roommate's name had been Brian. For a while I had thought he was the one I'd take home to Mom—until I'd discovered the pictures of movie stars under our mattress. Male movie stars. "You keep taking on other folks' problems all day, you're gonna be worn right down to nothing."

Sympathy. I sighed mentally, but kept my chin up like a real trouper. "Easier than blocking a running back's rush with my head," I said, and he laughed as he rose to his feet and followed me into my office.

"Guess that depends on what you got in your head," he said. "But hey, the day's almost over, and this'll help, huh?"

"I beg your pardon?" I said, and he raised his hand. I noticed for the first time that he held the neck of a velvet bag that looked as if it might contain a bottle of wine.

"My doctor said a shot an evening would do me good."

"Ahhh." I couldn't think of anything more clever to say. This was a new one on me.

"And it looks like you could use some, too." He stepped into my office and took two water glasses from the tiny table that stood below the Ansel Adams reproduction. I wasn't a particular fan of Mr. Adams, but the print had been free and added to the airy panache of the place. "Chic environmentalist," it said. Or maybe "too broke to buy more stuff." But the office was small and didn't need a lot of clutter, I'd told myself. Bomstad took up most of the available space anyway. He extended a glass toward me. His hand was the approximate size of my head.

"I'm afraid the board frowns on fraternizing with clients," I said, imagining what the board would actually do if I shared a drink with him. Tar and feathers came to mind, but maybe that was being unfair. Maybe they'd go straight to lethal injection and not fiddle around with poultry.

"I won't tell 'em if you don't," Bomstad said as I settled into the rollered chair on the far side of my desk.

"No, thank you, Mr. Bomstad. But it's kind of you to offer." Gosh, I sounded professional.

He raised his brows and laughed. For a second I wondered why, but he was a nice guy with a great smile and an even better body. And after the men I'd been seeing for the past . . . oh . . . decade or so, it was fun just looking at him. Not that I was interested in him for myself, mind you. The California Board of Psychology may frown on drinking with clients, but they'd grind me into pâté and serve me on whole wheat crackers if they found out I'd boinked one.

"You don't mind if I imbibe, I hope."

"No. Go ahead," I said. The truth was, I wasn't sure what the rules were about clients drinking during a session, but it seemed harmless enough to me.

He slipped the neck of the chilled bottle out of its burgundy bag. A small note dangled from the smooth green glass. It was Asti Spumante—my favorite. An odd coincidence, I thought, settling back into my chair as he poured.

"So how was your week?" he asked. Setting the bottle on the floor, he lowered himself to the couch.

I swiveled my chair toward him. "It was fine. How about yours?"

"A little hairy. Stocks are down."

"Are they?" Maybe I would have known that if I owned stocks. As it was most of my funds went to pay outdated school bills and a pessimistic banker. I owned an antiquated little cottage up in the valley. The yard looked like a rattlesnake habitat, Schwarzenegger would have struggled to wrestle the garage door into submission, and the entire place needed full time attention from a handy man with a sense of humor, but the house was mine, and I hoped to keep it that way.

"You don't worry about the market?" Bomstad asked.

"Not unless I'm making soup," I said.

He remained silent a moment, then laughed. Perhaps he wasn't the sharpest pin in the cushion, but I was hardly in a position to find fault. Remember Brian?

"So did your mother come down for a visit?" I asked to start the ball rolling. Mothers are always an issue, but for a man with an impotency problem . . .

"Yeah," he said, sipping his wine. "She came. Stayed for four days, then flew off to Seattle to yank my sister's chain. You sure you don't want a drink?"

"No, thanks." I really did. It's not as if I'm a big drinker. My weaknesses generally run toward chocolate and Virginia

Slims, but a glass of wine would go well after my last session. I wondered how Mrs. Lepinski ever managed to face the day sober. "So did you get a chance to talk to her?"

"Mom?" he said, then finished his glass in one gulp and poured more.

Wow.

"Yes, your mother. Remember? We discussed confronting her about how she treated you as a child. That perhaps her...insensitivity had something to do with your current problems." The woman was a card-carrying psychopath if half of what Andrew said was true. And I had no reason to think it wasn't.

He drank again, sighed, and settled his head back against the overstuffed cushion of my ivory-toned couch—homey but stylish. "My impotency, you mean?" I was surprised he said the word aloud. Most men would have been more embarrassed by such a disclosure, but Bomstad was a different breed. His blue eyes were soulful. His hair, combed in a perfect but casual do, gleamed like gold in the fluorescent light. His features were broad but lean, and his fingers on the heavy crystal were blunt, scrubbed clean, and square-nailed.

"That and other things," I said, trying to make light of it. Impotence is hell on men, I guess. *It drains them of their self-worth, often causing them to draw into themselves when they most need the support of others.* Or so the textbooks said. Regardless of that, however, I thought the board probably wouldn't understand if I told them I took him to bed in my ever-increasing desire to help a client rid himself of such a debilitating problem.

"Don't you never get tired of talking about other people's

troubles?" Bomstad asked and turned his head slightly. The tendons in his wide, suntanned throat pulled tight as he looked at me. His eyes were ultra blue and as sensitive as an angel's—a gentle soul in a gladiator's finely sculpted body. The kind of guy who could win the Super Bowl, cook a five course meal, then round off the evening by jotting down his deepest emotions in his tattered journal.

He had told me about his diary on more than one occasion. Originally, it had been my idea that he record those moments that were most important to him, but he assured me with a boyish spark of enthusiasm that he'd been doing so for years.

Since that day, I had filled many a spare evening with the thought of him sitting in front of his hearth, maybe on a bear rug, shirtless, of course, after a grueling day on the battlefield. His golden hair would gleam in the firelight as he bent over a leather bound notebook.

I had asked him if he'd like to share his diary with me sometime, for professional reasons only, of course. And he'd said he'd maybe like that, once we got to know each other better.

I stifled a girly sigh and brought myself back to the present.

"You must have problems of your own," he said and caught my gaze. "Don't you need to share them sometimes?"

I knew I should bring the conversation back to business. I knew it beyond a shadow of a doubt, but I felt something stir deep in my belly. It might have been hunger, but I had a bad feeling it had something to do with my glands, so I cleared my throat, shuffled some papers, and imagined being smeared with tar as the smell of chicken feathers filled my nostrils. "But it's my job to address *your* problems," I said, maintaining an admirably steady tone and managing to keep a good four feet of air space between us.

"But don't you ever just wanna..." He shrugged and lifted his glass. "Let your hair down?"

I could imagine the feel of those blunt fingers against my scalp, skimming through the heavy waves of my mahogany hair as it slipped from its stylish coif to my shoulders.

But wait a minute! The purple images screeched to a halt. Maybe I was thinking of a romance novel. My own hair was confined to the back of my head with enough hair spray to stick a cat to the wall. It was straight as a stick, tended to be overly fine and, without the assistance of Madame Clairol, strongly resembled the color of dirt. "Perhaps we should confine our discussion to your problems, Mr. Bomstad."

"You must have problems, too."

"But I'm not paying you a hundred and fifty dollars an hour to discuss them."

He laughed again. The sound was deep and tantalizingly masculine. My stomach did a funny little double loop. "Maybe I'd listen for free."

I sighed internally. It took me a minute to recognize the sound, but when I did I gagged it with manic haste and straightened in my chair. "That's very nice of you," I said, pretty sure my polite but dismissive expression was firmly back in place. "But I can't help you if you don't—"

"You've already helped me."

"I have?"

He glanced down. He exhibited endearingly boyish expressions sometimes, as if he couldn't quite meet my eyes.

"Immensely," he said, and raised his gaze.

"I'm glad to hear that. Still, I think—" I began, but then he brushed his jacket aside.

My eyes popped like peeled grapes and my jaw ricocheted off my desk top. There, between the spread edges of his jacket, I saw that his jeans were unzipped. He wore no underwear and voilà ... it looked as if that impotency problem was pretty much taken care of.

"Well?" he said. I raised my attention with a jerky effort. His elbows were propped casually across the back of my couch as he watched me. He grinned. "What do you think?"

"Damn," I croaked. "I'm good."

He chuckled and rose slowly to his feet, a big man fast losing his boyish demeanor. "Yeah, you are," he said, "and I'd like to thank you."

"You could double my pay," I suggested and rolled my chair cautiously backward. It was one thing to fantasize about an illicit affair with a hunky client. It was quite another to have that fantasy unzip in front of God and everybody.

"That's not the kind of payment I had in mind, Doc," he said, and placed his hands on the edge of my desk.

"As I've told you before, Mr. Bomstad, I prefer to be called Ms. McMullen." I sounded like I was lecturing a twelve-year-old. Or giving an order to the bartender. Not at all like I was talking to a guy whose genitalia was draped over my desk like berries on a vine.

"Whatever," he said. "You done good, and now I'd like to do a little something for you. Or should I say...a big something?" Removing one hand from my desk, he brushed his jacket aside again.

Crimony! It may have been smaller than a bread basket, but it blew a button all to hell.

He smiled as I stared. "I'll lock the door so we ain't disturbed."

It was those words that set the alarms exploding in my head. I reached for the phone, and his hand, still large and clean and square-nailed, thumped suddenly atop mine.

"Who you calling?"

I glanced up. The boyish expression had been replaced by something less appealing. My stomach pitched.

"I think you'd better leave, Mr. Bomstad." My voice was still steady, but my knees were bumping together like wind chimes gone mad.

"Leave?" he said, and wrapping his fingers about my hand, eased around the corner of the desk. I rose to my feet. I've never considered myself weak, but all things are relative. "After you done such good work?"

My heart was banging against my ribs and my head felt feather-light. "I'm flattered that you attribute your umm...newfound health to my services," I said, "but I'm afraid I still must insist that you leave."

He grinned and edged closer. "I like to hear you talk." I could feel the heat of his body now, and my own temperature rose so that my face felt hot. "All slick and high-class, but I wonder..." He touched me with his knuckles, brushing them against my cheek. "I wonder what you're like when you get riled."

"My secretary will be returning any minute." It was an out-and-out lie and not a very good one, apparently, because Bomstad didn't even acknowledge it.

"Always dressed so classy." He ran a hand over my shoulder. "Always smell so good." He leaned in, taking a deep breath near my neck. "But sometimes I think there might be a touch of animal in you. A little white trash." Bending his neck, he nipped at my throat. I was no longer sighing.

"Let go of my wrist," I warned. The words only warbled a little.

He grinned. "There's a stain on your blouse," he said, gazing down at my breasts but not loosening his grip. "Almost hidden. What else you got hidden, Doc?" Raising his free hand, he brushed his fingers down my throat, pressing my blouse aside during his descent. I shivered as he touched the slope of my breast.

"You like that, Doc?"

No, I didn't like it. Only a moron would like it, but I closed my eyes and dropped my head back slightly. A moan would have been a nice touch, but acting's not my talent. Still, I didn't need that extra drama, because apparently Bomstad was a big believer in his own overwhelming charm.

"Been a while for you, has it, Doc?"

I said nothing, but forced my muscles to relax.

"Good thing the Bomber took you up on your offer, huh?"

"Offer?" I opened my eyes, but kept my body carefully pliant.

He chuckled again. "Little late to be playing hard to get

now, ain't it?" he asked. "Little late when the Bomber is all hot and ready." He slipped his hand inside my bra, cupping my breast.

I gasped. My stomach heaved. What would happen if I hurled on his perfectly polished shoes?

"You like that?"

Like porcupines in my underwear, but I forced a sigh. It sounded more like a growl to me, but he didn't seem to notice, because he stepped forward.

I struck immediately, snapping my knee up with all the strength I could muster.

But even in his current state Bomstad had a professional athlete's reflexes. My blow made only minimal contact with his newly regenerated area before it was deflected by a tree-sized thigh. Still, he stumbled backward, holding his offended parts and cursing.

I didn't wait to enrich my vocabulary but bolted around the other side of my desk and dashed for the door. My hand closed over the doorknob, but there was a growl behind me and I was snatched away and flung across the room. I scrambled for footing, lost a shoe, and bounced off a wall, but I was still free and sprinted behind my desk, my breath coming hard.

"Don't do this, Andrew," I panted. "You'll regret it."

He was breathing hard, too. Still bent, he stalked me. "You're a tease is what you are, Doc."

"I'm not a tease," I said, searching wildly for my professional voice. "I'm sorry if you got the wrong impression."

"No wrong impressions," he said and lunged forward, grappling across my desk.

I shrieked like a B-movie starlet and bolted sideways,

making for the door again. He lunged after me. I skidded to a halt at the end of my desk, teetered on one shoe, and dashed off in the other direction. He was close behind. I screamed again. His hand closed on my jacket. Fabric tore. Buttons popped. I turned in desperation. There was no hope now. He was twice my weight and strength, but there was nothing to do but fight, so I swung with all my might. My fist thudded against his ear like the swat of a swallow's wing. He caught my wrist with little effort and grinned into my face as he pushed me toward the floor.

I was blubbering something incoherent, promises or threats or prayers. Who knows? Then suddenly, his grip gave a little. I scrambled backward, trying to gain my feet. He stumbled, grabbed his chest with clawed hands, and dropped to his knees. I lurched toward the phone, jabbing at numbers with spastic fingers and yammering into the receiver.

Bomstad rolled his eyes up toward mine. I dropped the phone and staggered against the wall. Then, like a melo-dramatic overactor, he fell to the floor, dead as a thumb-tack.

2

Even choosing the perfect dinner wine loses its
earth-shattering importance if your guests happen
to be cannibals and you, the unsuspecting entrée.

—*Dr. Candon,*
psych professor

*M*A'AM. MS. MCMULLEN."

I tried to concentrate. The police had arrived with head-spinning haste. Apparently someone had heard my scream and dialed 911. My own call had probably gone to a hang-glider in Tibet.

Everything seemed foggy and unfocused, except for the body lying immobile on my overpriced Berber. That was as clear as vodka. His eyes were open and vividly blue, his hands limp, his fingers slightly curled. He lay on his back, but his jacket had fallen across his crotch with blessed kindness. Still, my stomach threatened to reject both the yogurt and the dehydrated orange.

"Ms. McMullen."

"What?" I dragged my attention shakily away from Bomstad's blank-eyed stare and supported myself with a hand on the top of my desk. The oak grain felt coarse and solid beneath my fingers. But the world still seemed strangely off-kilter. Maybe it was because I was wearing only one shoe. Maybe not.

The man addressing me was dark. Dark hair, dark skin, dark eyes, dark clothes. "Are you Christina McMullen?"

"Yes. I'm . . . Yes." I sounded, I thought, about as bright as a Russian olive.

He stared at me for a good fifteen seconds, then, "I'm Lieutenant Rivera."

I said nothing. My gaze was being dragged mercilessly toward the floor again. Those sky-blue eyes, those large, open hands.

"I'd like to ask you a few questions."

"Uh-huh."

"You're a psychiatrist?"

I pulled my attention doggedly back to the lieutenant's face. It was devoid of expression, except possibly anger. A shade of distrust. Could be he looked cynical. Maybe devoid wasn't exactly the right word.

His brows were set low over coffee-colored eyes that matched the dark hue of his jacket, and his lips were drawn in a straight, hard line.

"Psychologist," I said. "I'm a . . ." My voice wavered a little on the vowels, making me sound like a prepubescent tuba player. "Psychologist."

He didn't seem to notice or care about the distinction. "This your office?"

"Yes."

"You work here alone?"

"Yes. No. I . . ." Three men were examining the body and muttering among themselves. A fat guy in a wrinkled dress shirt that was miraculously too large said something from the corner of his mouth and the other two laughed. My stomach heaved.

"Yes or no. Which is it?" asked the lieutenant. Patience didn't seem to be his virtue. Or empathy. Apparently, the fact that there was a dead guy staring at my ceiling didn't faze him much, but it wasn't doing a hell of a lot for my equilibrium.

"No. I usually have a . . . secretary." For a moment I completely forgot her name, but then she'd only been my best friend since fifth grade, when she'd kissed Richie Mailor and declared him to have lips like the spotted pictus our science teacher kept in his aquarium. "Elaine . . . Butterfield."

He was staring at me again. "Have you been drinking, Ms. McMullen?"

"I . . . No."

"There are two glasses."

"Ahhh . . ." My mind was wandering again. My focus crept in the direction of the corpse.

"Ms. McMullen."

"Mr. Bomstad brought wine," I said.

"How long have you two been lovers?"

My eyes snapped back to Dark Man. "What?"

"You and Bomstad," he said. His tone was as dry as Bond's martini. "How long have you been lovers?"

"We weren't lovers."

I can't actually say he raised his brows. Maybe one. Just a notch.

"We weren't lovers," I repeated, more emphatically. "He attacked me."

"Do your customers always bring...refreshments to their sessions?"

I stared at him. I'd worked my damn ass off to become a high-class psychologist and I didn't like his tone. "I can't dictate what my clients do with their time," I said.

"It's your office. I would think you could."

So that's the way it was. My brother Pete and I used to have spitting contests. I had been declared the indisputable winner. But perhaps spitting wouldn't be appropriate here. Just a stare-down, then. "You can think anything you want, Lieutenant..."

"Rivera."

"We weren't lovers, Mr. Raver."

Something like a grin appeared on his face, or maybe he was just curling a lip as he sized up his prey. There was a shallow scar at the right corner of his mouth. Maybe that's why his expression looked more like a predatory snarl than a smile. The romance novelists would have called it sardonic. I didn't read romance anymore. Now I was studying Tolstoy and thinking deep thoughts. Mostly I was thinking of giving up reading.

"What was he doing here after hours with no one else in the office?" Rivera asked.

"Elaine had a yoga class."

"Did she?" he asked, and I wondered if he actually saw some significance in my blathering. "There's a stain on your blouse, Ms. McMullen. Is it blood?"

"No." I had never had a stain that fascinated people to such an extraordinary extent. "Why would you think—"

"What was he doing here?"

I felt breathless. As if I'd run a long way. I don't like to run a long way. I'd tried it on more than one occasion. Every Monday, Wednesday, and Friday, in fact, if you call three miles a long way. I do. "What?" I said, struggling with the fog that threatened to engulf the interior of my cranium.

"Lover boy." He nodded toward Bomstad's body. "Why was he here?"

"For therapy," I replied, "like all my clients."

Two more men and one woman had joined the mob by the corpse. One of the men squatted by the body, suit crumpled, pen and clipboard in hand.

"What were you seeing him for?"

The fellow with the clipboard reached for Bomstad with his pen.

I jerked my attention back to Dark Man and raised my chin. I was pretty sure I looked like Hester Prynne. A first-rate martyr, but I felt a little faint. "Impotence," I said.

"Hey." The suited fellow's voice was loud enough to wake the dead. Almost. "Looky here. He's got a woody."

Rivera's eyes burned. I could almost meet them. "Damn, you're good," he said and my knees buckled.

I woke up in my own bed. I didn't remember much about getting there. My head felt fuzzy and my stomach queasy. It took a minute for the memories to come rolling back into my brain. It was a dream. A bad dream, I told myself.

But I'm nothing if not a realist. Which was what had convinced me to become a therapist in the first place. After years of depraved dating it had become apparent that all men are psychopaths. Therefore half the population needs professional attention. It was bound to be a lucrative field, and easy.

How many times could I be wrong?

I shut my eyes, trying to block out the previous night, but a dead body with a hard-on pretty much etches itself into one's memory. A noise distracted me and I rolled over, listening. My doorbell rang, making me wonder foggily if that was what had awakened me in the first place.

Questions rolled around in my head like BBs in a walnut shell but I fought off my bedsheets and staggered toward the door. It took me a minute to realize I was still wearing one shoe. It was a Ferragamo and matched my skirt. My jacket and blouse, however, were gone. I stopped dead in the middle of the floor. The doorbell rang again, drawing my gaze up from my not quite willowy body.

"Who is it?" I asked.

"Police."

A dozen thoughts garbled through me. Not one could be voiced in polite company.

"Just a minute," I yelled and plucking off my shoe, staggered back to my bedroom for a shirt. But once there I merely gazed around in disjointed uncertainty. I'm tidy enough, but I don't like to be obsessive about it. I'd thrown my robe over the foot rail of my bed and left my horoscope beside it before galloping off to work on Thursday morning. I was an Aquarius and yesterday was predicted to be my lucky day.

I dragged on the robe. Classy, it was not. Nor did it exactly match my rumpled skirt or the irritably discarded shoe that still dangled from my fingertips.

The doorbell screamed at me. I plowed toward it and looked through the peephole. Lieutenant Rivera stood on my porch, looking grim.

I braced myself and opened the door. He shouldered his way in. He wasn't a huge man. Six foot maybe, only a few inches taller than myself, and not particularly broad, but every inch of him seemed to be devoid of fat. And this time I mean devoid.

He wore jeans that had seen some life and a charcoal-colored dress shirt. His hips were lean, his eyes steady, and his wrists dark and broad-boned where his sleeves were folded up from his workingman's hands.

"Do you let just anyone in?"

I think I blinked at him. "What?"

"Your door," he said. "Do you let everybody in who rings your bell?"

"I saw you through the peephole."

"You didn't even ask for my badge."

The man was certifiable. Another candidate for the loony bin. Business was brisk.

"You thought I might forget you overnight?" I asked.

The almost-grin appeared, but Rivera turned, glancing around my foyer. It was really nothing more than a narrow entryway, but I liked to call it a vestibule.

"Nice place."

Was he trying to be civil? I wondered numbly, and decided to take a chance. "Would you like some coffee?"

He turned back toward me as if just remembering my presence. "Did you prescribe the Viagra?"

"What?"

"Bomstad," he said. "He'd taken a large dose of Viagra before visiting you. Did you prescribe it?"

I felt as if I'd lost a water ski and was now skidding across the surface of a lake on my face. "No. I'm—"

"Did you know he had a heart condition?"

"I'm a psychologist. I can't prescribe drugs," I said, still working on the last question.

"Even for a heart condition?"

"Not for anything."

"Then you knew he had a weak heart."

"No. I . . . No."

"So you didn't see any harm in trying to seduce him."

I took a deep breath and counted to five. "I didn't try to seduce anybody," I said.

His gaze drifted down from my face. Mine followed, then I snapped the wayward robe together over the top of my bra. It was black and frayed and had cost me less than twelve dollars brand-new. Why spend $49.99 on a garment no one would ever see?

Rivera's lips lifted.

"Why are you here?" I asked. My voice sounded angry. I hope. Maybe it was just a little bit breathless.

"I wanted to make sure you were all right. You seemed disoriented last night when I brought you home."

"You brought—" The truth dawned a little slowly, but I

was running on four hours of sleep and visions of a corpse with a woody. "What did you do with my blouse?"

"I was just trying to get you comfortable."

I stared at him, then lifted my right hand. The single shoe dangled between us like rotten fruit. "You left the shoe but took the blouse?"

He shrugged and walked into my kitchen. It wasn't a whole lot bigger than my vestibule. "Turns out it was a fruit stain. Cherry," he said.

"You tested the stain?"

He shrugged again. His movements were Spartan, as if each one was calculated. His gaze traveled back to mine. "How long had you and Mr. Bomstad been seeing each other?"

"I told you . . ." His attention made me fidgety. I hated being fidgety. Fidgety is not classy. "I wasn't *seeing* him."

A brow flickered. "I meant professionally."

"Oh. Yes." I cleared my throat. "Three months. Maybe four."

"And during that time how often did you have intercourse with him?"

He had taken a notebook from somewhere and flipped it open. I stared in disbelief. "I told you before, we didn't have intercourse."

"No. You told me before you weren't lovers."

I opened my mouth, then shut it.

"You were going to say something?"

It's not as though I have a temper, but sometimes, when I'm tired, it's best not to push me. Or when I'm hungry. I can get cranky when I'm hungry. And there are certain times of the month when I'm just better off left alone. "We weren't lovers," I said, keeping my tone admirably even. I *was* tired and hungry, but at least I wasn't menstruating. "Neither..."—I pronounced it with an elegant hard *i* sound and felt better for it.—"...did we have intercourse."

"Oh." He said it casually, as if it didn't matter. I ground my teeth and reconsidered the spitting contest.

"Were you aware of his activities?"

"Activities?" I said.

He shrugged. "What he did. Who he was."

"He was a tight end for the Lions," I said. "If that's what you're referring to."

"Did you know he was a Peeping Tom?"

"What?" The air had been squashed out of my lungs again.

"And an exhibitionist?"

"Andrew?"

"Do you address all your customers by their first names?"

"A Peeping Tom?"

"Howard Lepinski said you called *him* 'Mr. Lepinski.'"

"You talked to Mr. Lepinski?"

"I guess that answers my question."

"What the hell were you doing talking to my clients?" I asked, taking an involuntary step toward him. He didn't exactly cower away. In fact, his lips twitched again. I couldn't help but wonder what kind of an imprint a Ferragamo would make on his damned sardonic expression.

"Did you know he was a flasher?"

"Lepinski?" The shoe drooped in my fingers.

"Bomstad."

"Are you shittin' me?"

His brows did rise that time. I squeezed the edges of my robe together and remembered my professional image. "You must be mistaken," I said and lifted my chin in a haughty expression of pride. Start the bonfires, the martyr was back.

"I'm not mistaken," he said. "And neither . . ."—He pronounced it with a hard, elongated *i* sound.—". . . am I shittin' you."

I wandered into my living room and plopped down in my La-Z-Boy. It had once belonged to a man named Ron. Ron was long gone. The chair remained. Yet another way furniture is superior to men. "Bomstad?" I asked, and glanced up at Rivera. His eyes were deep set, like a sculpture's, and his hair was too long to be stylish. It curled around his ears in dark waves. "Andrew Bomstad?"

"The Bomber," he answered. "You're not the first woman he's charmed the pants off of."

"He didn't—"

"Then why did you send him the wine?"

I just stared this time, numb as a cherry pit.

"The Spumante," he said, and stared back at me. "Did you send it to him?"

I shook my head.

"Did you know he had a girlfriend?"

I nodded.

"That bother you?"

"I told you—"

"There were others, too. He liked them young, mostly. Teenagers. You're not his usual type."

"I didn't—"

"Not that I'm faulting his choice, but how did he happen to hear about you?"

"I'm telling you—"

"I mean, I would think a guy like Andy the Bomber Bomstad might find a psychiatrist with more . . . notoriety. But then, I guess he didn't pick you for your diploma. And maybe you didn't know much about his background. His handler was top-notch at keeping his indiscretions out of the papers. But you're going to have to come clean now. I'll keep it quiet. Make sure it doesn't affect your business. How long had you been sleeping with Bomstad?"

"I was not—"

"A month? Couple weeks?"

"Listen!" I growled and, shooting out of my 'boy,' stepped up close enough so I had to lift my chin to glare into his face. "I didn't sleep with him. I never slept with him. I haven't slept with anyone for ye—"

He was standing absolutely still, staring down at me, an expression of near surprise on his face.

Lucidity settled in at a leisurely pace. I took a deep breath and backed off a step.

"I didn't have intercourse with Mr. Bomstad," I said. If he so much as twitched I was going to spit in his eye.

"Ever?"

"Never."

"Oh." He nodded agreeably. "You have a boyfriend?"

"Not at the present time."

He snapped his notebook shut and headed for the door,

where he turned. "Years of celibacy," he mused. "It's bound to make a woman short-tempered."

I considered throwing my shoe at him, but I'm a professional. And he was damned quick in the face of a loaded Ferragamo.

3

Honest friends is kinda nice, but it's hard to beat a big-ass lie and a six-pack of brewskies.

—*Brutus O'Malley,*
Chrissy's first beau

I'M SORRY to bother you," I said. I was standing rather droopily on the spacious, pillared verandah of my friend and colleague, Dr. David Hawkins. A white wicker swing looked cool and elegant against the slatted railing at the far end of the gargantuan porch, making me feel even grittier by comparison.

"Chrissy," David said, stepping outside and pulling me into a hug. "Don't be ridiculous." His chiding tone was fatherly as he held my arms and leaned back to take a look at me. My mascara was smeary and my hair was wind-fried, but I was pretty sure my nose had stopped running. I was practically at the top of my game. "Come in."

I did, though I still felt shaky and disoriented. It had been a hell of a day, starting with Rivera's visit and persisting with a dozen ragged phone calls from various unwelcome sources. Elaine had canceled my appointments. I didn't quite feel up to discussing someone's reoccurring dream about mayonnaise when my own tended to include a hard-on and a corpse.

Instead, I had called David. *Psychology Today* had named him one of the leading therapists of our time. His house, a stately edifice, complete with stained glass and a triple garage, was nestled up against the San Rafael Hills, surrounded by wealth and good breeding. My own modest abode was some thirty miles and five social steps to the northwest. It was the approximate size of David's Jacuzzi. But I couldn't quite be jealous of him. He was like the psychiatrist I'd never had.

"Sit down," he said when we'd finally trekked the plush, endless hallway to his study. I took a seat on the leather davenport and laced my fingers atop my knees to keep them occupied. In the past I'd had a tendency to chew my nails in high stress situations, and in my experience, tight ends with postmortem erections tend to raise the stress level like nobody's business. "Tell me," David said as he settled into the chair opposite me.

Classical music played from some distant room. The airy sound of a flute wafted quietly through the house. I didn't play the flute, but I'd been hell on wheels with the tuba.

I shook my head, feeling stupid and hot. Whoever said L.A. has idyllic weather hasn't spent a day with malfunctioning AC in late August. I'd rolled the Saturn's windows down in self-defense as I'd trundled west on I-210, and the smog had saturated my wind-smacked hair like so much London soot. "I'm sorry," I repeated, for lack of a better segue. "I'm sure you've heard enough problems today already." And every day. David's clientele was both extensive and legendary. It was rumored he had once counseled Rush Limbaugh concerning his weight problem, but I guess even geniuses strike out sometimes.

"Nonsense." He leaned forward and took my hands between his own. "The day I'm too busy for a friend is the day I'm no friend at all."

Despite everything—the corpse, the lack of sleep, the electrocuted hair—I felt myself relax a smidgen. David had that effect on people. Maybe it was his voice—rich and soothing like French vanilla. Or maybe it had something to do with his age. He was a mature man, both physically and emotionally, which gave me some hope for the remainder of the male populace. His hair was silver, his face lightly tanned, and gentle lines marked his forehead and cheeks. But they were nice lines, the kind that make a face look comfortable.

"I just . . ." I exhaled carefully, holding onto my control by my, as of yet, unmolested fingernails. I couldn't help noticing that I'd now lost three acrylics. Damn it all, a dead body and now this. "It all happened so fast." I'd told him a pared-down version of my troubles on the phone. He had insisted that I come over straight away.

"What did the coroner say?" he asked, cutting to the proverbial chase.

"He died from a preexisting heart condition." I closed my eyes for a moment and tried to think of a way to soften the next words. Nothing clever came to mind. "Which was exacerbated by an overdose of Viagra."

"What?" He sat up straighter. "Andy Bomstad was taking Viagra?"

"Apparently."

"And you didn't know?"

"No."

"But...Even so...Viagra is perfectly safe, unless ingested in extreme doses."

"Uh-huh."

"Good lord," he said and tightened his grip on my hands before releasing them and rising abruptly. "You don't need a consultation. What you need is a drink."

"I'm just in time, then," someone said.

I glanced up. A goddess had appeared in the doorway. She stood about five four and couldn't have weighed more than a can of peas. Her hair was swept up in a complicated knot that would have made a sailor swoon, and her ensemble was impeccable; her slacks pressed just so, her silk blouse without a wrinkle. She even wore heels—in the house.

Generally when at home I'm a little more casual. In fact, the outfit I had worn during Rivera's last visit was a considerable improvement over my usual attire. Just now I was dressed in blue jeans and a T-shirt. Usually, I make it a point to look presentable when I'm out and about. But... the staring eyes...the ridiculously large erection...I was lucky to be dressed and coherent instead of running around stark naked, yammering about gummy bears in wine sauce.

Still, I tugged at my shirt, making sure it was well past

the bulge that overlooked my jeans. Some people become anorexic under stress. I don't have that problem.

"Ahh, Kathryn," David said, walking over and giving her a kiss on the cheek before taking the drinks she held in perfectly manicured hands. I curled my fingernails against my palms and noticed the glasses were cut crystal. Austrian probably.

"Chrissy, this is my fiancée." He beamed. First at her, then at me. "Kathryn LaMere. My dear friend and colleague, Christina McMullen."

She smiled. Her teeth were aligned like perfect, pearlescent soldiers. "It's so very nice to meet you. I've heard nothing but good." She had a faint but elegant accent, and she smelled delicious. Like high-priced heaven.

Reality dawned on me with belated brilliance: David was engaged...to be married. I let the fact sink slowly into my subconscious. It shouldn't have been surprising, really. After all, he was an attractive, intelligent man. But...I had bananas older than that girl. And maybe I had secretly fantasized about becoming the future Mrs. Dr. David. After all, he exuded kindness and good taste, while my own sprawling family leaned toward pranks involving flatulence and dead vermin.

"I'm sorry." I bobbled to my feet, feeling idiotic. Obviously they had planned to go out. It was Friday night, after all, and some people did that sort of thing on the weekend. "I'm interrupting your evening."

"Don't be silly," David said.

"Not at all," Kathryn chimed in. "This is the ideal opportunity for me to see to my work. Please, make yourself at home," she said and smiling, exited, closing the double French doors behind her.

We were left alone. David crossed the floor and pressed a Scotch into my hand.

"You're engaged," I said. Perhaps it sounded as lame to him as it did to me, but my fantasies are nothing if not tenacious and prefer to be smothered rather than drowned.

"Nearly a month now," he said, and motioned me back toward the couch. "Wedding's in May. Kathryn wanted to move it up. At least that's what she said. Personally, I think she was just trying to stroke an old man's fragile ego."

I stifled a sigh and dropped listlessly onto the cushy leather.

"You still look shocky," he said, taking a seat and studying my eyes. "You didn't see clients today, did you?"

I assured him I hadn't.

"Good. Take Monday off as well."

"I don't know if I can afford to—"

"Chrissy." He was the only person outside of my immediate family who called me that. My youngest brother still referred to me as Christopher Robin because of my former obsession with Pooh and the Hundred Acre Wood. But James was only thirty-six. Perhaps someday he would be as mature as David . . . if modern science lived up to its longevity promises. "Listen, you've just been through a terrible trauma. You need time to recoup."

"Maybe you're right."

He settled back, studying me carefully. "It's bound to happen every blue moon or so," he said.

I tried a smile. It felt ghoulish, but the Scotch made

me feel better. "I'm just..." I scowled into my drink. Glenfiddich. "They've been asking a lot of questions."

"They?"

"There's a lieutenant." Rivera's piercing eyes burned in my memory. "He seems to think I had a personal relationship with Bomstad."

"That's absurd." David sounded immensely offended on my behalf. I had considered calling my parents, but history and common sense suggested otherwise. Thirteen months ago a gale-force wind had taken the roof off my garage; Dad had immediately asked what the hell I had done. "How did he come to such an asinine conclusion?"

"Well..." I cleared my throat. "Mr. Bomstad had brought a bottle of wine."

"To his session?"

"I'm afraid so."

"You didn't drink any."

"No." My answer was quick. Explanations were about as pleasant as a full body wax, but I needed advice and he was on a first-name basis with the Board of Psychology. "No. But..." I swirled my drink and managed not to do the throat-clearing thing again. "With the Viagra, he..." When I glanced up I saw David was still watching me, scowling a little. "He—"

"Oh, no. Chrissy." He shook his head. "Don't tell me he was aroused."

I did clear my throat then. In my mind, David had always been a strange mix between mentor, friend, and the silver-haired guy on *Fantasy Island*. I'd been a kid when the show aired, but I'd always had a thing for that silver-haired guy. "I'm afraid so."

"Even after the police arrived?"

"Yes."

"But obviously they could tell there had been no relations. Even the dim-witted LAPD could deduce that much."

"He, uhhh..." I stared into my Scotch. "He had his pants unzipped."

David said nothing for a moment, but stared at me in silence. His eyebrows were nestled somewhere in his silvery hairline. "Did you—"

"I didn't do anything. I swear it," I said. "Sure, Bomstad was a good-looking guy, but..." I fumbled miserably for words.

"Perhaps you'd best start at the beginning," he said, and so I did, rambling through the entire humiliation from start to finish until I felt limp and exhausted. Like a first-rate psycho on the doctor's cushy leather couch.

"And he had given you no indication in the past that he was interested in you?"

"No. None." Although I had kind of wished he had. But I wasn't suicidal enough to admit that.

"And you were seeing him for an impotency problem." He shook his head. "Oh, the irony."

"Yes." I felt a little sick to my stomach. "I had myself a good laugh over that one."

He smiled gently, then leaned forward and tsked. "Well, you needn't worry. I'll speak to the board personally and vouch for your character."

"Would you?" I hope I didn't look like a love-starved puppy, but puppies need love, too.

"You didn't do anything wrong, Chrissy. We can't dictate what our clients do, much as we'd like to."

"That's what I said," I said, remembering my conversation with Rivera.

"I once had a middle-aged homemaker come to a session stark naked," he said.

"You're kidding."

He raised a well-manicured hand with an earnest expression. "God's honest truth."

"What did you do?"

He took a drink. "I suggested the Atkins diet."

Perhaps laughter really is the best medicine, because I felt instantly better. Screw therapy. I should just hire a stand-up comedian.

"It's good to see you smile again," he said, and rose to his feet.

I stood up beside him. "You've been a huge help."

"What are overpaid psychiatrists for?"

"I suppose I'll still have to file a report for the board?" I asked and bravely managed not to wince.

"I'm afraid so," David said. "But I'm certain they'll be lenient. When one works with disturbed people one has to expect disturbed behavior."

"He *was* disturbed. I just didn't realize how deeply."

"I was talking about you," he said.

I must have looked stricken when I turned at the door, but he laughed and took my hand again.

"I'm joking, Chrissy. You're one of the best therapists I know. Not all bogged down with that psycho-babbling mumbo jumbo. You're intelligent, empathetic, insightful..."

I suddenly felt all squishy. I'm a tough little soldier and all that, but it had been a hell of a week. "Maybe you could adopt me," I said.

He smiled with what I hoped was sincere fondness. If I can't have unbridled passion I'll settle for affection any day of the week. "I'll see how Kathryn feels about it."

I glanced at my shoes. Sincere emotion sometimes makes me uncomfortable. A former boyfriend had once told me I had no feelings at all, but then he had cried during *Toy Story*. "I really appreciate your help," I said.

"No problem. Really. The board will understand."

I gave him a plucky smile. "I hope the police are as enlightened."

"I am certain they will be," he said and kissed my cheek. "They'd have to be crazy to think you had anything to do with Bomstad's death."

I think you killed him," Rivera said.

"What!" I stood in my vestibule in my stocking feet. The door remained open behind him, letting in the Saturday morning sunlight. I was wearing my Eeyore pajamas. James had given them to me for Christmas and though my silk nightgown was more fitting for my professional persona, Eeyore was a hell of a lot cozier. Well, the top was, anyway. My bottoms had gone A.W.O.L. I had settled for a pair of nylon shorts that couldn't quite be seen past the donkey's dangling tail.

Rivera shrugged, as if he didn't really care if I had strangled Bomstad with my favorite thong. "I think you gave him the Viagra, then got him overexcited. Whether his death was intentional or not is yet to be determined."

"Yet to be— That's crazy." My heart was beating like a Sudanese war drum beneath Eeyore's hangdog expression. "I had nothing to do with his death. He—"

"He died in your office," Rivera argued. "Obviously you had something to do with the situation, even if it was merely adding stimulus."

"Listen..." I have some Irish blood in me and it was starting to heat up. "I didn't do anything to contribute to Bomstad's death. In fact—"

"Do you always dress so provocatively?"

I glanced down. My skin was as white as Elmer's glue. My leg hair needed harvesting and my socks didn't match. But it's funny what turns some guys on.

I looked back up at Rivera. He gave me a flat stare.

"I was referring to the dress you wore with Bomstad," he informed me.

"The dress..." I squinted at him. There were a half a dozen emotions bubbling around inside me. I could no longer sort one from the other. Suffice it to say, Saturday wasn't sizing up to be a hell of a lot better than Friday had been. "First of all, it wasn't a dress. And secondly, I was not *with*—"

"Were you aware he'd been arrested for statutory rape?"

I think I actually stumbled back a step, and I may have taken the Lord's name in vain.

"Is that a yes or a no?"

"No!"

"So you considered your relationship exclusive?"

I wanted to swear at him, but I thought verbally abusing a cop might be a bad idea at that juncture. So I plopped down on my steps and stared blankly. I'd been doing a lot of that lately. It had been about as effective as anything else in clearing up my current debacle.

"Listen. I don't want to see you hang for this," Rivera said, changing gears and firing up his good-cop tone. "You probably didn't mean any harm. I just need to know the truth."

"About what?"

"Everything."

"That seems like a lot," I said.

"I'm not your enemy, Ms. McMullen," he murmured, squatting in front of me. He rested one wrist over his knee. The denim there had faded to gray. "We can work together on this."

"On what?"

"Figuring out Bomstad's death."

I scowled. Something didn't quite add up. "I thought he died of a Viagra overdose."

"But that isn't generally lethal, is it?"

"Neither is breathing, but my great aunt died just last month. No known cause."

"How old was she?"

"A hundred and two," I said and nodded, thinking back. She'd always smelled vaguely of mothballs and garlic.

He gave me something that might have passed for a grin, in the canine family. "Bomstad was wealthy, success-ful, and . . ." He seemed to be searching his politically correct vocabulary for a moment, but coming up short.

"Truth is, he was a first rate dumb shit," he admitted. "But he wasn't quite bright enough to know it."

"I'm not sure I understand your point." Or any point. In fact, I wasn't sure I'd ever understand a point again.

"Why would he take Viagra when he knew he had a heart condition?"

I searched my well-educated memory banks. "Some men place an inordinate amount of value on their ability to..." I paused, scrambling for the perfect textbook phrase.

He waited, watching. "To what?"

"Copulate."

He could take the Lord's name in vain without blinking an eye, I noticed. Either he wasn't Catholic or his mother had seriously shirked her duty as primary guilt-giver. "Is that what you call sex?" he asked. "Copulation?"

"It's a professional term."

He snorted. "All right. What led you to believe he had trouble...copulating?"

"That's why I was seeing him. Remember?"

"I do," he said. "But the two hookers he hired on..." A notebook appeared from nowhere for the second day in a row. He flipped it open. "...Tuesday said he didn't have any problems in that area."

I know I should have been prepared, but I felt temporarily breathless. "He hired hookers?"

"He liked multiples."

But his shoes were Italian! "It doesn't make any sense."

"You ever tried it?" He had a deep, smoky voice. Probably perfect for bullying suspects and poor innocent psychologists.

I gave him a blank stare.

"Multiple partners," he explained.

"I meant, it makes no sense that he would hire me. Why waste his money, confess . . . things most men don't like to confess when he didn't even—"

"What kind of things?"

I paused. Had he intentionally gotten me riled before asking that question? "That's confidential," I said.

"What have you got to hide, Ms. McMullen?"

I stood up to gain the edge. He did the same, immediately looming. So I stepped onto the stair behind me, giving me the slight advantage of height. It didn't do much good. The nice-cop persona hadn't stayed around very long.

"I don't have anything to hide, Mr. Reever. What I have are clients that expect me to honor my agreement to keep their cases confidential."

"Deep dark secrets, are they?" he asked, leaning forward slightly.

I resisted leaning back. "Yes," I said and remembered Mr. Lepinski. Pastrami or ham. "And not to be aired to the general public."

"In case you haven't noticed, Ms. McMullen, I'm not the general public."

"No," I agreed. "Most people are far more congenial."

"I can be congenial," he said, but his present expression suggested otherwise. "Or not." There was a blatant threat in the murky depths of his eyes. But I pulled myself out of the quagmire with magnificent strength.

"I'm a professional," I said with dramatic conviction.

Eeyore's tail waggled a little when I spoke. "And I won't be bullied into divulging intimate details."

"How intimate?" he asked, crowding me a little.

I swallowed hard. I'm not a small woman, and I like to think I'm no wimp, but this guy probably ate psychologists as appetizers. Still, who was he to come barging into my house at all hours of the day? I raised my chin and stood my ground. Our faces were inches apart. For a cop he smelled pretty good. "How would you like to be charged with harassment?" I asked. My voice hardly shook at all, but he didn't exactly shrivel under the threat. In fact, he chuckled.

"Lady," he said. "I can tell you've never been harassed."

"I've been harassed plenty," I snarled back. In retrospect I see that it's kind of funny what gets my dander up.

"Of course," he said, and grinned.

"You ever juggle five margaritas, two Bloody Marys, and a zombie in a mob of middle-aged perverts?"

He gave me the old one-brow raise, and I immediately wished I hadn't started down that road. I was standing there with an Eeyore tail on my back, for God's sake. How much more did the man need to know?

"Either you were a circus performer," he guessed, "or you worked in a bar."

I glanced outside, but I probably couldn't outrun him even if I got a fifty-yard head start. "I was employed in a drinking establishment for a short time, to help defray my educational expenses."

"What establishment?"

I paused, but it didn't matter if he knew; he'd never recognize the name. "The Warthog," I said. "In Chicago."

"Sounds elegant. How long did you work there?"

"I don't think that's pertinent information."

He raised a brow. "How l—"

"Twelve years! Okay? Twelve years." I may have sounded a little defensive, although there is nothing at all wrong with working at a bar . . . if you don't mind having your ass groped like a Georgia peach.

His expression was predatory at best. "And in twelve years you never met a guy who rocked your world like Bomstad?"

"I met a thousand guys like Bomstad," I said and did my best to stare him down. "I met even more like you."

"Yeah?" He crowded again. "How so?"

"You don't hold the patent on arrogance, Rivers."

"You think I'm arrogant?"

The Irish in me bubbled. "And obdurate."

"Obdurate?" His lips twitched, and it was that damned suggestion of a rottweiler grin that got my back up.

"Controlling," I snarled, "and just fucking obnoxious."

Okay, my own control had slipped a bit, and in the back of my mind some tiny element of reason suggested that perhaps I should not be swearing at an officer of the law. But the words were out now.

"Fucking obnoxious," he repeated and moved in closer still, though I would have sworn it was impossible.

Angry? Was he angry? I hadn't meant to make him angry. The little voice mildly suggested that I take it back before I understood police brutality up close and personal, but my mouth wouldn't form the necessary words. So I stood frozen in place and wished to hell I had learned to keep my mouth shut when my brother Michael had shoved my face in our neighbors' sandbox twenty-some years before.

"Sometimes I'm obnoxious," Rivera said, "and if I'm lucky I'm fucking." I nervously reminded myself that he wasn't a huge guy, but he seemed pretty good-sized close up. His eyes had narrowed to dark slits. A muscle jumped in his lean, bristled jaw, and I found, strangely, that my lungs had somehow forgotten how to inhale. "But . . ." He leaned in. "I am never both at the same time."

His lips were nearly touching mine. My knees felt like Jell-O. His mouth quirked. My lungs ached. Nerve endings danced like fireflies up and down my frozen form.

Holy shit, he was going to kiss me!

"Don't leave town," he ordered and turning on his heel, left me standing on the steps like a beached trout, gasping for breath and wishing to hell I hadn't taken the bait.

4

Maybe curiosity did kill your cat. But it wouldn't hurt to keep an eye on the neighbor's rottweiler just the same.

—*Elaine Butterfield,*
wondering why her "steady"
suddenly smells like Shalimar

WHY?

It was three o'clock in the morning. Questions ran through my mind like tequila in a west Texan's veins. Why would anyone see a therapist for a problem that didn't exist? Why would a man say he was impotent when he wasn't? Why would that same man take an overdose of Viagra? And why, for pity's sake, would he choose my office in which to drop dead?

I had no answers. Only more questions that sent my mind spinning off in a dozen baffling directions. What had Bomstad hoped to achieve with his supposed subterfuge? Would the board blame me for this horrific fiasco, and did Rivera really think I was responsible for Bomber's death?

True, there was still a tiny, pathetic part of me that was flattered Rivera might think a man like Bomstad had been attracted to me, but mostly I was mortified to learn that despite thousands of dollars of tuition and a zillion years of night classes, my ability to judge men hadn't improved one iota. It was terrifying, as were Rivera's suspicions, because there was one thing I knew beyond the shadow of a doubt: Men like the lieutenant didn't care about anything except mounting a trophy on the wall. I knew the type. Any cocktail waitress worth her tips had witnessed the scenario a million times: A man saunters into her bar. He's feeling good, confident, on the prowl for the perfect woman, but as the hours slide by and Heidi Klum once again fails to appear, he becomes less particular. Willing, in fact, to settle for anything with boobs and a dab of mascara.

This business with Rivera seemed very much the same. And if there was one thing I knew for sure, it was that I didn't intend to be just another pair of tits in the LAPD's files.

It was 3:42 when I gave up on sleep and stumbled out of bed. My eyes felt gritty and my head throbbed like a bass drum when I turned on the lights. From the corner of my thumb-sized office, my PC glared at me with accusatory malevolence. It had been a while since we'd communed. I was, by no means, a techno genius, but I had learned a few things while writing my dissertation.

I typed in Rivera LAPD and waited. My system droned, then haphazardly presented a few options. For me, the Internet is a lot like fishing. It's anyone's guess whether you're going to wind up with a sunfish or a tiger shark. But I netted out one of my choices and subsequently found myself looking at a well-greased young man sporting a come-hither smile and little else. It didn't take me more than a minute of blank-eyed staring to remember that strippers are fond of impersonating police officers.

I moved on. My next feeble attempts garnered a mystery novelist, a snowboarder, and a guy who offered to clean my chimney for half the usual price. If I ever bought a chimney I'd have to look him up. But for the moment I settled back in my chair and glared at the screen. What I needed was more information if I was going to be able to anticipate the dark lieutenant's next move. So I kicked my foggy brain into gear and tried to recall every moment of the traumatic events of August 24. Someone must have spoken to Rivera while he was in my office. What had they called him? Sir? Lord and master? Supreme commander?

Jack.

The name popped into my head like Redenbacher's finest. I typed madly, made three mistakes on the four-letter name and tried again.

And voilà! Rivera's photo materialized before my very eyes. Or at least a vague fascimile of him. Gone was the beard stubble and dare-me-to-do-you attitude. In its place was a well-groomed businessman in a suit and tie. And he was almost smiling. I squinted at the screen for a moment, then scrolled down. Jack Franklin Rivera. I tooled down again. Commendations as long as my arm followed, but little else. No attempted murders, no harassment charges. Nothing. Maybe he saved his barbed threats for female psychologists who killed tight ends in their second-rate offices.

I tried a few other avenues, certain I'd net a few peccadilloes at least, but I was disappointed again. Frustrated, I moved into the kitchen, spooned up a bowl of double mocha inspiration, and wandered back to my computer. But my search for facts about Bomstad was even less productive, garnering me nothing but information about his warrior days on the football field.

How could that be? Rivera had said the man had been arrested. Had he been lying? My heart rate rose a notch. Maybe he had fabricated the entire story. Maybe Bomstad had been as clean as a nun's undies and the dark lieutenant was just yanking my chain. After all, Bomstad had been a highly visible personality in the community. Surely if there had been trouble, the media would have plastered it on the front page. Unless the Bomber's handlers really *had* gagged the news hounds. In which case it was going to be much more difficult to learn the truth. But there would be records somewhere. If only I knew how to break into police files, I could—

Solberg. The little hacker's image cluttered my mind like so much regurgitated SPAM. J.D. Solberg. I'd first met him in Chicago, but he'd since transferred to L.A. Short, bald, irritating. I didn't really know him on a first-name basis, but he had been something of a fixture at The Warthog. In fact, he had spent a good deal of time trying to convince me to check out his hard drive. There's nobody who can come up with clever come-ons like an electronics whiz and I had heard a million of them, which reminded me that the shrink business wasn't so bad, even with dead men cluttering up your office now and again. It was possible even Rivera's brooding attentions were preferable to . . . Crap. I still remembered Solberg's e-mail address—geekgod@unet.com.

I stared at my PC, considering, then clicked the screen into darkness and wandered back to the sanctuary of my kitchen. In a matter of minutes I had finished off the carton of ice cream and slammed my head against the wall enough times to convince myself to contact Solberg.

The task was quick and painful. When I flopped back into bed my clock said 5:55. At 5:56 I was out cold. At 6:17 the phone rang.

I blinked groggily at my clock radio, certain I couldn't possibly be awake. Not at such an ungodly hour on a Sunday morning. It was just a bad dream, I assured myself, but the phone shrieked again so I picked up the receiver and croaked an unintelligible greeting.

"Gorgeous," someone said. "I knew you'd come around."

I checked the clock again. Still 6:17. The nightmare continued.

"Who the hell is this?" Consider this an early morning modification of polite but dismissive.

"Come on. You don't recognize me?"

I had just about fumbled the receiver back into the cradle when he spoke again.

"It's J.D. Solberg."

My mind trundled along like a minivan at rush hour. I lifted the receiver tentatively back to my ear. "Solberg?"

"In the flesh."

I shoved the hair out of my face and scrubbed at my eyes. "How'd you get my number?"

"You e-mailed me, babe."

"I didn't e-mail my number." And it was unlisted—for several very good reasons, one of which was on the other end of the line.

He laughed. Yep, it was J.D. all right. He still sounded like an inebriated donkey.

"You know what they call me, babe."

An ass? It was just a guess, but I had a good feeling about it.

"The Geek God," he said, sounding inexplicably proud. "Give me a pair of initials, I can get you a green card."

"I don't need a green card." What I needed was nine hours of sleep and a lobotomy. What the hell had I been thinking?

"So what'd you want from the Geekster, babe? The usual?"

I refrained from venturing a guess about the usual. As far as I knew, Solberg's boasts of electronic genius were as overinflated as his self-reputed skills as a lover, but I had been desperate. Note to self: Desperation rarely fosters exemplary decision-making.

"I just need a little information," I said cautiously. "Thought maybe you could get it for me."

"You know it, babe."

I considered threatening his life if he called me babe again, but if the truth be told I was still pretty desperate, so I cleared my throat and let it slide. "The information might be, uhhh . . . classified."

He chuckled. "I'll pick you up tonight. Seven sharp."

"What?"

"Don't be late. The Geek God don't like to be kept waiting."

The phone went dead. I stared at it for a minute, then snorted and grumbled it back into its cradle. That pretty much disproved the theory that everyone grows up eventually, I thought, and went to sleep with the soothing assurance that he'd never find my house.

I awoke to the teeth-grinding ring of the doorbell.

Wandering hazily down the hall to the vestibule, I squinted through my peephole.

J.D. Solberg stood on the far side. Or at least I thought it was him, though he now sported a full head of curly dark hair and had lost the horn-rimmed glasses that had been as much a trademark as Zorro's mask. He was, however, still two inches shorter than myself.

I opened the door, but left the security chain in place. Nothing says friendly like a three-inch length of metal between you and your would-be guest. "What are you doing here?" Yes, my mother had taught me better manners, and although I prescribe to the polite-but-dismissive philosophy, sometimes I'm better at dismissive.

"Babe!" JD said, spreading his arms as if I needed a better view. "It's me."

"Uh-huh." I gave him a quick once-over. "What are you doing here?"

"It's seven o'clock."

I glanced down the street. The sun did seem to be

sinking toward the horizon. I checked my watch, and sure enough, I'd been sleeping for a good thirteen hours.

My next expression might have fallen a little short of gracious. "I didn't agree to go out with you."

"Sure you did," he said and leaned a shoulder against the brick outside my door. It needed sandblasting, and an exterminator. Although most pests weren't quite so well dressed as this one. His suit was Armani.

"Listen, Solberg," I said. Now that I'd looked at my watch, I was pretty sure I was no longer dead on my feet. So I stifled a yawn and tried to soldier my grumbling brain cells into submission. "I shouldn't have bothered you. It was my mistake. I had a bad—"

"Andrew Russell Bomstad, christened on April 3 of 1981."

My lungs felt suddenly tight. I let out a little air and stared at him. He was still five foot seven, so the world hadn't gone completely mad.

"What?" I asked and, sliding the chain from its slot, eased the door open another few inches.

He grinned. When he smiled like that he looked like the J.D. Solberg of old, before the store-bought tan and the extra hair. It wasn't necessarily a good thing. "I believe he was better known as the Bomb."

Maybe I was naïve, but I was floored. I hadn't told him who I wanted investigated, or even that I wanted *anyone* investigated. It made me ache to shake him until the truth fell out, but I played it cool. "What about him?" I asked, and he brayed again.

"What about him?" he repeated, slithering past me and

slinking into my vestibule. "You should know. He croaked on your couch."

"That's not true." My voice sounded raspy.

But he only shrugged. "Could be wrong," he admitted. "I got that last part from the papers."

"Where'd you get the rest?"

He grinned. "I ain't called the Geekster for nothing."

It felt strange in that alternate universe.

"Aren't you going to ask what else I learned?"

It hurt to voice the question, but he was already there, leaking into my living room like flan gone bad.

"He liked girls. Young ones. Not like me," he said, and grinned. I think a good description might be lascivious. Or maybe just creepy. "I like 'em aged. Like fine wine. *You're* lookin' good, babe," he said, reaching out.

I slapped his hand away, feeling winded. "Let's just stick to the facts."

His grin widened. "Fact is you asked for a favor. And the god come through for you."

"What do you want?" I asked, and slapped his hand again. It had started to rise like the living dead.

"Hey," he said, sounding offended. "I just wanted to buy you a little dinner, impart a bit of information."

I scowled. We have a maxim where I come from: Never trust a man who wears his pubic hair on his head. "Just dinner? That's all?"

He shrugged. "I'll understand if you can't keep your hands off me."

I gave him the evil eye, but maybe he's one of those guys who thrives on a good stiff challenge, because he didn't back down. "All right," I said, exhausted despite the lying clock. "Give me fifteen minutes, but I warn you..." I turned back, drawing out the silence for dramatic effect, "you try anything funny and I'll be wiping up my floor with your head."

*H*e drove a Porsche. An '04 turbo Cabriolet to be exact, and since all three of my primordial brothers had spent their adolescence drooling over cars, I knew a little about them. This one, for instance, was expensive. Wouldn't you just know it? The Geekster was rich.

"Dig the wheels?" he asked, grinning at me.

A chimpanzee would dig the wheels, but a chimp might also expect a little more subtlety from her dinner companion. For a man who had vowed to keep his hands to himself he was giving off vibes like Julio on a hot night.

"I don't mean to be rude," I began, and it was generally true, but it was harder at some times than others. "And I do appreciate your help, J.D.—"

"You can call me Geekster. I don't mind," he said, shrugging pragmatically. "Some guys, they got the looks and some guys, they got the charisma. Me, I got me a nice little job at NeoTech." He grinned as he shifted into fourth. The gears snarled like pit bulls. "And a Porsche." He stroked the steering wheel.

I shivered. "Listen—"

"A big-ass house in La Canada."

"I don't want you to get the wrong idea."

"A swimming pool."

"I mean, you're a perfectly nice guy...I suppose—"

"Couple mil in the bank."

"But you're just not—" I stopped, blinked. "How much?"

He grinned toothily. "Two million, four hundred thirty-three thousand, seven hundred and twenty-two. Not that I'm counting."

"Two million, four..." My voice drifted away, but I cleared my throat and managed to move on. "Listen, Solberg, you understand that this is just business, right?"

"I make five hundred an hour, babalita."

I felt the blood drain from my face. I couldn't even imagine what I would have to do to earn that kind of money, but I was pretty sure it would be illegal and probably physically impossible. "You do know that this is just a personal favor, right?" I asked, feeling weak.

He brayed a laugh. "That's what I always liked about you, babe. Great sense of humor."

Right. And the fact that the Warthog's uniforms displayed more cleavage than a porn flick.

Just now I was showing no cleavage at all. I had gone for a staid image with black slacks and a black, button-up blouse. Only the slacks had been at the dry cleaners. So I'd had to settle for a skirt instead. It was by no means a mini, but geek boy kept staring at my knees. I tugged at the unobliging fabric.

"Where are we going?" I asked. We were heading west at breakneck speed on the San Bernadino Freeway. Sunday night traffic was light and congenial. We'd only been flipped off twice since exiting Towne Avenue.

"Hope you like lobster," he said.

I don't think I'm overstating things when I say I'd kill

for lobster, but I felt it necessary to maintain my cool demeanor. Although I might have drooled a little.

The Geekster grinned. "So babe, what'd you do to the football player, huh? I heard he died of a heart attack."

At least news of the Viagra hadn't gotten out. "I didn't do anything to him," I said. I was going for hauteur, but my mouth was still pooling with saliva and it was beginning to pose an enunciation problem.

"Really? 'Cuz it's said he had a hard-on of colossal proportions."

I considered abandoning hauteur and going for smack down. "I had nothing to do with that, either."

He leered at my knees.

"I doubt that, babycakes. But don't worry. My ticker's good as gold," he said and put his arm across the back of my seat.

I didn't really mean to pull out my Mace, but I kept it on my key chain. Handy but bulky, like a baseball bat on a ring.

"Hey!" he said, immediately offended. But he retracted his arm. Apparently he was familiar with Mr. Mace. "What's that for?"

"The usual."

"You came to *me*."

Which wasn't exactly true, but true enough to cause a little spark of guilt to nibble at my psyche.

"Listen, Solberg, I've had a hard week. And I don't want any trouble. I just need some information."

He stared at me. "Okay, okay, just put that away," he said and turned off the freeway. In a matter of minutes he had pulled up beside an ancient-looking cottage.

Sycamore trees shadowed the parking lot, although a shingle beside the door called it the Four Oaks.

Elegance, from Solberg. Life was full of surprises.

He stepped out of the Porsche and gave his keys to the valet with an exaggerated word of caution. We were ushered into the restaurant. It was cozy and charming, but the smell of culinary delights distracted me. Old architecture is all well and good, but it can't hold a candle to a twice-baked potato.

We were seated in moments. J.D. offered to order for me but I declined, hardly snarling at all. In a few minutes we were settled back with our drinks. I had considered abstaining, since liquor tends to make me weepy and idiotic, but there are a few occasions when alcohol is strictly called for, and I was pretty sure this was one of them.

"So, how did you know I wanted information about Bomstad?" I asked, making my opening gambit.

He grinned over his martini. "Tricks of the trade, gorgeous."

"Are they tricks I could perform?" I asked, wondering if there was any possibility I could cut out the middle man. Namely, the Geekster.

"You got a password cracker and shh?"

"What?"

"How about keystroke logger?"

"Huh?"

He laughed. "Maybe you better not try it at home, dollface."

I drank and decided he couldn't possibly be as irritating as he seemed. It was probably just my stomach talking. I hadn't eaten since my predawn ice cream feeding. "What did you learn?" I asked.

"What do you want to know?" he countered, propping an elbow over the back of his chair.

I considered marching out my question: Was Bomstad impotent? Had he played threesies with hookers? And did he really flash his goodies in public? But somehow I couldn't quite force out the words, not here where they used cloth napkins and real metal flatware.

"The truth is . . . I'm concerned how this debacle might impact my career," I said, wowing myself with my linguistic genius. "I've got a reputation to uphold in the community, and—"

"He was banging your secretary."

The bottom fell out of my world. "What!"

Fourteen pairs of well-bred eyes turned to stare at the commotion, but I hardly cared.

Neither did Solberg. He grinned. "Three times," he said. "Unless you don't count the hand job in the parking lot."

"Elaine?"

"Elaine? No," he said, and made a circular motion with the bread stick he'd just pulled from its basket. "The other one. What's her name."

I was already shaking my head. "You're crazy." Elisabeth had only worked for me a short while, but she was as classy as escargot. It had been my main reason for hiring her. I thought she'd add panache to the workplace. "I can tell you categorically that she would *not*—"

"She e-mailed a friend. Graphic details. 'Bout sent my chubby into orbit."

"You're wrong."

"Sent from your office on, um . . ." He rolled his eyes up slightly as he slurped his drink. "Fifth and Everest. Unless the letter was from you and you were using her password."

I may have cursed, but I wasn't sure because I was feeling a little light-headed.

"Ahh, there you are," Solberg said, glancing up as waiters approached, bearing our plates like royal scepters. They deposited our meals, questioned our satisfaction, and departed. From the look of my lobster, their pretentious self-importance was well deserved, but my appetite was atypically lacking.

"*Bon appétit,*" Solberg said, flicking his fork toward my meal.

"Who else?" I asked.

He was already digging meat out of its shell and dipping it in butter. "What's that?"

"Who else was he sleeping with?"

He laughed and stabbed a piece of lobster in my direction with a leer. "I didn't say they were sleeping."

"Who else?" My tone may have been less than congenial, but my impotent client had been screwing my classiest employee! And I was hearing the news from a vertically challenged techno geek with displaced pubic hair.

"He had a couple of regulars. Sort of on-and-off-again affairs."

"You know their names?"

"I think there was a Sheri. No. Sheila?" He shook his head. "Might have been a Kayla."

God help me.

"Who else?" I asked.

He shrugged. "Anyone with tits. There were two high-school chicks. Apparently their parents weren't amused."

"They press charges?" I began to eat methodically. It seemed wrong to let it go to waste.

"I didn't see nothing about that. Got the idea there may have been a little payola going down."

Which might account for the reason I hadn't heard anything about it in the news.

"Who was his doctor?" I asked.

He had returned to his martini and glanced up. "Doctor?"

"Who prescribed the Viagra?"

He grinned with sharklike intensity. "You living under a rock, babekins? You want Viagra I coulda had it for you yesterday."

Of course. He was right. The little blue pill with the gigantic results. The thought of Bomstad's staring eyes and open pants made me feel queasy, but not queasy enough to quit eating.

"Was he seeing anyone else I should know about?" I asked.

"*Seeing* anyone?" He leaned across the table toward me. "You are one classy broad, babalita. Always was. Even at the Hog."

Yep, there's nothing classier than cutoff overalls and gingham shirts showing bushels of cleavage, but I let it go and slurped down the last of my lobster before starting on my potato. I like to give full attention to one detail at a time.

"Who else?" I asked.

"Well, there was some bad blood between him and

some of his jock buddies. Think there might have been some Humpty Dumpty going on with the Bomb and their wives."

"Really?" I managed to glance up from my potato. "Which ones?"

"Do I look like a guy who follows football, babe?"

He didn't even look like a guy who'd heard of football, but then he didn't look like a millionaire, either. Life was damned near hilarious.

"But you could find the information again?" I asked, feeling better for the meal and those tantalizing tidbits of knowledge.

He snorted and motioned for another drink. It appeared in seconds, and he started in on it immediately. He hadn't gotten far on his meal, but he was a martini's worst nightmare.

"There was one name I remember though," he said.

I finished off my potato and sat back. My waistband felt tight, as did my shirt. I wriggled a little, hoping to dislodge my under-wire from between my ribs, but Solberg was already staring at my chest, so I settled back and let it dig its way into my lungs "Who's that?" I asked.

He grinned, then shifted his gaze to my face before dropping it back to my boobs. "What'll you give me if I tell you?"

A reprieve from the kick in the groin you deserve, I thought. But I needed info and I needed it badly, so I propped my elbows on the table and gave him a sultry glance. Or maybe it was a post-consumption glare. My seduction skills had never been stellar and had pretty much rusted into nonexistence during my post-secondary education, but I thought I remembered something about men and breasts, so I squeezed my arms against them and felt my bosom swell forward. I should have been ashamed, but the ploy was so horrifically successful I couldn't quite manage it. In fact, I might have experienced a shameful little puff of pride when his eyes started to bug out of their sockets.

"Tell me her name and..." I fluttered my lashes like a llama with a retinal problem, but it was wasted effort. His eyeballs were still glued south of my chin. "I'll accompany you to your house," I crooned.

"Stephanie Meyers!"

It took me a moment to realize what he was saying, but when the truth struck home, my elbows bumped from the table and my own jaw dropped. "Stephanie Meyers!" She had been a rising starlet of sorts. But she'd OD'd on amphetamines some six months before. Not a huge shock to a community as self-involved as the actors' guild, but it had still made the news. "The actress?" I asked, but Solberg was already motioning rather wildly for the bill.

"Wait a minute," I said and, glancing around for a way to stall, snatched up my glass. It was still half full, but the ice had melted. Can't have that. "I need a fresh one."

He was already rising to his feet, albeit a bit wobbly. "Got a full bar at home."

"You won't regret it," I crooned.

He shot two half bent fingers into the air and the waiter disappeared, buying me a few more seconds of relative peace.

"You're sure?" I asked, my mind spinning. "About Meyers?"

He grinned sloppily. "The Geekster's always sure, babeta."

"How long were they seeing each other before she died?"

He broadened his grin, but only one corner of his mouth lifted. I was running out of coherency time. "That'd take more . . ." He eyed my chest and leaned closer. "Investigation," he said. "But I'm game if you are."

Our drinks arrived. I reached for mine and held it between us like a shield. But Solberg had already turned his attention to his. World class.

"What do you know about her death?" I asked, sipping sparingly.

"Offed herself, I think."

"Do you know why?"

He shrugged. "I wasn't the one doin' her. Course maybe that's reason enough," he said, then fired his fingers at his head and brayed like an ass.

"Yeah," I agreed, "probably."

"Time to go," he muttered and, finishing off his drink, struggled to his feet. Judging by the way he swayed, I believed he was right. If I didn't want to have to toss him over my shoulder and cart him out like a bag of turnips, we'd best hit the road. I led the way, but when I glanced back I saw he was having some sort of confrontation with the furniture. It refused to move, and he seemed unable to compensate. Tricky thing, those tables. I returned to his side, grasped his arm, and steered. The stairs were almost his undoing, but after a few close calls we managed to reach the sidewalk. The valet looked a little dubious as he trotted off, but he was back shortly and handing over the keys. I snatched them up first.

"Hey!" There is no one who can sound as offended as a sloppy drunk. "What you doing?"

"Driving," I said and got behind the wheel.

"This is my car."

I showed a little leg and leaned forward. From his vantage point, he'd have a bird's eye view. "I thought you were in a hurry to get home," I cooed.

He made it into the passenger seat with Road Runner speed and Wile E. accuracy, nearly slamming his foot in the door.

The engine hummed to reverberating life. I sighed at the throbbing horsepower and maneuvered onto Beverly Glen. Palm trees cast top-heavy shadows across the boulevard. The western sky glowed with gold. If one didn't venture too far into the heart of L.A., one could almost believe in the City of Angels scenario. As it was, the battle between good and evil seemed to be something of a draw.

"Where's home?" I asked.

He gave me the address, and sure enough, unless he was lying outright it was a posh part of town. I took a right onto Sunset Boulevard and headed west.

"Do you think you could learn more about Meyers?" I asked, picking up speed and sighing mentally at the rev of the motor. The Saturn could squeeze a good forty miles out of a gallon of petrol. But you didn't want to have to be anywhere too fast, or need to impress anybody while getting there.

Solberg mumbled something, but his voice was starting to slur in earnest. ". . . panties."

"What?"

"Can get you the color of her panties," he muttered.

Yeah, well, if I were a perverted little techno geek that might come in handy, but... "Can you find out who's investigating her death?" I asked. My mind was cranking along again. Could Meyers's suicide have anything to do with Rivera's reasons for hounding me? It was a huge long shot, but at this point any shot was a worthy one so long as it was pointed in the dark lieutenant's general direction.

"Easy as an East Side hooker."

I glanced at him from the corner of my eye. "Could I get info about the officer in charge?"

"Right down to the soles on his flat feet."

My heart was bumping along at a good clip. Solberg was staring at my chest again, but his head drooped against his seat which made him seem fairly harmless, if not comatose.

"How would I do it?" I asked, letting him stare.

The following dialogue was such discombobulated mumbo jumbo I was sure it was the booze talking. But I could have been wrong. Technospeak always sounds that way to me.

"How much did you say you charge by the hour?" I asked. Not that I was doubting my ability as a hacker, but...

"For you, babe?" he slurred and slumped messily toward me. I prodded him back toward the door with a stiff arm.

"Listen," I said. I was in dismissive mode again, but I was a little softer now. It's difficult to be really hard-nosed when you know the guy is going to spend the next few hours with his head in a toilet bowl. "I'll go home with you like I promised. I mean, I don't want to see you wrapped around a light post on the five o'clock news or anything. But let's face it, I'm not your type, Solberg." I couldn't quite force myself to look at him. "You deserve someone . . ." I searched for a kind euphemism. "Brilliant. Like yourself. Not me."

He whimpered and I winced. Breaking hearts was never easy, but I forced myself to be strong, to turn and look him square in the eye.

Unfortunately, his eyes had rolled back in his head. And the whimper I thought I'd heard was actually a snore. His fuzzy head lay half cocked against the rest behind him and his mouth was open and drooling.

Wouldn't you know it? I couldn't even keep the Geek God awake. Which was fine. I mean, it wasn't like my ego needed stroking or anything. Still, I have to admit, for just a moment I fantasized about reaching across the leather seat and twisting his nipple until he screamed.

But I was generally against torturing unconscious men, so I just skimmed the Porsche's sleek panels, pushing buttons until I found his GPS.

The drive was easy as pie then. I zoomed up the 405, zipped along the 101, and wheeled into Solberg's driveway like 007 on speed. We came to a shuddering halt in front of his three-car garage, where I turned off the engine and waited for him to be jolted into awareness. It only took a moment.

"Whir im I?" he grumbled, his head doing asymmetrical circles on his wobbly neck.

"Time to get out."

"I don't feel great."

"Really?" I said and hardly even grinned.

"Think I might be sick."

Panic struck. "Not in the Porsche," I rasped. The car and I had bonded. Lunging outside, I sprinted around the sleek grille, hauled open the passenger door, and yanked him out, but apparently the jerky movement didn't do much to settle his stomach, because in a moment he was ralphing into the azaleas.

I turned my back and tried not to follow suit. Finally Solberg moaned. I heard him flop down on the walkway beside the shrubbery and chanced a glance in his direction. "Maybe I shouldn't a had them shots before I picked you up."

I believe it's generally accepted that geniuses are the stupidest people on earth. "Come on. Let's get you inside," I said, trying to keep my eyes averted from the azaleas, but he had already slipped over onto his side.

I stared at him a moment, cursed in silence, and glanced around. It was a good neighborhood and a nice warm night. He'd probably be fine right where he was, I told myself. But my brother Pete had once passed out in my mother's peonies. I had spotted him beside the shrine of the Virgin Mary when I'd peeked out to see if anyone was necking in the backyard and I'd thought it an okay place for him to spend the night.

Mom had emphatically disagreed, and my bottom still remembered the lesson. In the McMullen clan, it's acceptable to drink yourself into oblivion but criminal to leave your brother facedown for the neighbors to gossip over in the morning. The irony didn't elude me then or now, and yet I still felt a need to haul the ragged-assed little geek to his feet.

"Come on," I said, dragging him along with an arm around his waist. "Wake up. I need your security code."

He just managed to mumble the numbers before his head slumped against my breast. I considered dropping him onto the concrete to make sure it wasn't intentional, but he seemed to be staring into the interior of his cranium, so I let it pass and pushed the door open with my foot. A chrome-and-crystal chandelier blazed in the gargantuan foyer. The house ran off in monochromatic sterility in every direction, not a couch or a blanket in sight.

"Where's your bedroom?" I asked.

He didn't answer. I gave him a little jiggle.

"Bedroom," I repeated. The word seemed to bump a few frazzled neurons together.

"Up," he croaked, and I stared up the mountainous steps and began to climb. By the time I'd reached the top I was breathless despite Solberg's minuscule weight and my own extraordinary fitness.

As I shuffled him down the hall, I noticed that only one of his feet was paddling. The other dragged behind him like a dead duck. I shoved open the bedroom door and tossed him onto the mattress.

Unfortunately, he dragged me with him, and with a drunk's unerring accuracy, landed with his hand on my right boob.

"Babe," he mumbled, squeezing.

My breath came back in a rush. I shot to my feet, and it could be I kicked him in the shin, but I'd hauled his bony ass all the way upstairs without so much as a word of thanks.

Grumbling to myself, I found a phone on his glass bedstead and picked up the receiver, intending to call a cab, but from that vantage point I could see his Porsche far below. It gleamed cobalt blue in the overhead lights, looking sexy and ultraelegant. But didn't it look a little lonely, too? Forsaken? Maybe I should take it home. Of course, if I did, Solberg would eventually show up to retrieve it, which meant another encounter of the weirdest kind.

On the other hand, I mused, if I had possession of his car, he could probably be convinced to do more investigating, despite the fact that I hadn't exactly lived up to his fantasies thus far.

Truth was, I was in deep shit. Rivera was heading up a lynch mob and I had no intention of being at the end of the rope when it swung. The more information I had, the better off I'd be, and if that meant I had to take a Porsche home for a visit . . . well, so be it.

5

Men are like beer. Some are bold and some are smooth. But every damn one of 'em has a big-ass head full of air.

—Lily Schultz,
owner of the Warthog, after
her husband's third arrest for
indecent exposure

MONDAY WAS A BITCH. Although I'd mostly agreed with David's advice to take the day off, I managed to force myself into a relatively dignified ensemble and drop the Saturn off at the dealership for a six-month-late tune-up. I took a cab home; then, after a few seconds of intense soul-searching, I fired up Solberg's Porsche and cruised to the office.

Elaine was there, fielding phone calls and rescheduling appointments, but she was wide-eyed and craning her neck at the parking lot when I walked in.

"Wow!" she mouthed, though she never quit her sympa-thetic *um-huming* into the receiver. Elaine is the kind of person who can write a dissertation while simultaneously finding the antiderivative of a polynomial expression. Unfortunately for the cerebral community, she has boobs big enough to ski on and eyes that scream bedroom in five different languages. She has a sultry voice, a nonexistent waist, and an ass that would make J.Lo cry. It was that lethal combination that had convinced her to head to fame and fortune in La La Land. I had no burning excuse to accompany her, except that I had received my Ph.D. while concurrently discovering my latest beau flagrante delicto with my ex-roommate. And seeing as how Schaumburg, Illinois, didn't seem particularly appreciative of my stellar qualities anyway, I'd packed my bags and headed to Hollywood, where everyone needs a shrink.

"Holy fuck!" she said, punctuating the words with the click of the receiver into the cradle. I stared at her. Elaine's father was a Methodist minister which had, heretofore, prompted her to confine her expletives to things like "ah, shucks" and "that's a darn shame." I could only assume she was practicing for one of the many roles she would never get. Elaine couldn't act worth a damn. "What the hell is that?"

"Oh." I'm pretty sure I had the good grace to look sheepish. "I'm just borrowing it."

She gave me a look as she hustled around the end of her desk. "Someone lent you his rocket ship?"

I may have grinned just a little, but I'm sure I was deeply ashamed of myself. "It's a Porsche."

"No shit! Was it the Bomb's?"

"What? No! Why would I be driving a client's car?"

"I thought maybe the rumors were true and you really were doing him."

"If your father heard you he'd turn over in his grave," I told her.

"He's not dead."

"Well, this would kill him. What kind of role are you up for?"

"One that pays," she said and turned toward me with a lusty sigh. When she did that around men, they slobbered like Pavlov's dog. "I need to get a decent..." she began, but just then the phone chimed up.

She answered it on the second ring. "L.A. Counseling."

I could hear the roar on the other end of the line quite clearly, and though the words were indistinct, the tone was self-explanatory. The caller seemed to be experiencing a high level of frustration. In other words, he was pissed as hell.

But Laney didn't even raise an eyebrow. "I'm sorry, sir," she said, her voice perfectly modulated to soothe, "it's extremely difficult to understand you when you scream at that decibel. What did you say your name was?"

The voice lowered to a dull shriek.

"Mr. Solberg, my apologies, but Ms. McMullen isn't in today." She lifted her electric green gaze to mine with absolute innocence. "Stole your Porsche. I'm certain you're mistaken, Mr. Solberg." Her tone was a perfect meld of unqualified certainty and quiet affront, which was amazing, because I'd seen her at auditions. She wasn't going to be the next Meryl Streep. In fact, Pamela Anderson had nothing to fear. "As I'm sure you're aware, Ms. McMullen is the consummate professional. But if you'll give me your phone number I'll make certain she calls you at her earliest convenience."

Thirty seconds later he'd given her six methods of contacting him and proposed twice. It was like that with Elaine.

She hung up the phone and crossed her arms over her gravity-defying chest. "Tell me."

"I just borrowed it," I said, but there was a twist of guilt in my gut that made me hungry for dark chocolate. Being fresh out, I shambled into my office, trying to ignore the spot from whence they'd removed Bomstad's dead body.

She followed me in. "Tell me everything and start at the beginning."

My head was starting to pound. "There's nothing to tell."

"Christina Mary McMullen, *nothing* is what's been going on with you for the last year and a half. *Something* is when you steal a guy's Porsche and park it smack dab in front of your office building!"

I considered arguing. In fact, I opened my mouth to do just that, but finally I plopped my head onto my desk and groaned through my eyeballs. "Holy crap, Laney, I'm in deep shit."

She grabbed a chair and scooted it across the floor. I could hear it being dragged along. "Because of the Porsche or because of the dead guy?"

I moaned again, but the front bell rang simultaneously, interrupting my pity fest. And it had promised to be a good one.

She lifted one finger in a request to hold that thought,

donned her professional persona like a feather boa, and marched through the door.

"Can I help you?" she asked, but the next voice brought my head up like a muskie on a hook.

"Lieutenant Rivera." There was a slight pause. I assumed he was showing her his badge. He had a tendency to whip the thing out like an Olympic medal. "I need to speak with Ms. McMullen."

"Lieutenant . . . Rivera is it?"

"Yes, ma'am."

"I'm sorry, but she didn't feel up to coming in today."

"That's understandable." His voice was unmistakable, as deep and dark as I remembered in my nightmares. "She's been through quite a shock."

"It's a terrible shame. I'm Elaine Butterfield, by the way," she said. I could imagine her extending her slim hand and wondered if he would pass out when her arm squeezed up against her breast. She'd dropped better men with a hello. "Elaine Butterfield."

"You're her secretary?" So he'd survived the handshake. Impressive, but I was still betting on Elaine. She'd been called Brainy Laney in elementary school. About the time she started filling out, the middle-school boys had thought of a few less cerebral monikers, but she'd had the last laugh; she'd only dated outside the district, operating on the idea that fraternizing with your schoolmates was tantamount to incest.

"Secretary and actress," she corrected, but her tone was, as usual, self-deprecating.

"Is that what you were doing on . . ." He paused as if to check his notes. "August twenty-fourth?"

"Audition," she said. "For one Silvia T. Gilmore, Attorney-at-Law, tough but with a soft side. You have a very nice smile, Lieutenant."

I rolled my eyes. Rivera's smile made him look like a cannibal at a fat farm, but maybe he'd given her the genuine article. I was almost tempted to peek around my door frame just to see if there was such a thing.

"So you weren't in the office when Bomstad arrived last Thursday?"

"Had to make it all the way across town. You know how the Five is once we working slobs punch out."

"But you've met Bomstad before. On previous visits?"

"He seemed like a nice guy."

"How nice?"

"Clean fingernails. Nice shoes, that sort of thing."

"And what about his relationship with Ms. McMullen?"

"She liked his shoes, too."

"Anything else she appreciated about Mr. Bomstad?"

"He paid his bills on time."

He paused a moment as if trying to figure her out. I almost wished him luck. Elaine was an enigma in 38C's. "So she never said anything about dating him?"

"Dating him!" She laughed. The tone was perfect. "Certainly not! She's the consummate professional."

"Bomstad was thought to be a good-looking man."

"Wasn't he just." Her voice sounded dreamy. "I have to admit to fantasizing about dragging him into the broom closet myself."

Her acting skills may leave something to be desired, but she could lie like the devil himself. Elaine needed another man hanging around her like I needed a tub of lard stuck to my ass.

"I didn't know there was a broom closet here."

"Luckily, there isn't," she said, and laughed again.

He chuckled in return. I canted my head at the sound, but I was pretty sure I had heard right. "So you'd say theirs was a strictly professional relationship."

"Ms. McMullen and Andrew Bomstad? Absolutely."

"And what of her character?" he asked. "Would you say she is, generally speaking, an honest individual?"

Elaine paused. I could almost feel him lean in, ready for the kill.

"Please speak freely, Ms. Butterfield. I'll make certain none of this gets back to your employer."

"Well, if you want to know the truth..." Another pause. "I think she's too honest for her own good. Do you know what I mean?"

"I don't think I do."

"Well, people like to be...flattered. You know, have their egos stroked. But Christina, Ms. McMullen, she just says things flat out."

"So she's confrontational?"

"Confrontational?" She seemed to consider that for an instant. "No. I wouldn't call it that. Just...forthright."

"Then, in your opinion, she's got nothing to hide?"

"Sometimes she bites her fingernails."

He laughed. "Nothing else?"

"The truth is, she's too good for her own good."

"Then you won't mind if I go through her office," he said, and suddenly footfalls were rapping across the floor.

My mind spun into overdrive, and although my professional image quailed at the idea of diving under my desk, my sense of survival insisted I do just that.

"Well. Ms. McMullen." He was standing in my doorway, his tone as dry as aged chardonnay. "I didn't expect to find you here."

And so I had been right again. He was a shitty actor and a sarcastic son of a bitch to boot.

"Mr. Riverman." I tried hard to imbue my tone with the same cocky nonchalance as his, but I might have fallen a bit short, since I was simultaneously dragging myself out from under my desk. My chair scooted away, but I managed to wrangle it under control and slip between the cushioned armrests. "I didn't realize we had an appointment."

He didn't bother to address that. "You should keep your employees better informed. Ms. Butterfield seemed to believe you weren't in today. But maybe you were under your desk when she checked. Did you lose something?"

My mind scrambled for a dozen excuses before I realized he was toying with me. So I crossed my legs as if I hadn't a care in the world and hoped my ears wouldn't burn off my head like fried tortillas.

"What can I do for you, Mr. Reverence?"

A tic jumped in his jaw. I almost smiled. "When I was reviewing my notes I realized I had neglected a few relevant questions. You don't mind if I ask them now, do you?"

"Well, actually—"

"Good," he said and, reaching back, closed the door in Elaine's face. Her expression as it swung shut was beyond surprised. Elaine hadn't been closed out since she was five years old and knocking on the "boys only" clubhouse. "I'm going to need a list of Bomstad's friends."

"As you know, Mr. ...." I shook my head. My father had once suggested that I was possessed by the devil. In the last few days there had been little enough to prove him wrong. "I'm sorry. What was your name again?"

He gave me a predatory smile. "Rivera," he said. "*Lieutenant* Rivera."

"Right. But as you know, Mr. Reever, I can't give out that kind of information. Client confidentiality."

"Which is, of course, superseded in a murder investigation."

"Murder! You said yourself that Bomstad overdosed on Viagra."

He shrugged with minimal effort, as though I wasn't quite worth the energy of real movement. "That was the original assessment. But further analysis suggests a trace of some additional chemical elements in the wine."

I felt sick to my stomach. "What elements?"

That carnivorous smile again. "I'm afraid that's confidential information, Ms. McMullen. But certainly you can understand my concern, and my need to determine who might have had access to the wine."

My first thought was to drop to my knees and beg him to believe my innocence, but I managed to stay upright.

He sat down on the edge of my desk and crossed his arms. "I don't believe he purchased the wine himself."

My throat felt dry, my hands clammy. "Any particular reason?"

"Several, actually. The Bomb made a good deal of

money, and while he had a host of personal foibles, frugality wasn't amongst them."

I waited.

"A seven-hundred-fifty-milliliter bottle of Asti Spumante retails at about thirteen dollars and ninety-nine cents. That's pretty cheap. But you'd know that, what with your previous experience."

I shrugged, feeling itchy. "I delivered drinks," I said. "That doesn't make me a drinker."

"Really? Even after all those years of being in such close proximity to it?"

"You're in close proximity with crime on a daily basis," I said. "That doesn't make you a..." I paused. "But I shouldn't jump to conclusions."

His lips twitched. "But you know something about liquor."

I shrugged. "Just what any woman knows. It makes men act like asses." I batted my lashes at him. "Might you be a drinking man, Mr. Rivven?"

He squinted his eyes, as if he might smile, but didn't. "What's your drink of choice, Ms. McMullen?"

"I like root beer," I said. "Mug. But I prefer it in ice cream." There was no way he could have known I liked Spumante. Was there? And why the crap would he care unless he really thought I'd killed Bomstad?

"I spoke with a—" He checked his notes. "Mrs. Lily Schultz."

"You called Lily?" Maybe I sounded as shocked as I felt, because his eyes were gleaming like a crazed werewolf's.

"She said you'd sometimes have a glass of wine after your shift." Perhaps he was waiting for me to confess and throw myself upon his mercy, but my mouth was too dry to speak and I strongly suspected he had no mercy. "She mentioned that you liked Spumante," he added.

I was going to be sick, right there in my own office. But I swallowed hard and raised my chin. "I didn't send Andrew Bomstad the wine," I said. "I didn't know he had it. I didn't tamper with it, and I certainly didn't kill him."

Rivera's eyes were as steady as a snake's. "Of course not," he said. "But I thought you might be able to help me ascertain who did so I can let you get back to work." He glanced around as if assessing every detail of my diminutive office. "Or whatever it is you do here."

"Shall I assume you disapprove of me?" I asked. "Or that it's mental health you detest?"

"Although I'm sure you did a wonderful job with the Bomb, I think sometimes your...profession...can do more harm than good."

"Would you suggest my clients all pull themselves up by their bootstraps instead, then?" I asked.

"Or have a stiff drink," he said, "maybe of Asti Spumante."

I tried to think of some snappy rejoinder, but I was out of spunky witticisms. He stood up, managing, once again, to loom.

"I'll need a list of Bomstad's acquaintances," he said. "Anyone he might have confided in."

"As I told you—" I began, but in that instant he pulled a plastic Baggie from his pocket. Inside was a piece of card stock, two inches by four inches and creased down the middle. He held it out to me, but there was really no need. I have excellent eyesight and I could see the words scrawled across the paper in dark, fluid letters. *"For tonight. C."*

"Someone sent him the wine," he said. "Someone with the initial *C.*"

Perhaps I should have responded, but the floor had just fallen out from under me.

"Any comments . . . Christina?"

Holy crap! Holy crap, holy crap, holy crap.

"Ms. McMullen?"

"I always knew I should change my name," I said.

He watched me.

"Maybe to Xenia. To avoid confusion."

"You're maintaining that you didn't send the wine?"

"Repeatedly." My mind was clicking away a mile a minute, but it was all ridiculous. What possible motive would I have to murder my own client? Which was a question the irritating Rivera must certainly have asked. I felt my blood pressure simmer down to a rapid boil. "But I'm sure you know that," I said. "Otherwise I would have already faced a firing squad. Most likely the highly acclaimed LAPD has already found the culprit."

He said nothing. I tried another smile and managed, yet again, not to ralph on my shoes.

"His diary would surely attest to the fact that he and I had a strictly professional relationship."

The silence lasted a second too long. I almost grinned for real as the truth of the situation dawned on me. He knew nothing about the journal Bomstad had begun years before I met him. The journal where he'd recorded thoughts and deeds. The journal which, I was suddenly sure, could exonerate me.

True, the Bomb had turned out to be a lying scumbag pervert, but even lying scumbag perverts keep notes for posterity. "You did find his diary, didn't you?" I asked.

I wasn't sure how to read his expression. There was definitely irritation, but there was wariness, too, and if I wasn't mistaken, there was a flicker of grudging surprise hidden carefully behind his double espresso eyes.

"There are several avenues yet to be pursued," he said.

Several avenues. I would have laughed out loud if I could manage to swallow.

His gaze narrowed the slightest degree. "You're a relatively attractive woman, Ms. McMullen. Did it ever occur to you that Bomstad may have employed your services simply because he wanted to get into your pants? That maybe every word he told you was a lie toward that end?"

In light of recent circumstances, I had wondered something disturbingly similar. And although the question certainly deserved some consideration, it was the words "relatively attractive" that I fixated on. It was childish, but the phrase made me want to yank out his short hairs with a tweezers.

"Whether that was the case or not," I said, pursing my lips and using my most professional/anal-retentive tone, "the fact remains that he did not, as you so tactfully put it, get into my pants."

"Terribly disappointing for you, was it?"

I almost said no. I should have said no, immediately and emphatically with a good deal of righteous indignation, but I'd been raised Catholic. Lying is tantamount to murder, and it was that moment's hesitation that lured that wolfish grin back to Rivera's lean face.

"Hoping he'd be the one to end the dearth?" he asked.

It took me a moment to realize he was referring to my sex life. I think it's safe to assume no one wants her sex life referred to in terms of deprivation.

"*If* you can manage to find the diary," I said, gritting my teeth around the words, "I'm certain you'll ascertain that my behavior with Mr. Bomstad was the epitome of professionalism."

He paused, doing nothing but watch me, and for an instant I was sure he could hear the blood pounding like panicked rhinos in my veins.

"If you think of anything to add to your statement, the L.A. Police Department would greatly appreciate it," he said and, turning away, walked out the door.

Elaine materialized a moment later, looking wide-eyed and a little discombobulated. Apparently, she was no longer Silvia T. Gilmore, Attorney-at-Law. "Remember when Zach Peterson said he'd found your panties in Matt Montgomery's car?"

Sadly, I did.

"But he was lying about the whole thing so you'd tell him how far you'd really gone with Matt?"

"Uh-huh."

"This is similar."

I thought about it in something of a haze. "Except a misplaced pair of panties isn't likely to get me ten-to-life in Folsom."

"True," she agreed, scowling into space. "And Peterson didn't have such a great butt."

6

Maybe knowledge *is* power, but it's damned hard to *think* a burglar to death.

—Glen McMullen,
in defense of the Beretta
under his pillow

THE NEXT FEW HOURS were a blur. By five o'clock on Wednesday my eyes felt gritty and my skull too tight for my brain.

Elaine opened the door a crack. "All is well?" she asked. Her enunciation was strangely stilted, I noticed. She wore her hair tacked up with knitting needles and spoke with the palms of her hands pressed together.

Either she was an imposter or she was practicing for the role of unassuming Japanese secretary.

"I'm fine," I said, too tired to inform her that she was neither Japanese nor unassuming.

She stepped in, mincing slightly. "You know, my friend, the drought only makes the lotus bloom brighter."

I already missed Silvia T. Gilmore, hard-ass attorney-at-law. "Uh-huh. But there's an irritating policeman who thinks the lotus killed its . . . client."

"I believe you are mistaken, madam."

I glanced up, hoping to believe despite her ridiculous diction.

"Indeed, I think he is, how do you say . . . crushing on you."

The singular lunacy of that statement launched me irrevocably back to reality. I laughed out loud. "I'll be lucky if he doesn't crush me into powder."

"Don't be crazy," she said, then drew herself back into character and corrected, "That is most unlikely, madam."

I sighed and managed to push myself out of my emotional quagmire for a moment. "When's the audition?"

"It is in three weeks' time."

God help us. "Tell you what, if I get the electric chair maybe you can watch the execution. It'll give you insight into the justice system."

She allowed a prim little smile. "All will be well for you. This I promise."

"Because of my good karma?"

"But of course. That and because the handsome lieutenant has a boner for you."

My jaw must have dropped, because she laughed, then gasped as she checked her watch. "Oh, crap! I gotta run, Mac. Sorry. Want me to stop over tonight?"

"No. No." I was trying to digest her words. "I'm fine."

She gave me a look, hand on doorknob.

"Really," I promised, but an hour later as I skimmed Solberg's Porsche up the 405 toward home, a thousand frazzled thoughts zipped through my overtaxed brain. None of them were ecstatically happy; I was basically being accused of murder, my car was still in the shop, and at any moment I might be charged with grand theft auto.

And yet, I wasn't ready to relinquish the Porsche. It was my most promising investigative tool and I had even more to investigate now. I needed to find some "*C*" person who might have wanted Bomstad dead.

Mind pumping, I pulled into my needle-sized driveway. Getting out on the cracked, slanted concrete, I wrestled my garage door into submission and carefully pulled the little blue roadster inside. It was a snug and somewhat aromatic fit. Maybe when my house had been built they'd only needed room for two goats and a wheelbarrow. As it was, I was hard-pressed for enough space to pull the door shut and pad around the sleek fenders to reach my kitchen entrance.

Once inside, I glanced into my fridge. Three pears and a carton of skim milk peered back. I opened the freezer, where a package of Snickers bars resided in cool comfort. I didn't really like Snickers bars frozen—why mess with perfection—but it discouraged me from impulse eating. I considered the pears again, then pulled out a Snickers and peeled back the wrapper.

Even frozen it had nutrition beat all to hell. I poured myself a glass of milk and munched contentedly as I peered out my living room window. The dirt in my yard was beginning to crack. I gave that some consideration, licked my fingers clean, and stepped onto the stoop, but something leaped at me from the bushes. I screamed and swung my elbow like a battering ram. The something staggered back, materializing, rather irrationally, I thought, into J.D. Solberg.

"Jesus!" he whined. "What'd you do that for?"

I glared at him as my brain cells filtered back into some semblance of a normal pattern.

"What are you doing here?"

"What am I doing here?" He pulled splayed fingers from his nose, checked for blood, then glared at me. "You stole my damned car."

"I did not steal your car." There was some blood, which immediately fostered a modicum of guilt on my part. "Technically."

"Then where is it?"

"It's . . ." I tried not to cut my eyes toward the garage, to pretend the little Porsche was a million miles away, but I'll never make an actress. A crocodile hunter maybe, or a pirate. Pirates are cool. "In a safe place."

"In your garage?" His voice was starting to squeak. "You got my Porsche in that stinking little hole?"

"No." Thirty-three years old and I still couldn't lie worth shit. It was disgusting is what it was. Probably even pirates could tell a decent lie.

He guffawed and strode stiff-legged up to the door. It listed toward the south as if tired. He grasped the rusted handle and gave it a mighty heave. Nothing happened. He glanced to the right, searching the stucco. "Where's your opener?"

"My—"

"Your opener!" he spat, fists propped on his scrawny

hips. "You might as well hand it over, I can override 'em all."

Ummm. "Not this one," I said. "It's a . . . deluxe ultra . . . ray."

He snorted. "I've never even heard of it."

"It's brand-new." Things as they were, a garage door opener was way down my list of necessities. First I'd need a garage door with more than one hinge. "State of the art."

"State of the art, my ass," he said and turned toward the battered little Beetle he'd parked half on the sidewalk. The residents of the suburb of Sunland use their sidewalks for a variety of purposes: lucky for him walking isn't amongst them.

"Listen, Solberg, I just need a little help," I said.

"I already helped you and look where it got me. I should call the cops."

Panic rushed through me. I'd been threatened before, mostly by prepubescent blood relatives, but still . . . "You're not going to call the cops," I said, and hoped I sounded as confident as I had when James had threatened to tell Mom about me and Micky Jay. But I had had first-hand knowledge concerning a shoe box stuffed with pot that was hidden under James's bed. Unfortunately—or fortunately, depending on your perspective—I'd never looked under J.D.'s bed, and he must have realized my disadvantage because he made a harrumphing noise and pivoted like an insulted Pomeranian.

I said the first thing that came to mind. "Ever heard of sexual harassment?"

He stopped like he'd been shot and turned back toward me. "I don't know what you're talking about."

Oh, yeah, he was familiar with the term, I thought, and I was hardly surprised. A guy like Solberg was probably charged with harassment every time he opened his eyes. "What would they think down at NeoTech if there was another complaint filed against you?"

He turned pale under his newly purchased tan and held up a placating hand. "Listen, just give me back my Porsche and we'll call it even."

It almost seemed fair, but I didn't want fair, I wanted the cards firmly stacked in my favor. "Even?" I shook my head. "I drive you all the way home so you won't wind up wrapped around a sycamore somewhere in Altadena and you end up copping a cheap feel."

"Well." He had the good graces to look chagrined. I wish I could say the same about myself. "That wasn't why you were supposed to drive me home, was it?" I tried to come up with a disclaimer but he was already yammering on. "And—hah! You're not going to call the cops, not with what you got hangin' over your head."

He made an interesting point, but I still needed help. "Listen, J.D.," I said, shifting seamlessly into wheedle mode. "I'm not asking much. Nothing you can't handle."

He snorted as if the idea of any sort of ineptitude was inconceivable.

"Just a phone number."

But he was already striding toward his Beetle. "I'll be back," he said, "and next time I won't be leaving without my Porsche."

From across the chain link fence erected to keep my yard wreckage at bay, Mrs. Al-Sadr stared at me, her dark eyes disapproving between the coordinated fabrics that hid practically every inch of human flesh. I gave her my everything's-hunky-dory smile, but she just turned away. I did the same a moment later, sliding into my little house and locking myself inside.

I spent most of that night searching the Internet for any sort of clues. I came up with basically nothing except a grainy, outdated photo of Bomstad and his ex-fiancée. Sheri Volkers was a blond woman with big hair, a big smile, and big boobs.

Digging through the phone book, I came up with Volkers's number, and although I didn't know what I was going to do with that information, I fell asleep feeling somewhat better for the knowledge.

The sun was shining through my window when I awoke, highlighting every streak of dirt to full advantage. But window-cleaning was low on the priority list, just below buying a chimpanzee and polka-dancing on the moon.

I showered in a fog, thanked God it was currently uncouth to wear panty hose, and shoved myself into a linen suit. My sling-back shoes matched to perfection. I hopped down the hall, dragging on the second one and grabbing a pair of Oreos from the cupboard. Opening the front door, I remembered my Saturn was not yet back from the dealer and simultaneously realized Solberg was sitting in his Beetle and pointing at my garage with something that looked like a remote control on steroids.

He caught sight of me through his open window and swore with some panache. I might have been impressed if I hadn't grown up Catholic.

"What's wrong?" I asked, still fighting with my shoe.

He got out of his vehicle, his contacts gone and his horn-rim glasses firmly back in place. His spidery hair reached out in all directions. "What the hell kind of opener did you say you have?"

I glanced down the street, hoping for some kind of help, but that damned knight in shining armor must have lost his trusty steed again because he was notably absent. I turned back toward Solberg. "Want to give me a ride to work?"

"What? Are you crazy?" His hair seemed to reach new horizons at the thought. "You stole my Porsche."

I found I liked him marginally better when he wasn't leering at me.

"Give me a ride and I'll give you a clue about the opener."

He was swearing again as I squeezed behind the Beetle's dash. I could understand why he wanted the Porsche back. The Beetle was like eating earthworms after filet mignon. Which inexplicably made my mind return to the thought of Sheri Volkers. Perhaps I should give her a call, see what she could tell me about Bomstad. Then again—

"So what kind is it?" Solberg asked, as he bumped onto the 5.

I pulled my mind from my current dilemma. "What's that?"

"The opener," he snapped, looking frazzled and making me wonder just how long he'd been working on my door. "What the hell kind is it?"

"Wouldn't it be easier to just help me out?"

We pulled into traffic. The sun was baking down on us from a faded blue-gray sky, and stinking, fuming vehicles were stretched out as far as the eye could see. The Beetle's fans were working hard enough to blow my eyes closed, but it was still hot on the passenger side where the unblinking sun hit me full strength. I lifted the hair from my neck and immediately felt Solberg's gaze slither in that direction.

"It ain't gonna work."

I blinked at him. "What's that?"

"You ain't gonna wheedle any more information from me with your woman's wiles."

Woman's wiles. Uh-huh. "Fair enough," I said and searched the hills for some sign of sanity. There was none, because houses were stacked like oatmeal cookies along the steep slopes. What the hell kind of a person would build a two-million-dollar home in the desert? I slumped down in my seat, feeling lumpy and lethargic. Traffic was struggling along like sun-baked Galapagos, and I could think of no good reason to refrain from sleeping. True, Solberg might decide to take me to some secluded beach and drown me, but I was too tired to give it much thought.

When I awoke, he was parked in front of the strip mall that housed my office. I yawned and slid upright, feeling groggy and rumpled.

"My buddy's got a yacht," Solberg said, his tone defeated.

I turned toward him and noticed that his magnified gaze had settled on my chest.

"He lets me take guests on it whenever I want."

I stifled a sigh. "I'll give you your car back," I said. "Just get me a couple phone numbers."

But apparently his car was a matter of pride now, because he shook his head like a petulant child. I disembarked and he puttered down the street, leaving me to wander dismally into my office building without the promise of a yachting weekend or the much-needed phone numbers.

7

There is none so troubled as one who thinks himself
perfectly sane.

—*Frank Meister, M.D.,*
professor of Psychotropic
Medications

*T*HE HOURS CREPT BY. Angie Fredricks talked about
her sexual fantasies, which were surprisingly inventive
considering she'd passed the seventy year mark nearly a
decade before. Melvin Osterman told me about the time
he'd bicycled down Owens Avenue wearing nothing but a
smile. It's amazing what some guys will do for a six pack
and a cheap thrill, and Mr. Ulquist, father of two, admitted
he had had a crush on his science teacher who happened
to be male and as handsome as a Greek god! Hormones
ruled the world, but none of their problems seemed to
compare to mine. Some kind of psychologist I was.

Around five P.M. Elaine drove me home. There, Solberg

was sitting across the street in his Beetle. I gave him a wave. He slapped a hand distractedly back at me, and I lumbered into my house.

The phone was already bleating by the time I locked the door behind me. I answered on the fourth ring.

"Chrissy?"

"Mom," I said, sliding into a nearby chair and prodding off my sandals. My toenails were now neon pink thanks to insomnia and lightning-bolt frustration. I prefer to consume a vat of cookie dough when frustrated, but I'd settled on a pedicure instead.

"What's wrong?" Mom's tone was tight, like it used to get when I told her I really *had* been at Molly's house *all* night and wouldn't dream of sneaking out to meet some boy.

"What do you mean?" Just the sound of her voice made me sweat, and I was pretty sure my acne was already reviving itself. "Nothing's wrong."

"You sound stressed."

Two thousand miles away and her maternal instincts were as sharp as a bloodhound's. "Just a long day."

"What happened?"

"Nothing out of the ordinary." Since breakfast. I crossed my fingers and said a half dozen Hail Marys.

"Tell me the truth," she said, her voice deepening like a boxer's.

"The air-conditioning went out on my car. It's a hundred and ten here."

"Well." She sounded relieved, maybe that my problems were so insignificant, maybe that she had proof that she'd been right about L.A. "It's beautiful here. Seventy-four degrees."

"In three months it'll be seventy-four below."

"Keeps the riffraff out. You should move back."

It was an ongoing disagreement. So far I had won, but there was no guarantee that would continue to be the case. I was only thirty-three and not quite ready to live on my own, at least according to Connie McMullen, who was made of no-fail instincts held together with barbed wire.

"What else is wrong?"

Damn.

"Chrissy?" There was already the threat of retribution in her voice. I winced, but at that moment the doorbell rang. Maybe I was being overly optimistic to feel relieved under the current circumstances.

"I'm sorry, Mom, I'll have to call you back. Someone's at the door."

"Who is it?"

I wanted to tell her I was a psychologist not a psychic, but I wasn't brave enough to give my mother lip. I'd almost rather face Rivera, who happened to be standing on my stoop at that very moment.

He wore dark sunglasses and seemed to be gazing into the Al-Sadrs' immaculate front yard when I opened the door.

He turned slowly toward me, removing his shades as he did so. "You an environmentalist?"

"What are you doing here?"

"Are you trying to save water, or do you just hate grass?"

I glanced into my yard, feeling immediately guilty. Growing up, Dad had maintained our lawn like the back nine of Pebble Beach and had duly implanted the idea that

I should do the same. "I've been a little distracted lately," I said. "What with being accused of my attacker's murder."

Rivera's lips flickered, making me wonder if that was his version of a genuine smile. "A little nitrous might help."

I tried to keep up but it had been a long day. Mr. Osterman had presented several photos of his cycling exploits. His belly had been as pale as an onion and just as round. The idea of him biking past elementary school kids like a hirsute root bulb had left me somewhat shaken. "Nitrous?"

"Something wrong?" he asked.

" 'Nitrous'?" I repeated.

"For your grass."

"Do the good citizens of L.A. know you drove halfway across California to give me lawn care advice?"

"We're a full-service police department now."

Was that a joke? Maybe I was staring at him like he'd grown tentacles, because he raised a cynical brow at me.

"I can take a minute out of my yard consultation if you want to make a confession, though," he said.

"Haven't found any of those elusive clues yet?" I asked.

His eyes were Spanish dark, but his hair, highlighted by the late evening sun, showed reddish tints. His lips twisted slightly, as though he found me mildly amusing. "I have *you*," he said, "looking disheveled and available at the scene of the crime."

"Motive?"

He shrugged. "Jealousy."

"Of what?"

"You tell me."

"Listen, there are ten million people in this city. Go talk to one of them. Or read his diary, or—"

He stopped me before I could say something that might make me wish I'd never been born. "I've been meaning to ask you about that," he said. "What makes you think there was a diary?"

I considered a half dozen smart-ass answers, but wisely decided on maturity. It was highly possible I hadn't shown enough of that recently. "Mr. Bomstad made numerous references to a journal. He started it years ago and told me of several entries."

"During your . . ." He tilted his head slightly as if struggling for the proper word. "Time together?"

"Yes. During our sessions." I gritted my teeth. He was intentionally baiting me. Knowing that didn't make it any less tempting to spit in his eye. "I'm a psychologist, Mr. Rover. Remember?"

"Didn't you think it rather odd that a tight end for the Lions would keep a diary, Ms. McMullen?"

"No, I didn't."

"Because he was such a sensitive soul?"

I pursed my lips and counted to ten. "I had no reason to believe he was anything other than what he said."

"Do you consider yourself naïve, Ms. McMullen?"

"Listen." My temper was rising again, which sucked, because El Charro was way across town and I always craved Mexican when my ire was up. "I'm not a criminal. Neither am I customarily in the company of criminals." I gave him the evil eye I'd inherited from my mother and honed in a cheap-ass bar four blocks from where I grew up. "He hired me as his psychoanalyst. I psychoanalyzed.

Second-guessing his every sentence would have made it impossible to help him."

"Maybe if you had questioned his statements instead of believing every half-assed lie, he'd still be alive instead of having his brains sucked out of his nose as we speak."

The image made me feel a little queasy, but since that was probably his intent, I continued on. "Projecting responsibility, Raver?"

"What's that?"

"The tendency to place your shortcomings on someone else. We call it projecting responsibility."

He leaned closer. I could feel the heat of his body. "Just what shortcomings are you referring to, Ms. McMullen?"

The oxygen was being sucked slowly out of my lungs. I leaned back. "I just meant—"

"Where's the damned diary?"

And suddenly everything was clear. I cocked my head to the side, granting myself a better view of his dark features. This was a moment I'd want to enjoy later, possibly while my cell mate etched her name into my biceps. "Let me get this straight," I said, savoring the words. "Did you come here to ask for my help?"

He shifted his gaze away from me for a moment, then looked back and smiled. "You have a rich imagination, Ms. McMullen."

"Ask nice," I suggested.

"I came here," he said, eyeing me cockily, "to find out if you have any kind of *logical* reason to believe there is a diary."

I laughed. I couldn't help it. And for a moment I actually wondered if he might reach out and throttle me. "Am

I correct in assuming, *Lieutenant*, that despite your best efforts, you have been unable to locate Mr. Bomstad's journal?"

"If there was a damned journal, we would have found it by now."

"Oh, there's a journal," I assured him.

"What makes you think so?"

"Because I'm a professional." And I had seen Bomstad's face when he spoke about it. He'd kept a diary, but I was beginning to believe it might not be filled with the kind of heart-wrenchingly sensitive prose I had originally expected.

"A professional," Rivera said and laughed. The sound made me want to shove a tube sock up his nose. It also made me hope to hell I was right. I turned away.

He caught my arm just above the elbow and I froze. I'd like to say I was affronted by his rudeness. But I hadn't been touched by a man since Dr. David's hug some days before, and the idea that my favorite mentor was engaged to Princess Di was still wearing at me a little.

Our eyes met. Something like lightning stroked my belly. I knew better than to fall for another cretin, but Rivera was looking at me with those smoldering eyes, and if I was the kind of girl to believe in chemistry, I'd have said there were enough sparks to explode the damned laboratory just about then. He was made of that lean, tight material that made my saliva glands go all goofy. But then he spoke.

"Withholding evidence is a federal offense, Ms. McMullen."

I gritted a smile and remembered why I hated him. "I

don't know where Mr. Bomstad kept his diary," I said, "but then, I don't have a task force and access to his living quarters, do I?"

He tightened his grip on my arm. "And if you did?"

"Then I'd have the advantage."

He dropped his hand and nodded toward the street with a terse jerk of his head. "Who's the geek?"

I looked over his shoulder, remembering Solberg for the first time. "Just an . . . acquaintance."

One brow rose fractionally. If he mentioned the dearth again, I was going to skip this month's mortgage and take out a contract on his pitiful life. "What's he doing?"

"I'm having a little trouble with my garage door . . . opener. Listen, Rivera, I don't know where the diary is," I said, and stepping quickly back, I closed the door. Or rather, I *tried* to close the door, but he stuck a foot in and pushed it back open.

"Did Bomstad have a safety-deposit box?"

I stared at him in some amazement. "Mr. Reeper," I said, "you believe we were ardent lovers; I maintain that our relationship was purely professional. Either way, it seems unlikely that the existence of a safety-deposit box would arise in our everyday conversation."

"Too busy with other things?"

"Yes," I said, and found I didn't really care what kind of idiotic suppositions he arrived at. "Now, if you'll excuse me—"

"Did he have any relatives he was close to?"

I eased the door open a few inches. "Surely, with the full force of the Los Angeles Police Department at your disposal, you could ascertain that information on your own."

"I'm just utilizing your...expert opinion. You must have spoken about his family on occasion. A mother complex or some such crap."

His phraseology fascinated me. "What kind of relationship do you have with your mother?"

"You thinking she beat me with a garden hose, therefore making me the hard-ass I am today?"

I gave only passing consideration to his hard ass. Really. "Actually, I thought she might be more imaginative. Use a vacuum cleaner attachment."

He gave me a smirk and leaned closer. "Maybe we should stick to the subject, Ms. McMullen."

"The subject being..." I really couldn't remember. He smelled strangely erotic for a hard-ass.

"Andrew the Bomb," he said. "And his relationship with his family."

Oh, yeah. According to Bomstad, he'd been a chronic bed wetter. He was eleven years old when his mother had stopped hanging diapers on the line for the benefit of his hee-hawing friends. "Once again, I'm afraid I'll have to remind you of a little thing called confidentiality." Maybe I really cared about the confidentiality thing, or maybe I just wanted to piss Rivera off. Either way, I was good.

"Ever considered making life easy for yourself, Ms. McMullen?"

What the hell was he talking about? I was Catholic. But I just shrugged, cool under fire. "I'm just doing my job," I said and tried to shut the door.

He blocked it . . . again.

"Hey!"

I can't say who was more surprised by the sound of Solberg's voice. We turned in unison. J.D. stood some thirty feet away, shuffling his feet on my sunken walkway. The garage door whatchamadingy bobbled in his hand. "What's going on?"

We both stared.

Solberg cleared his throat and pushed his glasses up with his middle finger. "He bothering you, Chrissy?" he asked.

Okay, as knights went, he was a little short, had a notable lack of shining armor, and was severely myopic, but still, I have to say, in my heart of love-starved hearts I was kind of touched by the fact that he had actually scrambled out of his Beetle to come to my rescue. And though he took a cautious step backward when Rivera lowered his brows, he didn't launch himself into his waiting vehicle like I had expected.

"LAPD," the lieutenant said, and flipped open his badge. "Who are you?"

Solberg took another step back. His eyes darted to mine, and I couldn't help but wonder if he was thinking about that sexual harassment charge I had mentioned. His mouth moved, but nothing came out.

"This is J.D. Solberg," I said. "A . . . friend of mine."

Rivera shifted his dark eyes toward me. His lips twisted just the slightest degree, suggesting thoughts best left unspoken. But I could see the word "dearth" tumbling around amidst his haphazard thoughts.

If I hadn't been so refined I would have voiced a few of the words zipping through my own head.

"Mr. Solberg," Rivera stepped past my dying arborvitae, "how long have you known Ms. McMullen?"

"Listen . . ." J.D. glanced fleetingly at his Beetle as if hoping to draw it kinetically toward him. "I didn't mean any harm. Maybe I had a little too much to drink is all."

I swear I could feel Rivera's damned brow rise with interest, even though he was turned away.

"How much *did* you have to drink, Mr. Solberg?"

J.D. tried a smile, first at me, then at Rivera. It looked a little green around the edges. At that point I maybe would have gotten him off the hook if I could have, but I didn't know what the hell to do. It wasn't as if my record was pearly white.

"Couple shots of vodka. A few martinis. But I didn't get behind the wheel. She drove me home." He gave me a nod, quirking his scrawny neck in my direction.

"Really?" Rivera turned, deadpan, toward me. "When was this, Ms. McMullen?"

I gritted my teeth. "Listen—"

"I wouldn't have made a move on her if I hadn't been drunk."

It was the closest thing to a real smile I'd ever seen on Rivera's face.

"Just for the record," Rivera said, sober as a monk again, "the two of you were on a date—"

"I wouldn't call it a date," I said.

He ignored me. "Would you call it a date, Mr. Solberg?"

J.D.'s loopy grin made me forget the fact that he had disembarked from his battered steed to come to my rescue. "She wore a little black skirt."

They shared a manly moment during which I considered pelting them both with dirt clods. "So you were on a date," Rivera said. "You overimbibed and made some advances."

Solberg nodded, seeming to think he had found a comrade.

"Which you wouldn't have done had you not been inebriated," Rivera finished.

"Absolutely not." Solberg shook his head vigorously.

Rivera turned toward me. His eyes seemed overly bright. I can honestly say I have never hated anyone more in my life. "Do you corroborate that story, Ms. McMullen?"

I considered telling him to take a long vacation someplace warm, but I cranked up a smile instead. "Mr. Solberg and I had a business engagement."

"To which you wore a miniskirt."

In the Catholic faith, we believe all sins are pretty much created equal. *In which case I might just as well kill him,* I thought, logic working overtime.

"Is it your habit to spend so much time considering a woman's wardrobe?" I asked.

The lip curled again, but he turned back to his new best friend. "What did you talk about on your date, Mr. Solberg?"

I tensed, but perhaps J.D.'s methods of obtaining information hadn't quite been on the up and up, because he lied, and fairly well, I discovered, for a lecherous little weasel. "She's been considering investing in some stocks."

"Stocks?" Rivera repeated.

"I'm senior executive for NeoTech Enterprises."

Rivera's gaze skimmed to the Beetle, and I tensed. "Make a decent income there?" he asked.

Solberg shrugged and puffed out his chest a little. "Got me a house in La Canada and an '04 turbo Cabriolet."

Rivera continued to stare.

"Oh . . ." Solberg jabbed a thumb over his shoulder at the mistreated Beetle. "You mean the car. She—" He shifted his eyes toward me. I gave him a glare that I hoped spoke of dire consequences and possible dismemberment. "She, the Porsche, that is . . ." There were five beads of sweat above his upper lip. "Is in the shop. This is just a temporary ride. Till things get straightened out."

Rivera nodded, friendly to the end. "And what exactly are you doing here right now?"

I felt my stomach lurch. "I don't believe it's any of your concern if a friend helps me with my garage door problems," I said.

Rivera shook his head. "Of course not," he agreed, but turned back to Solberg again. "How long have you two known each other?"

"February 1993," he said.

Okay, the idea that he kept that fact in his head was beyond creepy.

"She was wearing a little checkered top and cutoff overalls." The words spilled from him like bile.

"A pig farmer, Ms. McMullen?" Rivera asked.

"Cocktail waitress," I managed through gritted teeth.

Rivera's eyes were shining. "Ahh, that's right. And you followed her all the way out here to L.A., Mr. Solberg?

My teeth were beginning to hurt.

"I was here first," he said. "Come out most of four years ago to work for Neo."

"So I guess that means she followed you, then?"

Solberg was grinning like an idiot. I was tempted almost beyond control to strike their heads together like melons to see if they were hollow.

"Chrissy and I have something of an understanding," he said, hitching up his pants a little. "We live our own lives, but . . ." He shrugged. "You know how it is."

"I'm not sure I do."

J.D. pushed up his glasses. "Little nooky in the Porsche now and again don't hurt no one, huh?"

"That depends," Rivera said, his voice turning deep as he stepped toward Solberg, "on whether the nooky is consensual."

Solberg stumbled back a half pace, shocked by the speed of Rivera's mood change. Welcome to the dark side of the LAPD. "Sure it was. Wasn't it, Chrissy?" He glanced at me. I glared back. "I mean, we didn't do nothing much. Just a little . . ." Rivera was inches from him now, looming like a gargoyle. "I was drunk. Fell asleep on the way home. Ended up heaving in my bushes."

Rivera glanced at me, his face sober, his eyes still shining. I felt tired. "Is that how it was, Ms. McMullen?"

"I think she might have carried me upstairs," Solberg added in a panic.

Rivera's lips twitched.

"She's stronger than she looks."

"That how all your dates end?" he asked me. "With you carrying your conquest up to his room?"

"Don't you have some kittens to torture or something?" I asked, and he laughed, actually laughed. The sound did something despicable to my insides.

"So," he said, raising his voice slightly. "Would you like to press charges, Ms. McMullen?"

"Charges!" Solberg was jittering like a June bug. "Listen. She wore that skirt, and I was wasted, and—"

Rivera turned slowly back. "Sexual harassment is a serious matter, Mr. Solberg."

"Yes. Yes, sir. I know that."

Rivera nodded once. "I don't want to hear that you've crossed the line."

Solberg was shaking his head when Rivera turned back toward me. "If you have any idea where the diary might be, give me a call." His eyes darkened like dusk. "Or if you're tired of carrying your dinner companions upstairs," he added, and turning, strode past Solberg to his car.

I stared in dumbstruck disbelief. Had he just propositioned me? Was he attracted to me? Were we even the same species?

"Jesus!"

For one lovely moment I had forgotten Solberg still existed. But his panicky tone brought me back to the matter at hand.

"What an asshole!"

I failed to respond, but it seemed like we were both thinking of the same general area.

"No wonder you've been so damned bitchy."

Reality sifted slowly back in. I turned toward my tormenter. Maybe I looked as harried as I felt, because he drew back a little.

"Listen," he said. "Just give me my Porsche back, huh? I'll look into things for you."

I wasn't expecting good news. Not the way the millennium had been going so far, but I could dance to the music if I got a chance. "I'll need some information about Bomstad's football friends."

"Sure. I can do that. Anything else?"

Wow. A little police brutality and voilà. "Not right now, but keep in touch."

"Sure. Ummm..." He shuffled his feet again. "About the Porsche—"

I eyed the Beetle across the street and almost sighed. "Take it with you. I'll return the Bug when my car's fixed," I said, and turned away.

"But, the ahhh, the garage door..." He motioned with his mystical box, antenna bobbing like an alien's.

"There's no opener," I said. "Just stick your hands underneath and pull hard."

"There's no opener!"

I did sigh then. "Good night, Solberg."

I could hear his braying laughter as I closed the door. "You're a snooker, Chrissy McMullen. A real snooker."

8

I don't care what *Cosmo* says about exercise improving sex. Some things aren't worth the cost.

—*Eddie Friar,*
two weeks before he came
out of the closet

$\mathcal{M}$Y HEAD FELT SLOPPY the next morning. I rolled over in bed and groaned at the sunlight that streamed through my window. Chicago may be gray and smoggy and horrible, but at least you have an excuse to stay inside. In L.A., fitness has reached epidemic proportions. It's everywhere. I often recommend it as a stress reliever for my clients, but in actuality, there aren't many things I find more stressful than moving about for no good purpose. I'm never more relaxed than when I'm stretched out in front of the boob tube with a bowl of Häagen-Dazs and a vat of hot fudge.

Nevertheless, I pulled on a sports bra, shimmied into

my shorts, and strapped myself into my running shoes. The lawn crunched under my feet as I stepped off my walkway. Remembering Rivera's insulting comments and Mrs. Al-Sadr's disapproving stare, I wandered around the side of the house to turn on the hose.

Water arced out of the sprinkler, easing back and forth, and for a moment I was tempted to simply watch its hypnotizing rotation. But I could feel the fat coagulating around my waistband and finally forced myself onto the street.

The air was heating up already, but early morning traffic was light. I did two cursory stretches, thought "screw that," and pushed myself into a jog.

Mr. Harendez's roses were in full bloom on the corner of Orchid and Woodland. And up on Grapevine a dog jumped at its fence and barked ferociously. It looked like a cross between a grizzly and an orangutan. I feigned courage and lumbered on past.

Three miles later I was back home, my bra soaked with sweat and my body odor starting to wreak havoc with my still-functioning neurons.

There was a puddle on the lumpy soil beneath the sprinkler, but my lawn had yet to erupt into tropical glory, and though I was pretty sure I should move the sprinkler around, I was in desperate need of a shower and I had no desire to share the water pressure with the yard. I'm a strong proponent of survival of the fittest. It was me or the lawn. Stumbling around the corner, I bumped into someone and almost screamed.

Rivera glared down at me.

I clasped my chest in an effort to keep my heart from

erupting through my ribs. "What the hell are you doing here?" I asked, my voice an abbreviated croak.

He watched me for an instant. "I was concerned about the condition of your grass."

"My—"

He gave me a look that suggested my mind might not be functioning at warp speed. "I'm working on a case," he said. "Dead guy in your office." He took a step forward. I took a step back, remembering my peculiar post-running aroma. Rivera looked as crisp as a lettuce leaf. "Ring any bells," he asked, "or did last night rattle all that dull homicide stuff right out of your head?"

"Last night?"

"He make a habit of staying over?"

I scowled, not following his line of thought.

"Garage door man," he said, nodding toward the street.

And then I spotted the Beetle, still parked halfway on the sidewalk. So then I came to it. The first dilemma of the morning. Should I let him think I was so desperate even the Geek God hadn't wanted to stay, or let him think I was so desperate the Geek God *had* stayed.

"I'd have to check to be sure," I said, "but I don't believe my personal life is any of your concern."

"A guy was found dead in your office," he argued. "Everything's my concern. I have a few questions for him."

"Who?"

He gave me that look again. "Have you got more than one man in your bed this morning, Ms. McMullen?"

My mind rattled around a little more. I can exercise or I can think. Both at the same time is a bad bet. "Solberg?" I asked, reality finally filtering in. "What do you want to ask him?"

"You two so close you field his questions now?"

I wished to hell I didn't care that I smelled like pulverized fish guts or that sweat was dripping out of my saturated hair and into my eyes. "Ask him anything you like, Ribald."

He gave a sarcastic dip of his head, as if grateful he had my permission, and said, "I tried the door. It was locked."

"You tried to get into my house uninvited?"

He shrugged. "I knew you'd want to help with the investigation any way you could. Law-abiding citizen that you are."

The man had balls the size of cantaloupes. Maybe, I thought, and noticed that he wore dress pants today, dark blue, belted low on his rock solid waist. Crap.

"You have a key," he asked, "or is lover-boy supposed to let you in?"

Still didn't know what to say. Still was debating the age-old question about size. Rivera was looking at me funny, like maybe I'd lost my mind.

"I tried the doorbell," he said. "No one answered. You didn't kill him, too, did you?"

My mind clicked back to the matter at hand. Better late than never. "They must think you're a riot down at the precinct."

He gave me that almost smile. "In a scary sort of way."

"Uh-huh."

"You going to invite me in?"

"Uh-uh."

"Afraid I'll be intimidated by your man's sheer . . . magnetism."

I gritted my teeth. "Solberg is not my man."

"Just out for a little nooky like he said, then?"

It dawned on me at that precise moment that he was having entirely too much fun. "I do have some information for you, after all," I said.

"Yeah?" His eyes sharpened.

"Yes. Turns out you're an ass."

His eyes gleamed. "Rouse Don Juan," he ordered. "I'll only take a minute."

And so we finally came to it. I took a deep breath. "He's not here."

There might have been a flicker of surprise in his expression. In fact, there might have been something else.

"Lost him?" he asked. "Running?"

"He . . ." I remembered Solberg's lies from the night before, and since they tended to cover my own rather exposed ass, I decided to corroborate them. "He took a cab home and left the Beetle for me. My car's in the shop."

"An epidemic," he said.

"His vehicle's going to be done today."

"Ahh." Something sparked in his eyes. I didn't like it.

"What does that mean?"

"Nothing. Just ahh."

"It just so happens Solberg and I are no more than friends. In fact, we're not even friends."

"Business acquaintances, I believe you said."

"Exactly," I agreed, and remembering the pond in my front yard, bent to shut off the water.

When I straightened and turned I couldn't help noticing that Rivera's gaze was just skimming up my body to my face. His eyes were smoldering. I swear they were. My stomach did a funky little double loop. But I was sure it was just hunger.

"You run every morning?" he asked. His voice was deep and primordial.

My heart rate jumped up another notch, which it didn't usually do because of hunger. Still, I couldn't possibly be attracted to this man. I was a psychologist. He was an ape. But I'd always thought the ape was the sexiest of the lower primates. I moistened my lips and remembered to breathe. "Most days," I lied, and couldn't help but notice there was a bulge just to the right of his fly.

A muscle jumped in his jaw. He clenched his fists, eyed my chest and took a step toward me. "Got any protection?" he asked.

And in that precise instant my hormones fired up like a kiln. It was stupid. Asinine. But I hadn't seen a man look at me like that for a couple of lifetimes, and if I wasn't ready to apply for renewed virginity I should do something about it quick. Maybe I should have been glad he was concerned about protection, but right then I really couldn't think about anything but the tingle in my shorts. "Yeah." It was all I could manage.

His gaze raked over me, hotter than hell. "Where do you keep it?"

I was breathing like a racehorse.

"Dresser drawer," I managed.

Chemistry burned like a torch between us.

He scowled. "You run alone and leave your pepper spray in your bedroom?"

"Pepper spray?" My voice sounded hoarse. My mind clipped disjointedly back to reality. Pepper spray! Holy crap!

He was staring at me as if I was one bean short of a hot dish. "You don't have a gun in there, do you?"

Oh, fuck!

"Most firearm accidents are perpetrated by their owners on themselves."

"I . . ." I felt faint. And a little sick. "No. No gun."

He took a step closer. My face felt hot. Hell, my knees were blushing.

"Do you know the penalty for lying to an officer of the law?" he asked.

"I don't have a gun. I swear it." If he produced a warrant and found the aging condoms stashed away beneath my underwear I'd have to kill myself—with the rubbers, since I didn't own a firearm.

He was looking at me funny. "But you do have self-defense spray."

God save me. "Of course."

"How old is it? Sometimes the propellant goes bad. The chemical's still viable, but it won't do you a hell of a lot of good if it doesn't spray."

"I'm sorry," I said, wishing quite fervently that I was dead. "You'll have to excuse me. I have a ten o'clock appointment." I turned like an automaton, hoping the earth would swallow me, but it was pretty doubtful, even in L.A.

"I have some questions for you."

"Just bought it a couple months ago," I jabbered. Digging my key out of my shoe, I shoved it into the hole. "Zapped the mail carrier just last week. Worked like magic," I said and escaped into my house like a squirrel into a nuthouse.

9

Booze and boys, ain't nothing in the universe that'll make a girl stupid faster.

—*Lily Schultz,*
when she bailed her husband
out of jail for the fifth time in
as many months

$\mathcal{M}$R. ANGLER." I stuck out my hand like a real grown-up.

Vincent Angler didn't reciprocate. Instead, he stared at me, head tilted back slightly, dark eyes hooded. He was tall, black, and as broad as a freight train. He was also a defensive lineman for the Los Angeles Lions. Solberg had dug up a list of the team's phone numbers as promised and had subsequently given it to me. I had started calling immediately, thinking there was no time like the present.

The first two players had been polite but unhelpful. The third had spouted profanity like poetry. Angler was fourth on the list, and while he had been less than ecstatic to meet with me, he had agreed. Thus my excursion across town to a squat, graffiti-riddled bar called the Hole. Just looking at it made me miss the aristocratic class of the Warthog.

"You McMullen?" I wasn't sure why my name seemed to amuse Mr. Angler, but his expression suggested that it did.

"Yes. I am." My hand was beginning to feel self-conscious.

He nodded and his ebony eyes roved down my midline.

I withdrew the hand. "I appreciate your willingness to meet me."

He gave me a lazy-eyed smile. It was the kind of expression one might see on the face of a cat. But there would invariably be feathers involved. "Was wonderin' 'bout you," he said. He had high cheekbones and arms that bulged like pythons beneath the short sleeves of his tomato red T. He nodded with a thin snort, and his gaze rested on my breasts for an elongated moment.

There's a saying about not letting them see you sweat. I had never thought of it in a literal sense before. Always good to broaden one's horizons, I thought, and wished to hell I had changed out of my office suit. Once again, I was hardly dressed provocatively, and yet I felt strangely exposed in the thin ivory rayon and Gucci sandals. But full-body armor might have been incongruous with the Hole's decor—early pigsty. I had only given his bar of choice a cursory glance upon arrival, but I was feeling paler by the minute and beginning to suspect the clientele hadn't originated on some drafty, northern isle, like that from which mine tended to descend.

Angler leisurely met my gaze. If I encountered him on a

football field I'd run like hell. If I met him in a dark alley I'd be lucky not to soil myself.

He lifted one hand, motioning me toward the bowels of the establishment. I steadied my knees, slipped past him, and slid into a vinyl booth. He eased into the other side, his movements strangely graceful as he draped an arm across the back of his seat. "So you was Bomber's shrink." Something about the way he stretched his arm out across the cracked vinyl reminded me of Bomstad—before he had me racing around my desk like a broken-down greyhound. My bladder felt weak.

A half dozen pair of dark eyes were watching me. All male, all steady. I kept mine on Angler. As if I had a choice. I'd seen snake charmers with less magnetism. "His psychologist. Yes," I said.

He nodded, still staring. I tried a smile. He didn't reciprocate.

"Figures."

"Really?" I tried to sound intrigued but casual. I may have managed coherent. "How so?"

His gaze dropped again. "You got tits."

For a moment I was certain I had heard him wrong. In fact, I turned my head slightly to hear better. "I beg your—"

"Fucker couldn't keep his dick in his jock long enough for sprints."

I tried to think of some sort of response. A question, an answer, maybe a hand gesture. Nothing came to mind. I just stared, and before any earth shattering witticisms sprang into my head, a server appeared.

"Mr. Angler," he said. I creaked my neck to the side. He

was in his early twenties and had a million-watt smile. Even in my current state I could tell he beat the hell out of me in the adorable department. Had I not been sitting across the table from Conan the black barbarian I would have felt like an overgrown troll. "Good to see you again."

Angler gave the waiter a curt nod. "Bring us a pitcher of draft, will ya, Jeff?"

"Right up," said Cutie, and turned away.

The feminist in me cleared her throat before I could throttle her. Damn feminists! You can never trust them to keep their mouths shut. "I'll have an iced tea." Another couple pair of eyes turned toward me. Cutie raised his brows in unison with the corner of his lips. "With a twist of lemon," I added. Because hell, if you're determined to get your throat cut, why not do so with panache?

The waiter raised his gaze to Angler's for just a moment, then turned away with a grin. Angler was staring at me.

"So . . ." It was as good a way to start as any, I thought, and tried to pretend this was just another business meeting. But the word "tits" had eroded the genial atmosphere. "How long did you know Mr. Bomstad?"

"How long you fuckin' him?"

My mind bumped to a screeching halt, then scurried along like a rat in a maze. Should I cut and run, act offended, pretend I hadn't heard him? After a brief internal debate, I settled on a professional tone—no nonsense, but patient. "As you probably know, Mr. Bomstad died in my office."

His lips rose again, showing unreasonably white teeth and a questionable sense of humor. It gave me the chills. "So I got you to thank, maybe," he said, and slipping his arm from the booth, propped both elbows on the table as he leaned toward me. "But that don't answer my question."

I blinked, my mind stalling. "I take it you weren't overly fond of Mr. Bomstad?"

His eyes narrowed, his smile eased back. "Figure that out on your own, did you, Shorty?" His gaze shifted to my breasts again, lingered. "Must be why he hired you." He pointed to his own cranium. "Sharp as a blade." He watched me in silence for a moment. "Where'd you go to school? One of them fuckin' ivy places?"

The professional image is hard to maintain when you're sweating like a stallion. "I don't believe my education has any correlation—"

He laughed, then leaned close and mimicked me. "'I don't believe my education—' Shit, yeah. You're the one he'd choose all right. 'Cuz he could sure as hell put on a show, could the Bomb. You musta thought you got yourself one of your own."

Panic was beginning to bubble closer to the surface, and it was getting harder to breathe. "If I could just ask you a few questions—"

"Dinners at the country club." He put his index finger and thumb together as if gripping crystal stemware. His forearms were as big as my neck. The air felt close and cloying. "Weekends on Daddy's yacht."

If I were in a session I'd say his mood was deteriorating rapidly. As it was, I was wondering what the hell I had been thinking coming here. I *would* like dinner at the country club. And a weekend on someone's yacht sounded fabulous! I forced myself to breathe. In and out, just as if I expected to continue living. "There have been some discrepancies surrounding the circumstances of Bomstad's death."

"Sipping champagne out of your damned—"

"Shut the hell up!" I snapped. I wasn't sure who was more surprised, Angler or me or one of the dozen patrons who stared at us from nearby, but I was too damned mad to care. "I didn't work my ass off just to listen to some overpaid jock yak about something he knows nothing about."

His eyebrows were somewhere in his hairline. "Shit, girl," he said, and grinned again, but it was different now. A little less cannibalistic. He leaned back, stretched both arms along the booth, and seemed to relax a bit. "You got yourself a pair of balls on you."

I cleared my throat, feeling stupid. My professors had been very clear about the necessity of keeping cool in high-stress situations. Dr. David would probably have known Bomstad's shoe size by now and have Angler scheduled for anger therapy two times a week—Mondays and Wednesdays without fail. "I'm sorry. I've been a bit . . . overanxious since Mr. Bomstad's death."

"Overanxious." He snorted as if mildly amused. "Yeah, I 'spect a dead guy in your office can do that." He eyed me for moment, his gaze narrowing. "You have a thing for him?"

His expression was sober now. An honest question. I decided on an honest answer. Just to see how it went. "He'd been a client for several months. Came in for therapy every Thursday night." I drew a careful breath and steadied my nerves. "The last time, he tried to rape me."

Something shone in the recesses of Angler's bottomless eyes. I wasn't sure what it was, but I changed my mind about that dark alley scenario. If he ever accosted me, I'd just slit my wrists and get it over with. He could kill you with a glance anyway.

"Tried?" he said.

I exhaled carefully, keeping my hands steady. "I screamed, kneed him in the crotch..." I planned to go on, but it was harder than I expected. There seemed to be a lack of oxygen in the room.

Silence descended. I fiddled with my napkin, despite postgraduate education. Go figure.

"What you want to know?" he asked finally.

I glanced up. There was a change in his tone. But damned if I could figure out what it was. Still, my grandfather, a wizened little farmer from North Dakota, had admonished me more than once to make hay while the sun shines. "How well did you know him?" I asked.

Angler tilted his head a little, narrowing his eyes. "Know he fucked my old lady."

The words "holy crap" zipped through my mind. I wasn't sure if they reached my lips. "Did you... I mean..."

He watched me, eyes half closed. "Did I see them together? Yeah. At his place. She was humpin' him like a bitch in heat."

My eyeballs were popping out of my head. I felt like the other occupants could see through my skin. Role reversal sucks.

"I'm sorry." It was the best I could do.

"I was sorry I couldn't put a cap in his ass," he said, but

his voice hitched a little. He glanced away. I looked at my lap.

"But I got me a kid. Just turned four. Don't need me no more time in the pen."

"You've spent time in prison?"

"Eleven months in the ant farm. Fucker wasn't worth going back there for." His jaw flexed. I wondered if he had gotten any psychiatric help, but doubted if he'd appreciate my asking.

"Were you friends?"

He snorted. "What do I look like? A fuckin' whack job?"

"Why were you at his house?"

The jaw flexed again. "He said he needed a ride. I was goin' right by and he'd picked me up a couple times."

I didn't mention that it sounded like they were friends. "So..." My mind was spinning like a whirlpool. Bomstad was a piece of work. "He knew you were coming."

"Fucker set the time up himself."

"Any idea why?"

"You're the minimizer."

I gave him a glance. Then, "Ahh," I said, "the shrink."

Our drinks arrived. Beer and an ice tea. Getting drunk was sounding better. Unfortunately, it was not sounding smarter.

"Anything else I can get for you?" The waiter smiled at Angler, then at me, which meant he had to be gay. My luck didn't run that way.

Angler rumbled something I couldn't quite understand. I expressed my thanks. We nursed our drinks, careful not to look at each other for a minute.

"Did you know?" he asked finally. The question seemed

like a complete thought. Luckily, he went on. " 'Bout him. Did he tell you the real shit?"

I felt like an idiot. After all, I had been Bomstad's therapist—there to analyze and assist. But when your client ends up deep-sixed in your office, you tend to wonder if you failed somewhere. Still, I parried. "Sometimes patients are so damaged they find it impossible to share the truth—even with their therapists. There's no way to ascertain why, exactly, but they seem unable to admit the true—"

"What the fuck you talkin' about, woman?"

I looked at him, feeling tired and wondering the same thing. "He didn't give me the real shit," I said. "Just a load of crap."

He nodded, drank half a mug of beer, and nodded again. "You fuck 'im?"

I opened my mouth. He shook his head. "I gave you the real deal. You do me the same."

"No," I said. "I didn't."

"You want to?"

I opened my mouth again. He raised a brow as if he knew I was about to hedge. For a gladiator, he had excellent insight.

"Yeah," I admitted. "I did, kind of."

He smiled. "You're all right," he said, downed enough beer to sink a battleship, and poured himself another. "For a white bitch."

$\mathcal{T}$en minutes later, it was that ringing endorsement that kept me feeling warm and fuzzy as I made my way out of the bar. Angler hadn't offered to walk me out, but he hadn't ground me into sausage, either. So I figured I'd won. I glanced back at him and saw that our server had returned to the table. They were laughing together, and for one paranoid moment I wondered if the joke was at my expense, but it didn't look like that, really. In fact, it almost looked like . . . flirting. Angler glanced up. His eyes were lazy, as if he'd known I'd be watching him. I dropped my gaze and scurried outside. Five or six young men were clustered by the door, opinionated, loud, and intoxicated. As far as I could tell, none of them shared my anemic color, but there was no shortage of intriguing coiffures. They eyed me with interest as I made my way between them. Smoke hung thick as jambalaya in the heavy darkness. California's air quality might be toxic in large doses, but we weren't about to allow nicotine to contaminate our bars, and even the young rebels weren't brave enough to buck that system. But neither were they about to give up smoking. It was a filthy habit. Disgusting, I thought, and tried to remember the slides I'd seen in high school showing smokers' lungs. But lungs looked pretty disgusting under any conditions, and the message had been rather lost on a teenager dying to look cool.

I breathed appreciatively of the blue haze and sidled between the addicts. They barely moved aside enough for me to squeeze through. In fact, one lanky fellow's shoulder brushed my left breast. Maybe it was my own desensitizing profession that made me doubt it was an accident. Maybe I was naturally jaded, but either way I decided to forego all that lovely smoke and hustle toward my car.

I burst past the bubble of humanity and turned the

corner. My chic but professional heels clicked against the walkway. The light dimmed somewhat as I marched into the parking lot, but I had left my newly repaired Saturn as close as possible. Still, I pulled my keys immediately out of my purse, an instinct honed from late nights at the Hog. My purse strap crossed my chest and hugged my bag snugly against my right hip.

I exhaled, relaxing a little. All right, the expedition hadn't exactly been an afternoon poolside, but it had been informative. According to Angler, there was no shortage of people who hated Bomstad. In fact, if I were looking for a murder suspect, it sounded like I could start at the top of the Lions roster and work my way down. Which made me wonder if Rivera was doing just that, or if he had all his guns trained at me. Which—

"Kinda far from home, ain't ya, honey pot?"

The words rasped against my ear. I spun around. Or rather, I tried to spin, but there was already an arm across my throat, dragging me backward. I screamed, but the sound was muffled by a hand. Fear strangled me as much as the attacker. I tried to think. To yell. My throat hurt with the effort. I tried to stab him with my heels. But he was carting me backward, making it all but impossible to stay on my feet, to keep up, to breathe. I clawed at his sleeve, trying to fight free, but my efforts had no effect.

Mace. I remembered it with a jolt and realized I still held my car keys. It was right there, dangling from the ring. I rolled my eyes, trying to see it, but it was no use: he had a stranglehold on my neck. So I'd have to just grab it and spray.

The overhead lights faded as I was dragged backward.

Shadows swallowed us. He slammed me into a car. The door handle dug into my abdomen. I could feel his erection through my skirt and wondered what would happen if I had to vomit.

"Lookin' for a little action, were ya?" he asked and licked my neck, lapping my ear lobe.

I whimpered, feeling sick with terror and nausea.

"I can help ya out with that."

Reaching around me, he yanked the door open. I fought in earnest now, trying to wrestle free, but he was pushing me down and in. I twisted wildly, managing to turn, but he shoved himself up against me again.

"So you want it missionary-style, huh?" he asked, grinding into me.

I opened my mouth to scream but he slapped his hand over my face, splaying his fingers across my nose and mouth, suffocating me. "Shut up!" he hissed. His face was too close to see. He smelled sticky sweet, like pot laced with sweat. "Or we won't get no time alone." I could feel his other hand groping between our bodies, fumbling with his belt. "And you wouldn't want that." His buckle dug into my hip. "'Cuz I'm all the company you're gonna need."

He tried to shove me backward. I fought like a woman possessed, flailing with my arms, but he was too close, too large, too strong. *Think, think,* my mind screamed. But animal instincts had taken over, scrambling my mind, stiffening my muscles.

I remained on my feet as long as I could and then, whether it was dumb luck or some kind of frantic plan, I collapsed backward, folding myself onto the seat behind me. For a moment I could breathe, an instant reprieve, a tiny bit of space, and then I was moving again. Yanking my knee up, I kicked with all my strength. Maybe I was going for his groin, maybe I didn't care, but I caught him in the face. I felt my heel strike home. He roared and stumbled backward. I sprang out, but he was already stumbling forward, spewing curses as he came at me. I screamed, jiggling my keys, juggling the Mace.

My hand closed around it. My fingers shook on the trigger, but I managed to squeeze. There was a hissing sound. He paused for a second, waiting, then chuckled.

I stared in horror at the worthless plastic in my hand, then spun around and darted away. His fingers snagged my blouse, yanking me back. I fell to my knees. He clawed at my back. Ripping my arm forward, I slammed my elbow into his nose.

He wailed like a trapped animal. Limbs pistoning, I scrambled to my feet. He was still down. From the bushes behind him something rustled. Friends? Maybe. But his or mine? Skittering on wobbly heels, I bolted across the parking lot to my car. I jabbed wildly at the keyhole, cursing and praying and crying until the lock turned and I was inside. I don't remember shutting the door or turning the ignition. I only remember screeching out of the parking lot and onto the street.

Something crashed against my bumper, but I didn't care what it was. Unless it was my attacker. Then I hoped to hell it was his head.

10

Life is what you make it. Unless some guy finds you with his girl. Then the ball's pretty much in his court.

—Peter McMullen,
upon being caught with
Mary Lou Johansan

MY HANDS WERE still shaking when I reached home. The house seemed ungodly dark, even when I turned on the lights. All of them. Including the one in the oven. I wiped my nose with the back of my hand, locked every door three times, and limped into the bathroom. Toeing off my shoes, I sat down on the toilet seat and examined my knees. They were black with tar and coagulated blood. My nose was out of control. Reaching over, I tore off a square of tissue and tried not to cry. It was no use. So I plugged the bathtub drain and turned on the faucets, thinking I might as well just weep into the water.

Stripping down was ridiculously painful, as if I'd been

flayed. Every muscle screamed. Bruises marred my lily skin in the most unlikely places. I slipped carefully into the tub and hissed as the water enveloped my scrapes. But eventually the pain eased. I sniffled to myself, slid a little deeper, and finally fell asleep.

Sometime during the night I must have awoken, because I found myself in bed in the morning light.

It was early. I could go back to sleep, except I couldn't, so I got up, stuck bandages on the worst of the abrasions, and got dressed, choosing slacks and a long-sleeved blouse to cover the bruises. Putting on my brave little soldier face, I looked in the bedroom mirror and decided I didn't look too bad.

Elaine didn't agree.

"Mac! Oh, crap! What happened?"

I hadn't even gotten through the door before I started to cry. She came around the desk like a mother hen, folded me under her wing, and deposited me onto my own couch. I crumpled onto the cushions like a broken doll.

Feathering my hair away from a bruise I didn't know I had, she searched my face. "Oh, Mac. Who did this?"

I couldn't come up with anything but a hiccup for an answer. I figure if you're going to feel sorry for yourself, you might as well lean into it.

"Was it Rudy?!" She said the name with sudden conviction. "Damn his sorry ass. I'll kill him."

Rudy. The name rang a distant bell in my fuzzy brain. He had been the center of my universe about two years back, but the memory hardly even registered anymore, even though the final months of our relationship had been less than congenial. Compared to the parking lot incident, his bullying seemed like poetry. I shook my head and attempted to pull myself together. It was like trying to box up the wind.

"Why didn't you call me? Where were you? I would have come. Did you tell the cops?"

The thought of the police brought on a fresh bout of self-pity. I'm not sure why. Maybe I still had enough Midwest naïvete to think they should have protected me.

"You have to call—Oh, no!" Elaine said. "It wasn't that lieutenant guy, was it?"

I shook my head and exhaled carefully, feeling stupid and shaky in equal measures. "I was at a bar."

"With who?" She rose to her feet like a playboy pugilist. "Give me his name. He'll be sorry he was ever born."

It might be that I actually laughed, but the noise I made sounded a little gruesome. "I'm all right."

"No, you're not, honey," she said, and sat down cross-legged on the floor beside my feet. "You're a mess. What happened?"

I gave her the short version. It was more fun than the long version, and not so long.

She was shaking her head and holding my hand when I finished. "You've got to go to the police."

I think I cringed. I'd had my share of L.A.'s finest in the last couple days. "And tell them what? That I was jumped by a guy I couldn't see, couldn't identify, and probably have never met before?"

"You must have some idea how he looked."

I shook my head. It hurt. "He was . . ." I took a brave breath. "So close. And it was dark. I couldn't seem to . . ."

"You should go home."

"I have appointments. Don't I?"

"I'll cancel them."

"No." I straightened. Man, I was one tough chick. "I'm all right."

"Mac—"

"I don't want to go home," I said, and that was the truth. She must have seen it in my expression, because she finally dragged out her super-size makeup kit, covered my bruises to the best of her considerable ability, and sent my clients in one by one.

Actually, listening to other peoples' problems turned out to be rather therapeutic. Maybe I should have offered to pay them. But I didn't bring up the suggestion.

Elaine insisted on staying late, despite her yoga class, but in the end I made her leave. After all, I'd been accosted twice in a week. What were the chances of a third time? They must be astronomical.

Mr. Lepinski showed up right on time, looking nervous as he took his usual spot on the couch, crushed up against the right cushion, bony knees pressed together, fingers curled atop them.

"I can't believe he's dead. The Bomb." He shook his head, eyes wide behind thick, round spectacles. "What happened?" His whiskers twitched. "I heard he had an overdose."

"Yes." I felt drained and ancient. "It's a terrible tragedy." But my lying skills were improving.

Mr. Lepinski left at 7:56. By the end of his session, I felt like falling face forward onto my desk. I thought I heard him talking to himself on his way out the door, but at that point I didn't hold it against him. There are worse things.

"Long day?"

I almost screamed as I jerked upright. Damn the odds! They were obviously stacked against me.

Lieutenant Rivera stood in the doorway, his brows furrowed like storm clouds. "What happened?"

I felt immediately self-conscious, as if I'd done something wrong. As if I shouldn't have been in that bar, that part of town, with those people. As if it were my fault that I'd been attacked. I needed my head examined.

"What are you talking about?" I asked, and was glad Elaine had never convinced me to try acting. They'd have run me out of L.A. on a rail.

Rivera took a step forward. "Who hit you?"

"No one. I . . ." I searched for a lie, though I really didn't know why. "I thought I heard something in the kitchen last night. I fell down the . . ." Not the stairs. That story was as old as dirt. "I ran into the chair . . . in the dark."

"Really?" he said mildly, but his eyes were as black as sin and he was already reaching across the desk and jerking up my sleeve. I winced at the exposed bruise, though I couldn't guess how it had gotten there. He raised his gaze to mine. Anger burned like a bonfire. "Table attack you, too?"

I jerked my arm away. The movement hurt like hell.

"Who did that?" His voice was deep and low and for a moment I almost thought he might actually care. But then I'd once fallen for a guy whose name was Brutus. Really. On his birth certificate and everything. Enough said.

"I just . . ." I paused, trying to think. It was hard. "Went out for a couple of drinks. After work last night . . ."

He waited. Damn. I was hoping he'd get bored and go home.

"When I went outside . . ." My voice cracked. I cleared my throat. "You're right about the Mace." Clever segue. "It was outdated after all."

As swearing goes, he was aces at it. I listened for a while, impressed despite my Catholic education. "What the hell were you doing out alone at night?"

I stared at him. Somehow that hadn't been the aspect I thought he'd fixate on. "Still America," I said. "Remember?"

"Where were you?" His eyes looked flat and steady.

I rose to my feet, brusque but polite. "I'm so grateful for your concern, Mr. Lieutenant," I said, "but—"

"Where the hell were you?" he asked, and grabbed my arm.

I must have cringed because he looked almost guilty as he loosened his grip.

"East side," I said. Guilt. From this guy. I couldn't help but be fascinated. Maybe he thought he should have protected me, too. And he wasn't even a midwesterner.

"Where at?"

I couldn't quite meet his eyes anymore, even if he was looking guilty. "I believe the establishment was called the Hole."

The room went uncomfortably silent, so much so that avoiding his gaze became more difficult than holding it. A muscle flicked in his jaw. I thought he was probably swearing again, but it was silent this time. That must be why he was so good at it. One can't overestimate the value of mental preparation.

"Why?" he asked.

I considered pretending I didn't know what he was talking about but figured he'd just explain himself, and I was getting more fatigued by the minute.

"I met a . . . friend there."

"Who?"

"Listen—"

"Who?"

"Vincent Angler."

It took a moment for the name to register. When it did, I thought I saw his face flush a little. Hmmm. "Lineman? For the Lions?" he asked. His voice was suspiciously devoid of inflection.

I nodded.

He drew a breath through his nostrils. They flared. I was pretty sure it couldn't be sexy. "You going to explain why you're meeting a known felon at a bar in a shitty part of town, or should I guess?"

I was right. It wasn't sexy, and I hated his patient tone. "It just so happens that a man died in my office a week ago today," I said. The view looked better from my high horse. "I simply hoped to ascertain—"

"Ascertain!" The muscle in his jaw jumped again. "You're lucky he didn't ascertain your pretty ass."

I didn't know what to address—the fact that his statement made no sense whatsoever, or the fact that he'd just complimented my ass.

"He wasn't the one who attacked me."

He took a deep breath and seemed to steady himself. "Who was it?"

"I don't know."

He paused a second, then, "How'd he look?"

And here came the tricky part. "I don't know."

"What do you mean you don't know? Someone beat the hell out of you less than twenty-four hours ago. You must have a physical description."

"I was preoccupied. With surviving."

He didn't find me amusing. That happens sometimes.

"How tall was he?"

I thought about that for a moment, though the images made me feel shaky again. "About my height. Maybe an inch or two taller."

"How old was he?"

"Really, I don't—"

"How old?"

I blew out a martyred breath. "Twenties, thirties?"

"White or black?"

And here was the really funny part. "I'm not sure."

He looked at me like I'd lost my already questionable mind. "Now's not the time to be politically correct, Ms. McMullen. Was he black?"

"It was dark," I said. "He might have been green for all I know. And . . ." The thought came to me suddenly. "I think he might have been wearing a mask."

"A mask?"

"Yeah." My mind was tumbling over itself suddenly trying to unravel the facts. "The type skiers wear."

"What color?"

It seemed like a strange question. "Black."

"Was his skin white around his eyes?"

I really couldn't remember and told him so.

"How about his speech patterns. Ghetto? Middle-class? Latino?"

I thought about that for a minute. "Kind of African American. Or more—ghetto wannabe."

"Was he waiting for you when you got to your car or did you see him cross the parking lot?"

"He just..." It was getting harder to breathe. "There all of a sudden. Right behind me."

"And you never saw his face."

"No."

"What made you think it might be a mask?"

"When I kicked him, it didn't quite seem like I struck skin."

His brows rose. The room went silent. "You kicked him in the face?"

Was that against the law? I mean, he had been trying to rape me. Surely even in L.A. self-defense was considered acceptable behavior.

"You'd better start at the beginning," he said, and though I argued, he finally won out.

Forty minutes later I was feeling like a whipped poodle. Rivera was sitting a few inches away in the roller chair I'd abandoned. He'd pulled it out from behind my desk and prodded it up to the couch where I huddled.

"Your life always this exciting?" he asked.

I figured a romance novel heroine would tell him this had been a dull week, but I wasn't feeling either romantic or heroic just then. "Do you still think I killed Bomstad?"

He didn't answer. "Where's your receptionist?"

I vaguely wondered if he was already in love with

Elaine. That would just about cap off the night. "Yoga," I said.

"And you didn't think to lock your door? Even after last Thursday?"

"I was playing the odds," I said. "What are the chances?"

He looked at me funny. Go figure.

"Come on. I'll drive you home." He rose to his feet, leaving me staring at his crotch.

"Ms. McMullen?"

I realized the direction of my gaze and jerked to my feet. "Oh. No. I'm fine."

The funny look had expanded. I turned away, looking for my purse . . . or something.

"You're one entertaining woman. I'll give you that."

I stopped my search and stared at him. "I'm glad you find me amusing."

He laughed. The sound was deep and quiet, and almost . . . admiring. But not for a minute . . . not for one damned second did the sound intrigue me. Really.

11

Analyzing dreams is much like walking on water.
There are a limited number of people who do it well.

—*David Hawkins, M.D.*

I DREAMT ABOUT RIVERA that night. He was Batman.
Unfortunately, I wasn't Catwoman, all sexy and sleek in
black leatherette. I wasn't even Robin. I'm afraid I may
have been the Joker, but that part was a little fuzzy. I
know, though, that Rivera looked really hot in his cod-
piece and cape.

"Solberg," I said, speaking directly into the receiver. It
broke my heart that I had the Geekster's phone number on
my Rolodex, but then the rest of the week hadn't been that
great, either. "It's Christina."

"Hey!" He sounded happy to hear from me. Apparently
he was the forgiving sort, but I was afraid that wouldn't

last long. And how depressing was it that a guy like J.D. Solberg would get tired of me? "You talk to those football players?"

"Yeah, I did."

"How'd it go?"

Well, I'd been attacked, bruised, and nearly raped. Not so good really. "All right."

"That info wasn't easy to come by. For big macho guys, they're sure private 'bout their numbers."

Uh-huh. "I need some more information on Rivera."

The line went silent, then, "No way."

"Listen, Solberg—"

"Absolutely not. That guy's just looking to put me away."

Okay, Rivera could be a little hard-edged sometimes, but still, the seeping drama seemed a bit over the top even for a Geek God.

"Put you away? What are you, some kind of desperado, Solberg?"

"Laugh if you want to."

"Come on. I let you have the Porsche."

"It's my car." His voice had gone all squeaky and self-righteous.

"I just want a few details."

"Why?"

And now we came to it. I wanted to tell myself that I needed to understand my nemesis—to figure out how best to outwit him. But as some poor sap had once said, we've met the enemy and he's us—or something like that. I wondered vaguely if the author's hormones were out of control, too, if he'd dated a couple dozen losers who'd taught him better than to fall for the wrong sort. If, perchance, he'd felt it necessary to investigate anyone he'd had a wet dream about just so he could stave off any idiotic emotional attachments. Sigh.

"He thinks I killed Bomstad," I said.

"What?"

"Come on, Solberg." I was tired and crabby and pretty sure I was premenstrual. "Don't be an ass."

"I'm not the one who stole your car."

"And I'm not the one who's being charged with sexual harassment." It was a cheap shot. Did I mention that I was premenstrual?

There was a prolonged silence that boded ill. Note to self: Never let a techno geek think too long. "What'll I get out of it?"

Oh, crap! Visions of me naked on the Internet danced in my head like sugarplums, whatever they are. Or maybe he'd go for the big one this time. Instead of him ralphing in the azaleas, we'd be—

"I'll do it if you'll hook me up with your secretary."

My X-rated visions screeched to a halt. "What?"

"Eileen, Arlene—"

"How do you know Elaine?"

"Saw a picture of her on the 'Net. She's scorchin'."

I couldn't get him a date with Elaine. I liked Elaine. "Sorry," I said. "But she's not . . ." I paused, searching for a euphemism.

"Brilliant? Like me?" He brayed. "Hey, don't sweat it. I'm tired of brainy chicks anyway."

I had been going to say she wouldn't be interested in an irritating little monkey with bad hair. But sometimes it's best to try to control our hormones no matter where we are in the mad cycle. "She's seeing someone," I said.

"Well . . ." He laughed again. "I ain't going to ask her to bear my children. Though with my brains and her looks." Bray. "Or vice versa . . ."

I was starting to get a headache. "I'm afraid you're going to have to make your own conquests, Solberg."

"Hey, you can leave the conquesting up to the Geekster. I just want you to put in a good word for me."

But I couldn't think of any good words. "I'm sorry, really—"

"Yeah, and I'm sorry you've been accused of murder."

He may be a weasely little geek, but he was sneaky, too.

"Get me the info," I said. "I'll see what I can do."

Some therapists take Fridays off. So apparently some therapists don't have sewage systems that are older than God and periodically threaten to erupt like Mount Vesuvius gone mad. Personally, I need money and generally put in extra hours on Fridays. Clients often want special help to get through the weekends—when they spend time with their loved ones, a phrase often used rather loosely.

Still, sometimes things work out. Sometimes my occupation has a purpose. Sometimes people's lives actually improve.

"I told Kelly I couldn't see him anymore."

It was late afternoon. I was behind my desk. Angela Grapier sat on the couch with her legs curled under her like a lost puppy. Her latest boyfriend's name was Kelly. He'd introduced her to Ecstasy and unprotected sex. Kelly should be shot with a tranquilizer gun and turned loose in Tanzania with the rest of the wild animals. But I kept that opinion to myself.

"How'd that go?" I asked instead.

"Oh." She sighed. At sixteen, she was cute as a button and small as a pin. She had a tiny ring through her left nostril and a cluster of stars tattooed below her right ear. Generally, I'm against piercing living flesh, but she made it look so appealing, I had to repeatedly fight the urge to pick up the hole punch. Of course, I could always call Tats "R" Us, but I'd been to that particular establishment some years before and learned a valuable lesson from the experience: Do not, under any circumstances, visit a man called Whack when you're drunk and infatuated.

"It was hard, you know, but I don't wanna..." She fiddled with the strap of her backpack. I let her fiddle. It was tough being thirty-something, but it was hell being a teenager. Don't ask me why. It seems like they have everything, and maybe that's the problem. Maybe Homo sapiens were meant to be fighting off saber-toothed tigers while foraging for berries. We have no idea how to be happy when things are swell. "Ally ran away from the halfway house again."

Ally was her older sister. She was officially a lost soul. Bringing her back from the abyss was going to take more than therapy. Direct intervention from God might not even do it. But there was still hope for Angela. Her mother was a first-rate twit, but her father cared—enough to send her to me anyway. Enough to tell her to stay away from Kelly the animal. Folks had to be damned brave to become parents these days. Or drunk.

"I thought she'd maybe make it this time," she said, referring to her sister again. "I thought, you know . . . she was gonna be all right." She glanced at the Ansel Adams. There were tears in her eyes. "But she's not gonna be, is she?"

Shit. "I don't know," I said, carefully keeping my tone in that beige, neutral zone.

She turned her gaze to me. She had eyes like a beagle puppy, big and brown and soft. If I were her dad I'd have moved to the Antarctic with her by now. Keep her in layers of goose down and feed her whale fat.

"But I do know this," I added. "The choice is her own. Just like yours is. You can make anything you want out of your life."

She watched me as if assessing the honesty there. Luckily, the past few days had drained me of lies.

"You really believe that?"

"Bill Clinton grew up poor and fatherless."

She thought about that for a second. "I've got enough people hounding me. No way I need the Secret Service on my ass."

She had the ability to make me laugh. Even when things were really grim. And things were often pretty grim for her.

"Eminem's classmates put him in the hospital," I said. "Now he's a millionaire."

"You listen to Eminem?"

"Me? No. Strictly polkas."

She smiled. "How old are you, Ms. McMullen?"

'Bout ninety, going on Methuselah. "I'm thirty-three."

"Hmmm." I wondered if she could imagine what that meant. "Did you ever . . . you know . . . screw up?"

Oh, man! "I made some mistakes," I said. I may have been all out of lies, but I could hedge like the devil himself.

"Yeah?" She cocked her head at me. My profs had been pretty clear about the importance of refraining from sharing too much information with clients, but this one's eyes were still misty. A misty-eyed beagle puppy. That's hard to fight. "Like what?"

Screw the profs. "Well, for starters, I had an eating disorder."

"Like anorexia?"

"Not exactly."

"Bulimia?"

"I was a compulsive overeater."

"No way!"

"My father called me Pork Chop."

"He did not."

"God's truth," I said. No one could accuse Glen McMullen of being overly sensitive.

"You were fat?"

"My brothers suggested using me for a cage ball." My brothers should have been hung up by their thumbs and beaten with a broom.

She gave me a look. "But you're so skinny now."

I sat there for a moment, let the ragged feelings of inferiority wash away, and contemplated adopting her. Screw her father and his good intentions. "I don't think I'm skinny, but thank you."

"My mom's always fighting her weight. Says I'll get fat someday, too. Like she can't wait."

"It's just another choice, Angie. Like drugs and school

and boyfriends. Sometimes people like to believe the stars are aligned against them or something. But it's just because they're scared, or weak."

"I'm scared," she said. Her voice was very small and a little broken.

I could convert my office into a bedroom for her, I thought. I could read her stories and make her popcorn. It wasn't as if I ever had overnight guests anyway. "It's a scary world sometimes. But you're not weak," I said.

"Ecstasy makes you forget all the shit."

"But all that shit's still there when you come back," I reminded her. "And then you have the shit and a drug addiction."

"Yeah." She sighed.

"Tell you what, maybe you can just stay clean until I see you again," I suggested.

"A week?"

"Yes."

"Then what?"

"Then we can talk about it. See how you feel. Figure out what needs changing and how to change it."

She gave that some thought. "Okay."

The Hallelujah chorus blasted through my mind. "Good," I said and managed to refrain from begging her to move in with me.

I mowed my lawn on Saturday. Or rather, I mowed my weeds and did some swearing as I paced behind my antiquated Yard-Man. I believed what I'd told Angie, that we make our own destiny and all that crap. But I didn't like the direction it took my thoughts. Because if I was going to make my own destiny, I'd damned well better do something to keep my ass out of jail.

But there wasn't that much I could do besides talk to people. And the last time I'd done that had been something of a disaster. Who had attacked me? And why? Was it just some random hooligan or did it somehow tie into Bomstad's death?

The memories made me feel queasy and paranoid. I glanced over my shoulder. Mr. Al-Sadr was staring at me from across his fence. I wasn't sure if it was because my grass was nine inches long or because my shorts were approximately the same length.

I didn't give him my hunky-dory smile because I had discovered a terrible truth. I was scared, too, and it was time to do something about it.

12

A pig's a pig, until you really get to know 'em. Then he's a pig with a soul.

—Cousin Kevin McMullen,
porcine expert

MS. VOLKERS." I extended my hand. Sheri Volkers took it in her own. She had once been Andrew Bomstad's fiancée and apparently wasn't mourning his death enough to abstain from adhering little pink hearts to her fingernails. She gripped my hand as though she were afraid they might fall off. "Thank you for meeting me."

"Yeah, sure. What'd you want?"

"Just to talk," I said. We were already being ushered to a table. The Elephant Ear was fairly empty for a Sunday afternoon.

" 'Bout Bomber?"

"Yes." I slid into the booth across from her.

"You was his shrink?"

I was becoming a little tired of the word "shrink." I felt like I should pull my hair atop my head and put a bone through my nose. "His psychologist. Yes. For several months."

She nodded. Her hair was platinum blond but for the dark roots, and her face was plump and pretty. "You boink 'im?"

Wow. Another recurring theme. Who would have expected that?

"No," I said. "My relationship with Mr. Bomstad was purely professional."

She looked at me from under her kohl-black lashes and smiled as if she knew something I didn't. I decided I didn't like Sheri Volkers very much. I also decided she probably didn't know a whole lot I didn't. But maybe that was just the bitch in me. I'd been right the other day. I had been premenstrual. Now I was dangerous.

A chipper little waitress trotted up. We placed our drink orders. Sheri had a whiskey sour but I, classy to the end, stuck with iced tea. If I was going to be attacked in the parking lot again, I wanted to be fully cognizant. I also wanted to have an Uzi handy. Unfortunately, I hadn't even managed to pick up a new can of Mace. But it was full daylight, and the bogeymen seemed fairly distant. Besides, I was menstruating. The boogies would have to be suicidal to try anything.

"What's good here?" Sheri asked, opening her menu.

I wondered if I would seem cheap if I suggested the soup. Probably.

In the end she ordered a porterhouse. Damn her. I love

porterhouse. I ordered a chef salad with dressing on the side and almost felt more haughty than jealous.

"So?" She finished off her first drink, glanced around for the waitress, and eyed me again. "What'd you wanna know?"

"Nothing very specific, I'm afraid. As I said, I had been seeing Mr. Bomstad for several months, and some of the information he gave me didn't quite match up with recent events. I'm simply trying to justify—"

She snorted, halting my clever soliloquy. I gave her a moment to explain. She took a slug of her drink instead.

"Something wrong?" I asked.

"I heard he died with a hard-on big as my pocketbook."

Ahhh, good, the news was out.

I gave her a somber expression. "I was seeing him for an impotency problem which—"

She snorted again. The waitress appeared at our table and Volkers handed over the glass without glancing up.

"The Bomb," she said, leaning forward as if we had a secret, though she failed to lower her voice, "...was a friggin' animal in the sack."

Good to know, I thought. And I was sure the other patrons were just as appreciative as myself. I refrained from glancing around to confirm. "So you don't think he had any...difficulties in that department."

She snorted again. I fantasized about sticking an ice cube up her nose. "He didn't have much upstairs. Ya know?" She tapped her skull, as if hers was chock-full of government secrets. "But his main floor was well stocked." She grinned. "Only..." The grin faded, replaced by peeved resentment. Her drink appeared. She slurped it down. "He couldn't keep his front door locked. Ya know what I mean?"

Cryptic, but I thought I could decode it. "How long did the two of you share an apartment?"

She shrugged. Appetizers arrived. Mozzarella sticks. There are days when I would gladly sell all three of my moronic brothers into slavery for a mozzarella stick. This was one of them.

"Most of a year," she said. I eyed the appetizers and tried not to drool. "The bastard couldn't go a full month without boinking some bimbo."

"Is that why you left him?"

She licked cheese fat off her fingers. "That and the fact that I met Matt."

"Matt?" I said.

"Friend of Bomber's. He didn't have the Bomb's ammunition, but he was loaded just the same. You know what I mean?"

I was pretty sure she was mixing metaphors, or maybe she was just into guns. "How did Bomber take your leaving?"

She scowled, which made me guess that the Bomb hadn't cared all that much. I could commiserate. Sometimes you had to kill them or leave them, but it never hurts if they beg a little. "Turns out he was doin' some high-school slut."

"Did he tell you that?"

Our meals arrived—my fodder and Sheri's cow. Luckily, she could eat and talk at the same time. I had the same talent, but I didn't like to show off. "Locker room gossip," she said and sliced into her meat. Some restaurants won't serve beef rare. This wasn't one of those places.

"Was he still seeing her when he died?"

She shrugged and ate.

"Do you know her name?"

She scowled as if trying to think. If her expression was any indication, the process was brutally painful. "Druella or Duane or something."

"Duane?" I'm not a sarcastic person by nature, but judging by the last million people I'd met, the name seemed unlikely.

"Something like that," she said, speaking around the half-masticated side of beef. I considered snatching away the remainder and holding it for ransom.

"Did her name start with a D?" I guessed.

"Yeah."

"Denise, maybe?"

"Naw."

"Dena?" I realized this process could take a while, but I didn't have any better ideas.

She canted her head, chewing madly. "Deannnn. Dana!" She said it with some pride and took a giant gulp of booze to celebrate.

"Dana? Are you sure?"

"Yeah."

"Do you know her last name?"

She rolled her eyes. "We weren't exactly pen pals, if you know what I mean."

"I don't remember hearing about her," I said. "On the news."

"News!" she said and snorted so loud I was afraid the

cow might come charging out of her nose. Maybe I wasn't as hungry as I thought I was. "Bob woulda taken a slug to the heart before he let a juicy tidbit like that slip out."

"Bob?"

"He was a coach or something, but if you ask me he was nothing but a friggin' pain in the ass. Bomber couldn't take a piss without Bob knowin' 'bout it."

"Would he know where the Bomb kept his diary?" It was my prime question, my number-one reason for watching her slurp down the steak I was paying for. It was casually couched between a delicate bite of lettuce and an elegant sip of tea.

"Diary!" she said and cackled like a demented laying hen. "The Bomb didn't keep no friggin' diary. He could barely write his own name."

*I*t was dark when I got home that night. Armed with the coach's full name and a little more knowledge than I'd started the day with, I checked the street twice before I unlocked the Saturn's door and scurried up toward my house. My security light was dim and the trek murky.

"Shorty."

I gasped, spun toward the sound, and dropped my keys. They clattered on the concrete like shattering glass. A giant shadow stepped from the darkness beside my front door.

"Stay back! Stay right where you are!"

The shadow didn't listen. "I had me a visitor, Shorty."

I recognized him in a second, but the realization did

little to soothe my skittering nerves. "Mr. . . ." My chest was crushing my heart like a squeeze box. "Mr. Angler?"

"I gotta tell you, girl, I don't like cops."

"Oh, shit!" The words slipped out on a breath. "Rivera?"

"Yeah." He was close now, sharing the stoop, so close I couldn't bend to pick up my keys, even if I dared shift my gaze from his. "Rivera." He stepped closer still. "You send him by?"

I managed to shake my head.

"He said you been attacked. Thought I might know something about it. You give him that idea?"

I shook my head again, but he grabbed my arm.

I gasped at the pain and he eased up, glaring at me as he yanked the sleeve up to my elbow. Even in the semi-darkness, the bruises were impressive.

He stiffened. "You think I did that?"

"No!"

"Don't lie to me, bitch!" he warned, and it was that word that set my teeth and straightened my spine.

I snapped my arm out of his grasp. "I never thought you did it."

"Yeah?"

"Yes," I said. "If you'd wanted to hurt me you would have done it without the mask." He watched me, eyes narrow as a cat's. "And I'd be dead."

A smile twitched his lips as he studied me. "So, this Rivera, he your boy?"

"No." It was still hard to breathe.

"What's he to ya, then?"

"Nothing."

He flashed his teeth at me as if he knew better. "He look like he could be a mean motherfucker if he get riled."

I didn't know what to say to that.

"You have trouble again, you let him know right off."

"Okay."

He gave me a nod and turned away, but a moment later he stopped. "And if you hear who done you that way, you give me a call. I got me a few things to say to him."

Then he was gone, disappearing into the darkness.

My fingers managed to scoop up the keys, my knees got me into the house.

It was my bladder that failed.

By morning my nerves were stretched to the breaking point.

The scab on my knee broke open when I tied on my sneakers and my tendons groaned like a mummy's when I did my two-second stretches. I stepped out onto my stoop and locked the door behind me.

"Where's your spray?"

I screamed as I spun around, holding my keys in front of me like a semiautomatic.

Rivera simply stared.

"Holy crap! Can't you just leave me alone?"

"I didn't mean to scare you," he said, but his expression suggested he wouldn't lose any sleep over it.

I kept my keys aimed at him. "Then why the hell are you here?"

"Do you tell a friend when you go out?"

I was trying to marshal my senses back into working

order, but he wasn't making it easy on me. "What the hell are you talking about?"

"You should let someone know when you go and when you plan to return."

I threw my hands up, crazy as a loon. "Don't you have a job to do?"

"I'm doing it. Protecting the good citizens of L.A., remember?"

"So, what? You've decided I'm innocent?" I wanted to walk away from him, but I was afraid my legs weren't ready for that Herculean feat.

"Until proven guilty," he said, and I scoffed, remembering his former words, his general attitude. "How far do you run?"

I would have liked to have lied, but I didn't feel up to the effort. "Four miles." Huh! Guess it didn't take that much energy to lie.

"Do you vary your course?"

"What?"

"You don't run the same route every day, do you?"

"Of course not." Another lie. Wow. I was on a roll.

He gave me a look. "What if someone's watching your house, figures out your schedule?"

I felt my toes curl inside my sneakers. "Why would anyone do that?" I asked, but I couldn't help scanning the bushes.

"Why would someone attack you in the parking lot of a fine establishment like the Hole?"

I forced my gaze back to his. "Do you have a purpose for being here?"

"I have a few questions."

I waited. Apparently my mind still wasn't working at full capacity.

"Why would someone attack you?" he asked again.

Oh. "Isn't that your line of work?"

He stared at me. "Did he say anything about Bomstad?"

"My attacker?"

"Yes." He was in patient mode. I hated that even more than cocky mode.

"We've been through all this."

"I thought you might have forgotten something."

"Believe me, it's all pretty vivid," I said and stepped off the stoop in an effort to act casual. My knees wobbled like a toddler's.

He turned and followed me, catching up in a few long strides. "So you believe his purpose was just to rape you?"

Just rape! I stumbled. He caught my arm, drawing me to a halt. His eyes were like lasers. Okay, I've never actually seen a laser, but if I had, I'm pretty sure that's how it would look.

"Yes," I said and found that my teeth were gritted. "Just rape. Nothing horrible." I jerked my arm out of his grip.

He caught it again. "Listen," he said, "I'm just trying to help you."

"You're just trying to frame me for a death I had nothing to do with."

We stared at each other like two rabid hounds. He leaned in.

"Bomstad was in your office with a bottle of wine and a hard-on."

I leaned in. "I had nothing to do with the wine . . . or the hard-on."

We were inches apart. My sports bra was one of those clever little numbers that zip up the front. He dipped his gaze in that direction for a fraction of a second. "I'm pretty sure you had something to do with one of those." His tone was gruff, his eyes hawkish when he lifted them to mine.

My chest felt tight, my stomach ticklish, and for a second I wasn't sure if I should skitter off like a scared bunny or drag him into my dying tea roses and have my way with him. I stood there trying not to pant while I debated.

"Here," he said and taking my hand, thrust something into it. "In case condoms aren't enough protection," he said and turned away.

I stood staring after him, then opened my hand and glanced at the contents. It was a big-ass can of pepper spray. Don't ever let it be said that size isn't important.

13

If I wanted to catch the damned worm I'd get outta
bed.

> —James McMullen,
> *seconds before his mother*
> *doused him with the scrub*
> *water*

I HAD SENT an official sounding letter to the Board of
Psychology on August 30. But apparently I hadn't pacified
them with my five-dollar words, because they still wanted
to meet with me in person. Evidently most therapists
don't have clients drop dead in their offices, and the powers that be were wondering why I felt a need to buck the
system.

I was looking forward to the interview about as much as
I would have enjoyed being diagnosed with the clap.

As it turned out, the clap would have been considerably
more fun, but I fenced and parried and tried to act as if my
world hadn't come undone. I left the interview feeling

marginally better. I would still have to file a half million idiotic reports and one of the board's gray-faced drones had said something about a probation period. But if I kept my nose clean they weren't likely to yank my license.

The following day, Tuesday, I had Elaine cancel my appointments and I drove out to the Lions training complex in Napa. I was wearing black rayon slacks and a form-fitting black blouse to cover my blossoming bruises.

By the time I reached the backfield I felt hot and irritable, but I'd consoled myself all morning with the idea that I'd get the opportunity to see hunky men in football gear.

Instead, I saw two guys throwing up and a three-hundred-pound nose tackle guzzling Gatorade. Most of it missed his mouth and ran down his bare belly like water down a flume.

The ugly side of professional sports.

I shifted my gaze to the front of the field and soothed my own fractious stomach. Sunglasses are lifesavers. You can stare like the village idiot without anyone being the wiser. Unless you lose the battle with your stomach and hurl on you shoes.

Or drool.

Off to the left a trio of guys were dressed in black and silver. The closest one wore shorts and a full-body sweat. He was pointing across the field. Muscles danced like magic in his upper arm. Without even turning my head, I could see he was built like Tarzan, all long, sleek muscles that gleamed in the sunlight.

I was just considering how to inform him that I was Jane when I spotted Bob Limmerman. He was a stocky little man with a flattop haircut and a stride too long for his stubby legs. His picture on the Internet had made him look like a toad. As it turned out, the photo had been flattering.

He was just dismissing a harried middle-aged woman when I approached him.

"Mr. Limmerman," I said, and smiled as I thrust out my hand.

He glared at me. "Who are you?"

"I'm Christina McMullen."

The glare deepened. "The broad on the phone."

At least he hadn't called me a shrink. "The psychologist," I said.

"I told you, I got nothing to say."

In fact, he had said just that, but I had called his secretary and informed her I was a reporter doing a story about the Lions' charity work. She had told me where I could find Mr. Limmerman. The trickster in me, created by genetics and honed by desperation, had come out to play.

"I'll only take a few minutes of your time," I said, withdrawing the hand. These people were not, it seemed, avid hand shakers. What kind of WASPs were they?

"I don't have a few damned minutes," he said, and turned toward the two story brick building behind him.

"I'd like to talk about Dana," I said.

There was a hitch in his stride, but he kept walking.

"To you or the press," I added.

He turned like a bulldog, his head tucked into the folds of his neck. I felt my mouth go dry and tried not to pee in my pants as I held his gaze.

"In my office," he said, and I went, head held high as I stepped out of the blistering heat. It was cool and dim inside. Linoleum tapped beneath my heels. To my right a fan burred softly from someone's office. I still had my sunglasses firmly in place. I couldn't see a damned thing.

"What's this bullshit?"

When I removed my shades, I found that Limmerman had entered his office. I did the same. He seated himself behind a battered metal desk. Two battered metal chairs occupied the opposite side and one battered metal stool stood against the wall. Consistency. I liked that.

"I don't want to make any trouble for you," I said. "I just have—"

"Then get the hell off my field," he snarled, and smacked his palm against the top of his desk. It echoed like thunder. So that was the advantage of all that metal. Intimidation. And it was working marvelously. My bladder felt like a nine-year-old's water balloon.

"One of your players is dead," I said and was quite relieved that my larynx still functioned. "I would think you would want to know why."

"I know why," he rasped, leaning onto his desk like a hyena over a fresh kill. "It's 'cuz Bomstad couldn't keep his dick in his pants."

"So he didn't have an impotency problem?" Maybe it's strange that I kept returning to that question, but I had been counseling the man for months for impotency.

"Impotency!" Limmerman barked a laugh. "You must be one hell of a psychiatrist."

"Psychologist," I corrected. "Someone sent him a bottle of wine. Any idea who might have done that?"

He snorted through his nose. I wondered vaguely if it had once been broken or if he should just be considered congenitally unfortunate. "There were half a dozen bimbos spreadin' their legs for him every time he left the field." He glared at me as if my entire gender was to blame, but I didn't feel like shouldering the burden. Even for a Catholic that seemed unjust.

"What were their names?" I asked instead.

"What?"

"Their names," I repeated patiently, as if I were talking to a deranged psychopath. It wasn't much of a stretch. "Even bimbos who spread their legs have names."

"Get the hell out of my office."

"Was he seeing anyone whose name began with a C?"

He leapt to his feet. I quivered to mine. He strode around the corner of his desk, but before I could dash for the door, it opened behind me.

"Mr. Limmerman." A Hispanic man stood there. He was about my height, and stood very straight. He wore a full linen suit. The creases in his pants were as straight as little Marines. It's amazing what you notice when your eyes are about to pop out of your head. "I was told we have a guest."

Limmerman stopped about six inches from me, fists clenched and eyes disappearing into the folds in his face. I wasn't sure but I thought there was a little bit of spittle escaping from his lips. My gaze sprinted from one to the other. The room went absolutely silent, then, "Get her outta my sight," Limmerman said, and lumbered from the room.

I considered trying to stop him but I was too busy calming my giddy bladder.

The Hispanic guy inclined his head. "My apologies," he

said. His elocution was very formal, almost old-world, and hell and gone from Bob's angry growl. "I fear Mr. Limmerman took Andrew's death very hard."

I stared at him, trying to determine whether or not he really planned to sell that line.

Apparently he did, because his expression never changed.

"I don't want to cause trouble." I'm not sure why that idiotic platitude seemed worth repeating.

"This is very comforting," he said and raised his hand, palm up toward the door. "Please, accompany me to my office. We can speak there."

His office matched his personality. It was neatly decorated in Southwest art and old artifacts. An asymmetrical pot of rusts and browns occupied the corner of his antique desk. He motioned toward a plush chair upholstered in earthy tones, then disappeared through an open doorway and returned with two SoBes. I'd always appreciated the lizard wisdom. "Please, sit," he said and handed me a bottle. It felt wonderfully cold against my palm. I wondered if I looked as flushed as I felt. "Tell me what I can do for you."

I blinked. I couldn't quite remember the last time someone had said those exact words to me and it took me a moment to dredge up an appropriate response—God bless you, kind sir seeming a bit over the top.

"I am—was . . ." I corrected, "Mr. Bomstad's therapist."

"Ms. McMullen," he said and took the chair not far from mine.

I must have given him my stupid look, because he laughed.

"I prefer to be well informed."

"About what?"

"Anything that pertains to my team."

"But he'd been off the team for some months, hadn't he?"

He spread his hands and smiled fondly. "He was still part of the family."

I couldn't help remembering how Bomstad had looked as he'd sat on my couch, his pants open and his cock as big as a prize plum. What kind of family was this man raising here?

"Good," I said, "then you're just the guy I want to talk to."

He inclined his head graciously, as though he couldn't wait to be helpful, and though I tried to shift gears, it kind of threw me off my stride. I won't say I missed butting heads, but at least in that game I knew the rules.

"Were you aware that Mr. Bomstad was seeing a therapist?" I asked.

"Indeed, yes," he said. "While he was with the team, at least. I had, in fact, encouraged him to do so, as I do with all our players."

No shit. "May I ask why?"

He shrugged, just a slight lift of well-proportioned shoulders. "Football is a very physical game, Ms. McMullen." He sounded a little like the *Fantasy Island* guy when he said my name. Have I mentioned my obsession with the *Fantasy Island* guy? "It is demanding. Exhausting. Brutal even. And that is not considering the effects of the fans."

"The fans?" I thought I knew what he meant, but I liked listening to him speak.

He gave me a smile. His eyeteeth were a little crooked and his molars were sharp. It gave him almost a Tom Cruise look. Tom Cruise with a tan and an accent. Yowsa.

"I'm sure you are aware of the difficulties associated with...How is it said? Stardom." He waved a hand. "The fame, adoration, the money."

I thought about my cracker-sized abode and failing septic system. "It sounds hellacious."

He laughed. He had a nice laugh.

"Our players are not..." He paused, thinking. "Let me say only that they live by the strength of their arms, Ms. McMullen—" He made a fist. "And not by their mental prowess."

"I'm not sure I see your point, Mr...." I paused for him to fill me in.

"My apologies again," He spread his fingers across his chest and inclined his head. "Where are my manners? I am Miguel Rodriguez. You may call me Rodney if you like."

But I really liked the name Miguel. And he had great eyes. I gave myself a mental slap before I forgot why I was there. "And what exactly is your position with the Lions, Mr. Rodriguez?"

He smiled, maybe because I had refused to use his pet name. But I secretly hoped that it was because I was so damned adorable he couldn't help himself. "I am the community relations director. My job is to make certain our players stay out of trouble. A task at which, sadly, I often fail."

I remembered my panting terror as Bomstad chased me around the office, jeans undone and my success fully exposed.

"Indeed," he continued, "I have been meaning to speak to you, Ms. McMullen."

"In regard to . . ."

"To offer my apologies."

Just how much did he know? "For what exactly?"

He looked troubled, as if he didn't care to touch on such a delicate subject, but whether it was for my benefit or his own was impossible to guess. "I consider the players' failures my own failures."

I could remember the feel of Bomstad's hand on my breast. "Ever have trouble sleeping at night?" I asked.

He smiled again, but his eyes were sad. "Indeed, quite often," he said. "But there are not so many failures as one would think. The press . . . they publicize the bad and often forget the good. For while our players may be sometimes boisterous, they are, basically, good at the heart."

"And what of Mr. Bomstad?" I asked, and remembered screaming as he dragged me backward by my hair. "Was he basically good at the heart?"

His soulful gaze held mine. "You are, perhaps, better equipped to answer that than I."

"You know how he died," I said.

He spread his hands. "Sadly, yes."

"You know about the statutory rapes."

For a moment I thought he might argue, say something stupid like "alleged" statutory rapes. But he didn't.

"Again, yes."

"Why didn't you do something?"

"I sent him to seek help."

Ahhh. And how to explain this. "I'm afraid Mr. Bomstad

was not entirely honest about his troubles, Mr. Rodriguez."

He sighed. "I feared as much. Indeed, I suggested . . ." He paused.

"What?" I asked, but he shook his head.

"My intentions matter little. I failed Andrew and I failed my employers."

"I don't think you can take your clients' failures as your own, Mr. Rodriguez."

"And you," he said, watching me with his dark, soulful eyes. "Do you not do the same?" He had that Spanish pathos that tends to make American women go soft in the head. "But I digress. You have come here for a specific purpose."

I firmed up my cerebellum and nodded primly. "Yes," I said. "I had a number of questions to ask."

"Then, by all means, ask away."

Really? I thought, but caught myself before I spoke. "Do you know who, if anyone, Mr. Bomstad was currently seeing?"

He looked troubled again. "I fear Andrew's relationships were rarely monogamous."

I almost laughed. Knowing what I now knew about the Bomb, I would be surprised to find he limited himself to one species. "A list of names would be fine," I said.

He watched me in silence for a moment. "May I take the liberty to ask why?"

I considered a host of answers and settled tentatively on the truth. "Since he died in my office, of rather . . . irregular causes, some suspicion has been laid at my door. I would like to absolve myself of that suspicion."

"Yes, of course," he said slowly, "but how would this information you request help you in your endeavor?"

"He came to his final session with a bottle of wine." I exhaled carefully. In for a penny, in for a pound. "The wine had a card signed with my first initial."

I hurried on, feeling an irresistible need to explain myself, though God knows I should have learned better by now. "I had nothing to do with Mr. Bomstad's death, Mr. Rodriguez."

He actually looked offended on my behalf. When the Lions hired a PR man, they went all out. "Of course you did not. The police, they are simply . . . overzealous at times."

"Overzealous," I agreed, remembering Rivera's looming accusations.

"Again," he said, taking my hand in his. His eyes were intense and full of old-world sorrow. "I apologize for any troubles Andrew caused you."

But apologies, no matter how charmingly delivered, weren't going to keep my ass out of jail, or get me back into the good graces of the Board of Psychology. "I need information, Mr. Rodriguez," I said.

He studied me in silence for a moment, then nodded. "I will look into the matter and telephone you . . . unless you would rather call me." He relinquished my hand with seeming regret and pulled a card from his coat pocket. "A lady like yourself, you must be cautious, yes?"

For a moment I didn't understand his meaning, but when I gave it some consideration, I thought I remembered getting a compliment sometime in the distant past. This might be one of those, I thought.

"I, ummm..." If I blushed I was going to kill myself. "I'll give you my office number," I said, and bending over the cavern I liked to call my purse, I drew out a card. It was smeared with lipstick. At least I hoped it was lipstick. I shoved it back into my handbag, gave Ricardo Montalban a smile, and handed over an unstained copy.

"Christina," he said. "A lovely name."

He was flirting with me, I realized, and resisted the temptation to giggle like a ninny. "I'd appreciate any information you could give me," I said.

He nodded. If he was disappointed by my ultramature professionalism he didn't show it. "If there is anything else I can do for you, Ms. McMullen, you've but to ask."

His eyes were earnest, dark, and entrancing. I swallowed. It's not as if I have an older-guy fetish or anything, but... Well, hell, this guy owned a suit and hadn't once accused me of murder.

"As a matter of fact, there is," I said, my mind kicking in. "Do you happen to know if Mr. Bomstad kept a diary?"

"A diary?"

"Yes."

"I very much doubt it, Ms. McMullen." He spread his hands atop his desk and explained. "You see, our Andrew... he could not read well."

14

Chocolate may be cheaper than a psychologist, but the latter doesn't generally adhere to your ass for the rest of your natural life.

—*Christina McMullen, Ph.D., in defense of her chosen profession*

SCREW THE DIET, I thought. I'd gone running. What more did the world want from me? I took another scoop of Raspberry Rhapsody straight out of the carton. It tasted like Sunday mornings, before Bomstad had ruined my life and I hadn't been able to sleep in without wondering if I'd still be a free woman on Monday.

Where the hell was his damned diary? Okay, I realized I was fixating on that one thought, and maybe it was because I was desperate to believe I hadn't been completely fooled by the Bomb. Maybe it was because my life was sliding down the tubes, and I needed some means of keeping it from flushing away. Something to hold on to.

But damn it all, why would he lie about a diary he had seemed so sincere and enthused about?

A half dozen possible reasons came to mind: He wanted to impress me with his sensitivity; he was a pathological liar; he liked toying with me ... But instinct told me that none of those answers quite jived. And if I couldn't trust my instincts, what could I trust?

Ice cream.

I took another scoop, nodded at its succulent honesty, and sighed. One could always trust ice cream.

And one's self. It was Thursday morning. I didn't have any appointments until twelve forty-five and I was feeling philosophical. Never good.

Resolutely thumping the lid on the carton, I tossed the spoon in the sink, marched to the fridge, removed the lid, took one more scoop with my finger, and shoved the rest into the freezer. A waft of cold air swooped past the glacier growing inside and cooled my face, but it did my brain little good. Nothing made sense. I still believed, despite everything, that the Bomb had kept a diary. But where? If I could gain access to his house perhaps I could figure that out. But Rivera and I hadn't exactly hit it off thus far. So I'd best pursue other avenues since breaking and entering seemed both difficult and idiotic. I thought hard for thirty seconds, got tired of that, and went to gaze in my cupboards for something that might pass as nutrients. A box of raisin bran and a bag of dried apricots were the only foodstuffs that wouldn't require any sort of preparation. A moth flew out of the raisin bran. I put the box back, took out the apricots, dragged the yellow pages from under the sink, and sat down at the kitchen table.

Five apricots and two minutes later, I knew that one could rent a safe-deposit box at Sunwest Bank for twenty-five dollars a month if one had an account with them. I did. Unfortunately, I didn't have anything worth putting into a safety-deposit box. But odds were good that Bomstad had.

I chewed on that and another apricot for a moment. It was entirely possible, of course, that the Bomb would have kept his diary safely hidden away as Rivera had suggested, but the idea of a super-sized ex-football jock sitting on the tile floor of Sunwest Bank as he scribbled in his diary was a little mind-numbing. So where would he keep it?

No great ideas came to mind. If I had ever gained any honest insight into Bomstad at all, maybe I could venture a guess, but it seems he had lied like a Protestant since the day I met him.

The apricots bag was half empty and I'd discovered two things: I hated apricots, and I needed some unbiased information about Bomstad. But how would I garner that info? It seemed likely that anyone who had met the Bomb had probably formed some pretty strong opinions of him.

I trundled back to the cupboard and scanned the contents again. Still nothing. So I removed my sneakers and limped off to the bathroom, my knees hurting from asphalt burn and unwanted exercise.

A warm shower generally helps me think. It didn't. But as I was driving to the office, my brain started popping. What I needed were police records. I was a respected member of the medical community after all. Surely the LAPD would welcome my input.

*N*o." Somewhere along the line, Rivera had given me his business card. And somehow I'd convinced myself to call him.

"Listen." I was sitting behind my desk, in my power chair, wearing my power suit, and drinking PowerAde. Actually, I was drinking orange pop but that's neither here nor there. "You asked for my professional opinion about the diary, and I'm willing to give it to you, but I can hardly ascertain where he may have kept such a personal item if I don't have the facts about his—"

"Like I said, Ms. McMullen, I don't think there is a diary."

I curled my lip at the receiver. If I wanted to be interrupted, I'd call my mother. "And what has caused you to arrive at that conclusion?" I asked.

I could almost hear his feral grin through the telephone line. "I realize you were his psychiatrist, Ms. McMullen." I didn't correct him. If Reivers was infantile enough to try to annoy me with improper terms, I'd just let him enjoy himself. "And that you were, above all, professional, but I'm afraid Bomstad may have been less than one-hundred-percent forthcoming with you in this regard."

Bite me, I thought, but kept my tone level. "Perhaps you are unfamiliar with the idea that there is generally a grain of truth in every lie, Mr. Repper."

"You're not acquainted with a lot of known felons, are you, Ms. McMullen?"

"Regardless of what you might think, the theory is correct. And I believe that if I were allowed access to Bomstad's records, I could better evaluate his personality."

"Or maybe, if you were allowed access to his records," Rivera began, "you'd find a way to screw up my investigation."

"I'm innocent," I snarled. "I'm not going to screw anything."

"My loss, then," he said. "Why so eager to help, Ms. McMullen?"

I forgot to breathe for a moment, concentrating on the "loss" statement, but I found my train of thought and jumbled an answer. "Some of us truly are law-abiding citizens, Mr. Reebler, despite your jaded opinion."

"Then this has nothing to do with saving your own ass?"

"Absolutely not." And that was just a stupid thing to say. I doubted if even Rivera was dumb enough to believe it. His laughter pretty much proved me right.

"Thanks for the offer, Ms. McMullen, but I think the LAPD will just have to muddle along without you."

I wanted to swear at him, but I didn't. I was mature, even-tempered, and professional.

I hung up and made another call immediately. "Solberg," I said, "Christina here. Give me all the dirt you have on Rivera."

The process was fairly simple from then on. A few more phone messages, a couple favors called in, and voilà, I found myself in the dog park on the following Saturday—

the very dog park Rivera's ex frequented during the weekends.

True, the greyhound I accompanied was not mine; I had gotten lost twice and driven forty-five minutes to arrive at a green belt filled with dog poop; and I felt, somehow, like I was trading secrets to Al Qaeda, but still, I was there.

Sophie, the greyhound in question, glanced at me, her eyes shining as I pulled to a halt in the gravelly parking lot. There were already a fair number of animals loping about and she gave a little cock of her head, maybe telling me she wanted to be amongst them. I don't speak dog. My mother had once owned a cocker spaniel that was in serious need of exorcism, but that was as far as my canine knowledge went. During my girlhood, the dog had mostly peed on my carpet and tried to remove my fingers when I suggested he do anything contrary to his wishes, such as abstain from peeing on my carpet.

Sophie seemed more amenable. And Eddie, her owner, had raved about her on more than one occasion. But I wasn't sure one could trust the opinion of a man who called his dog Princess and bought her tasseled pillows proclaiming her name and title. Eddie was like that. We'd dated briefly, and truth be told, he was one of the good guys, but he'd come out of the closet some months later and it didn't look like he was going back in any time soon. Wouldn't you just know it.

"You ready to go?" I asked, turning toward the dog. Sophie tipped her head at me and gave me a cool smile. You gotta like a dog that smiles. Especially one that does so coolly. Snapping on her leash, I opened my door and wondered what the hell I was doing. But thoughts of sharing a communal shower every day for twenty-to-life urged me to get out of the car.

Sophie stepped regally out behind me. A couple was sitting on a bench to my right, talking baby talk to a hairy mongrel I couldn't identify. I looked at the greyhound, wondering if I should do the same. She glanced back. I swear I could see one eyebrow shoot up, a subtle suggestion that I keep my baby talk to myself. All right.

Solberg had said Rivera's ex-wife usually arrived at the park sometime before ten and stayed nearly an hour. It was now nine forty-five. The sun was out. The air was clear. It was the kind of glowing morning only California can dish up. I wished to hell I was still in bed. I wished more that I had never met a psychopath named Andrew Bomstad. But since I had, and he had shown the bad manners to die in my office, I felt a need to learn all I could about the LAPD's irritating lieutenant who wanted to put me away for the rest of my natural life.

In the end it was quite simple meeting Tricia Vandercourt. I'd seen a photo of her standing next to Rivera as he accepted a commendation. *She looks younger in person,* I thought, as I watched her cross the park, but she'd subsequently left Rivera and that was bound to put a spring in any girl's step. The golden retriever Solberg had told me about, on the other hand, looked exactly as I'd pictured him. Golden and retrieverish. Set free of his leash, he loped after a tennis ball she tossed out. He snatched it up on the run and returned it to his mistress, who took it with a smile and tossed it back out. She was wearing blue shorts. Her legs were tan and lean, her blond hair pulled back in a bobbing ponytail. If she'd hit the thirty-year mark she hid it detestably well.

I took a deep breath, gazed across the park at the other patrons, and wondered what the hell to do next. Intellect suggested that I get my ass back in the Saturn and take Sophie out for ice cream. Paranoia, or whatever force was driving me, reminded me that Rivera was the type of guy who had tested a fruit stain on my blouse.

I walked around a while longer, trying to look casual. *Here I am. Just me and my borrowed dog* . . . enjoying a Saturday morning when I could still be in bed. Sophie seemed content enough to glide along beside me like a runway model with her 'droid, though I was pretty sure she too was wondering what the hell we were doing. Eddie had assured me I could turn her loose within the fenced confines of the park, but I had no way of knowing if the little princess would return when called, and I was pretty sure that telling Eddie I'd lost his royal hound would be worse than admitting I was indeed Bomstad's murderer.

Glancing surreptiously about, my eyes cleverly concealed behind dark glasses, I saw that Tricia had taken a seat on a park bench nearby. Seeing an opening, I made one more circuit of the park, then sat down on an adjacent bench. Sophie gave me a look that suggested I might be the laziest slut to ever walk the face of the earth, so I decided to turn her loose. I tried to think of some doggy kind of thing to say to her before the emancipation, but in the end I just said "bye" and unclipped the leash.

It was then that the retriever returned. The two dogs did a little butt-sniffing, which the regal Sophie seemed to find surprisingly inoffensive, then galloped off together. Huh.

I gave my throat a mental clearing, turned toward Vandercourt, and threw out my opening gambit. "Is he yours?"

Tricia Vandercourt turned to me, her lips curved up in a half smile. What cradle had Rivera robbed to find her? "What was that?"

"The retriever," I said, sure she could use her cop-wife vision to see straight through to my quivering viscera. "Is he yours?"

"She. Yes, she is."

"Oh, sorry. She's beautiful."

"Thank you. Yours, too."

This was going great.

"Did you rescue her?" she asked, and my mind screeched to a sudden halt.

"Sorry?" I said, stalling.

"She's a greyhound, right?"

"Ahh, yes."

"Was she raced?"

"Oh, ummmm . . ." *Lie, you idiot. Lie your ass off.* "Yes."

"How long have you had her?"

"Just, ummm, four years." Holy crap! Why hadn't I prepackaged a few likely answers?

"So how old is she?"

What was she, the dog police? "Six. Just coming up on six."

"Really?" The pair was loping toward us in tandem. "She doesn't look more than two."

"She takes good care of herself," I said. Crap! I was so

screwed. I glanced about, half expecting Rivera to come roaring out of the bushes, handcuffs at the ready, but he didn't seem to realize as of yet that I was digging into his past like a daft terrier.

I desperately tried to think of something intelligent to say, but Tricia was laughing, as if I were clever. As if I'd made some kind of joke. I gave her a half-assed grin. She was scratching the retriever behind the ears and spared a hand for Sophie. My mind balked at the idea, but I had to think she might be a genuinely nice person. No wonder Rivera had married her. It had to be nearly impossible for a Neanderthal like him to convince a decent human being to even talk to him. And hell...I couldn't help noticing that her thighs were completely bereft of cellulite. I'd marry her myself given half a chance. But no, wait, I was here to lie to her and try to pry out information about her ex-husband.

"I'm Tricia," she said and thrust her hand toward me. "Tricia Vandercourt. I don't think I've seen you here before."

I almost reared back, almost glanced into the bushes again. This was too easy. Life wasn't supposed to be easy. Hadn't she ever heard of Catholicism? But I struggled through the simplicity. "Hi." For a moment I couldn't quite decide if I should pet Sophie or reach for her hand. I opted for her hand. "I'm—" And then I realized the ugly, glaring truth. I'd spent the drive over debating whether to give her my real name or an alias, and I'd never come to a firm decision. Maybe I hadn't actually expected her to show up. Maybe I'd thought I wouldn't get an opportunity to talk to her. Maybe I thought I would be smarter than to just sit there and stare at her like a concussed dumpling. But my mind was spinning hopelessly, screaming suggestions. *Don't lie. Make something up. Keep it simple. Lie, you moron!* But it wasn't as if she'd have heard of me. Unless she and Rivera spoke on a regular basis. Unless he liked to trot out all the psychologists he accused of murdering tight ends with Viagra. Unless—Oh, crap. Our hands were already parting. She blinked at me. Her smile was starting to fade at the corners.

"I'm Carla," I said. "Carla . . . Going." I have no idea where that name came from.

"Nice to meet you," she said, and roughed up the retriever's ears again. "What's your dog's name?"

"Sissy." It didn't occur to me for several seconds that the dog probably wouldn't need an alias, but I was on a roll. Quick reactions. That's what I needed, although intelligence would have come in damned handy. "Sissy Walker." I don't know what was wrong with me. Now that I'd gotten a good start, I couldn't seem to stop.

"She must be registered."

"Yes." Why the hell not? "With the greyhound . . . club." For a moment I actually hoped Rivera would appear and shoot me dead. But wouldn't you know it; the loser didn't show up.

"They're so elegant. Greyhounds," Tricia explained. "And so loving. It's a shame how they're treated."

Why was I there? Why the hell was I there?

"I thought about adopting one, but my husband wanted to get a rottweiler."

Husband! That's why I was there. To learn everything I could about Rivera. To get my ass out of the sling.

"Or something equally terrifying." She made big eyes at me.

I tried to look seminormal. "Why would he want something terrifying?"

"He's a cop. Was a cop. Well..." She shrugged. The retriever laid its head on her lap and gave her adoring eyes. "He's still on the force, but we're not married anymore."

"Oh." I felt like a voyeur, but my plan was working. I couldn't have been more surprised if I'd fallen off the edge of the earth. "I'm sorry." I wanted to run screaming, but I was there for a purpose, if I could just focus on what it was. "But..." I actually forced a sigh as I glanced away. "I know how it is."

"Are you divorced?"

"Yes." And I was going to hell. "Three years now."

"It's so hard on everyone."

Everyone? For one wild moment I imagined the worst; Rivera had spawned offspring. "You have kids?"

"No. I'm sorry. I meant the dogs."

"Oh, yes. Of course." I gave an intelligent nod. Sophie lay down, crossed one elegant ankle across the other, and looked at me as though I was the village idiot. The dog was smart. Damn smart.

"Was she really attached to your ex?"

I must have given her a sappy expression, because she laughed. "Sissy," she explained.

Was she calling me names? Was she...Oh...the greyhound! "No. She didn't know him long." Holy crap, I couldn't remember when I said I'd gotten her. "Not long at all." I had to quit lying. Absolutely no more lying.

"I know he wanted to take Rockette with him. But he let me keep her."

"Rockette?" I was floundering hopelessly, like a bloated cow at high tide.

"He wanted a macho dog with a macho name. Butch or Killer or Rocky. I wanted something sweet. We settled on something big." She smiled. If I didn't know better I'd think little Tricia wasn't quite over Rivera. But stranger things had happened. "So he called her Rockette. Because she's a girl." Her smile could kill. "It was kind of a joke."

A joke, from Rivera. Hmmm. It sounded suspicious to me.

"How long have you been divorced?" I asked, trying to give my mind a chance to start functioning.

"Just a couple years." She gazed at the dog. "We were separated before that. It was really hard. I mean, he's a great guy and everything."

It was that statement that made the truth dawn on me; I had the wrong Tricia Vandercourt.

"But he's so . . ." She made a fist and gritted her teeth. "Irritating."

Okay, maybe I was on track after all.

"Intense." She shook her head. "He worried all the time."

"Worried?"

She shrugged. "About current cases. About work. Not that that's a bad thing. I mean, he's a cop and everything. And it wasn't like he didn't have time to worry about *me*." She rolled her eyes. "I could barely get out of the drive-way without him running me down to make sure I had..." Her hands fluttered. "An assault weapon and a gallon of Mace."

I couldn't help but think of the pepper spray in my purse.

"Something like this." She motioned from herself to me. "Us. Just sitting here talking. This would have driven him crazy. He thought I was too naïve. He didn't trust anybody. He thought everyone I met was out to get something from me."

She sighed. I squirmed and tried to refrain from being zapped straight into hell.

"Maybe he was jealous," I said, because I was jealous. If I had legs like hers, I might even keep them shaved. If she were my client I'd call her ingenuous. In real life she was just damned cute.

"Jealous?" She thought about that for a moment. "No," she decided, and shook her head. "He was just so ... suspicious. And I'm ..." She widened her eyes again. "Well, I'm like this." She made talking motions with her right hand. "He always said I could make friends with a cactus. At first I thought that was a good thing, but he said a cactus can kill you." She looked sad and momentarily distant.

Wow. I searched for something to say and came up with, "I suppose being a cop could make him that way."

"Yeah," she agreed, sounding dubious. "But I blame it on his dad."

Father issues. Now we were getting somewhere. The therapist in me perked up. Or maybe it was the cocktail waitress. Both thrive on gossip and emotions, and sometimes I can't tell them apart. "What was wrong with his dad?"

"He was a bastard. Excuse my French. Still is, probably."

I nodded, thinking of a half dozen clients. "Fathers are often damaging influences on their sons."

Her lips parted slightly as if puzzled. "Are you a... social worker or something?"

Shit. "A psychologist." There was no way that could hurt me, and I wasn't nearly imaginative enough to think up more lies.

"Oh, man." She brushed back her bangs, looking ridiculously young. "And here I am talking your ear off. I'm sorry."

"No. No, that's fine. That's why I do what I do. I like to listen."

"Then we could be great pals. 'Cuz I like to talk." She laughed.

"It's therapeutic."

"Gerald didn't think so. But then, I left him just a few months after starting therapy. Maybe he associates the two. But the problems were already there, of course. I just needed... validation, I guess. In fact..." She continued, but I failed to hear her for a moment.

"Gerald?" Holy crap, I thought, panicked. I really did have the wrong woman.

She laughed. "He hates it when I call him that. Everyone else calls him Jack. I thought Gerald was a perfectly good name, but it was his father's and God knows he didn't want anything to do with that."

I relaxed marginally. At least I had the right ex-wife, I thought, and maybe, in the back of my mind, I was quite sure no one named Gerald could be all that dangerous. "Did he resent his dad?"

"I don't know." She sighed. "His father was in politics. A big advocate for tougher laws and the death penalty and trying kids as adults. Responsibility for all ages or some such rot, but when Gerald got in trouble..." She shook her head.

My heart was racing. Our Gerald—in trouble. God forbid. I searched for a means of urging her to go on. "Parents often see other people's kids and their own kids in an entirely different light."

"I suppose it's hard. Me..." She laughed. "I'm even protective of my dog." She gave the retriever another scratch, but her gaze was distant. "His dad managed to keep him out of jail, but sometimes I wonder if he wouldn't have been better off..." She shambled to a halt, but my eyes were probably bugging out of my head by then.

Jail! Rivera!

"He just never let Gerald forget it. You know? Nothing he ever did was good enough."

My mind wouldn't adjust.

"What had he done?" My mouth spoke without my mind following along.

"Nothing... terrible," she said and gave a charming little shrug. "But he was young." She was starting to balk. The therapist in me insisted that I let the session wind down, the cocktail waitress suggested that I call her a cab, and the murder suspect told me to shut the hell up unless I wanted to spend the next twenty years sharing a toilet with a woman named Lancer. "And he got into the wrong crowd. You know how it goes."

No. Tell me. I might have been drooling a little. "Adolescence can be difficult."

"Tell me about it."

She was probably still an adolescent herself.

"Anyway, the senator got him off the hook, but he never let him forget it. Held it over his head like an ax. Probably still does. He was this giant believer in *discipline*." She made little quotation marks in the air with her fingers.

"So . . ." I tried to sound casual. "Is that why Gerald went into law enforcement. To discipline like he'd been disciplined?"

"Oh, no." She looked shocked. Horrified. "He truly wanted to make a difference, to make L.A. a better place to live. Maybe even to keep us safe from what he'd once been. But . . ." She sighed. "God have mercy on anyone who steps out of line, especially if they hurt someone he cares about."

15

Beauty is only skin deep, but who gives a shit what's
under their skin anyways?

—Michael McMullen

THE NEXT FEW DAYS seeped by like stagnant mo-
lasses. I took appointments, chugged up Chestnut Hill,
and fought with my yard. But I didn't sleep much. Visions
of Rivera slow-cooking me in a giant pot with the rest of
L.A.'s criminal element haunted my dreams. But the reasons seemed to shift oddly. One moment he was charging
me with invading the privacy of his family life, or ex-
family life, and the next he was convinced I was responsible for Bomstad's engorged death. Either way, being boiled
with vegetables was a bad way to go.

I woke up tired and strangely hungry for stew.

But since the scale was stubbornly insistent that I was

not yet of Twiggy proportions, I packed up my lunch, boysenberry yogurt and plums, and headed off to work.

Three weeks had passed since Bomstad's death. They had been the strangest weeks of a relatively strange life. It was a slow Thursday, so I updated files, bought a pack of Virginia Slims, and spent the day thinking of reasons I should smoke it.

By evening I'd opened the package four times and finally thrown the thing in the toilet.

I was just blowing it dry when Mr. Lepinski arrived. I shoved the hair dryer and the smokes in my bottom drawer and ventured into the lobby to meet him.

He looked as wrinkled and timid as ever when he entered my office, but L.A. Counseling had hardly been the stress-free zone I'd intended to make it. Two of his sessions had ended with visits from Bomstad and Rivera. He probably wondered who would drop in tonight.

"Good evening," I said, giving him my professional smile, all warmth and intellect.

He didn't smile back. Instead, he twitched his whiskers and sidled into the room.

I waved graciously toward the sofa, hoping to soothe him with my melodious professionalism. He perched on the edge of the couch like a fidgety sparrow and looked like he was ready to fly out the window. Sometimes I'm better at melodious professionalism than others.

"I've been thinking about the Bomber," he said.

I heaved a heavy mental sigh. "What have you been thinking?"

"How he died. Right here." He shifted his gaze to the floor and back. "It's just . . . confusing."

No shit. "How so?"

"He's gone. And I'm still..." His myopic gaze skittered over to me. "Well, I'm still alive, aren't I?"

I stared at him and carefully pent up my fractious sense of humor. Some find my sarcasm amusing, but I have reason to believe there are others who would be willing to strangle me with a shoelace. Best to keep my cleverness to myself while in session, I decided, especially since it almost seemed as though we were moving past our usual conversations about sandwiches.

"I mean, I was... When I was a kid I was asthmatic." He bobbed a nod in my general direction, though he could no longer meet my eyes. "Did I ever tell you that?"

"No. I don't believe you did."

"Father..." He paused, seemingly not quite ready for the father speech, and began again. "Mother and I were alone. I was..." He glanced at his knees. They were as knobby as newel posts. "Small. Of course. Frail. We didn't have much. But it was my birthday. Mother got me a jacket. Lions jacket. I was a fan. Football players—they're so..." He tightened his hands into fists and gritted his teeth like a fierce bunny. "Rugged. I loved that jacket." He blinked behind his glasses. "So did the other boys. I was on my way home after school." He was starting to breathe hard as he remembered. "And they—"

"Mr. Lepinski." I interrupted him as quietly as I could. "How old are you?"

He blinked. "I turned fifty-two last May."

"What do you do for a living?"

"I'm an accountant." He scowled at me as if I'd lost my mind. The idea had some credence. "You know that."

"An accountant," I repeated, speaking slowly, giving him time to calm himself. "It's a good job, wouldn't you say? An adult job. You're educated, intelligent. Responsible."

He still looked confused, but he seemed to have caught his breath and pushed out his chest a little. "I'm doing Daniel Dalton's books this year."

I didn't know Daniel Dalton, but I'd heard the name associated with money. "You have a house in Covina. You don't beat your wife and you pay your taxes on time."

He straightened his narrow shoulders. "Estimated and paid quarterly," he said. "It's the only way to do it."

So this was it—the number-one reason I'd given up Dairy Queen for months at a time to pay my education bills: the opportunity to see a withered little man pull back his shoulders and remember what was right about himself. Of course, I'd seen the same kind of results while wearing cut off overalls and a gingham blouse at the Warthog, but now my clients weren't hearing my advice through an alcohol-induced haze.

I gave him a smile. Mr. Lepinski wasn't always an easy man to like. But just then I liked him quite a lot. "You're a good person, Mr. Lepinski. The very definition of a solid citizen. Dependable, intelligent, decent."

He knew what I was getting at. I could see it in his eyes, but he refused to admit it. Fear is like that sometimes. Evasive, enduring, destructive.

"But the Bomber was a warrior," he said. "An animal."

"Yes," I agreed, and perhaps a bit more honesty crept into my tone than necessary, but he didn't seem to notice.

"So what chance do I have?" His shoulders were beginning to slump again.

"Well . . ." I shrugged, trying to act casual, but the image of a scrawny boy in a Lions jacket was strangely haunting. "Do you make a habit of ramming heads with giant men who want to pulverize you?"

He scowled at me. "That's absurd."

"How about your diet? Are you taking steroids, eating massive amounts of meat, drinking to excess?" How about screwing your large friends' wives? I added mentally.

"Sometimes I'll have a glass of red wine in the evening."

I smiled at him. "The answer would be no, Mr. Lepinski," I said. "You don't do any of those things."

"Pastrami's high in saturated fats and—"

"My point is this," I interrupted before things got out of hand. "One often makes one's own luck. Don't you agree?"

He stared at me. For a moment I thought he hadn't heard, but finally he spoke. "Was the Bomber on steroids?"

His voice was very small, and I found it indescribably strange that a scrawny little boy who'd doubtless been tormented for his shortcomings would still idolize the very type of personality that had plagued him.

"I believe he was," I said. "Not to mention a good many other dangerous substances."

"But he was so . . . forceful."

"Yes." I remembered the suffocating feel of his hand against my breast and felt my own shortness of breath. "He was also cruel."

Maybe I shouldn't have said that out loud. Maybe I should have kept my thoughts to myself. But I said it again. "He was cruel, he was self-absorbed, and he made poor choices."

Lepinski stared at me, then blinked, not quite able to give up his illusions. "But he was a warrior."

I didn't sleep any better that night than I had on the previous two. In fact, I did a lot of staring at the ceiling and some fantasizing about those Virginia Slims I'd left at the office. My mind was as busy as a two-dollar prostitute.

But he was a warrior. Lepinski's words kept rolling through my head like a foggy mantra. Bomstad *had* been a warrior, and one who had chosen to die in my office. Okay, maybe chosen wasn't quite the right word, but he'd died, damn him, and my world had been loopy as hell ever since. Actually, it had been loopy for several minutes before that, I thought and spooned a little more brain power out of a frosty Häagen-Dazs carton.

He'd died and left one idiotic lieutenant believing I had something to do with his demise.

Which was ridiculous, of course. Why would I kill a warrior? A warrior with soulful eyes and clean fingernails. With a self-effacing laugh and Italian loafers. A warrior with a diary that had yet to be located and perhaps had never actually—

My mind clattered to a halt as one sterling truth came marching into my chilled brain. A warrior wouldn't hide his diary away in some safe-deposit box or a relative's musty basement. A warrior would be proud of his conquests, pleased with his antics.

A warrior would guard his diary with his own body.

Probably in his bedchamber, where he took his many conquests. His many conquests he would later lie about to his poor, underpaid therapist. The very therapist who...

Ahh, to hell with it. The point was, the diary was in his house. All I had to do was find it.

16

Just remember this, Missy, escargot ain't nothin'
but snails with their noses stuck in the air.

—Connie McMullen,
upon learning of her
daughter's desire for higher
education

THE PRECINCT STATION was large and loud. I had
thought of a half dozen ways to break into Bomstad's
house, but they all involved a cat suit and skeleton keys. I
didn't have a cat suit and I didn't know what skeleton keys
actually were, so I settled on a somewhat more sedate
method. I would offer Rivera my professional services. If
that didn't work, I could resort to blackmail. After all, it
seemed unlikely that his juvenile transgressions were
something he wanted bandied about.

I gave some consideration to dropping in at his house.
But the precinct offered a modicum of security. Even if
Rivera had learned I had invaded his ex-wife's privacy, I

would be safe from his wrath if surrounded by other police officers. Wouldn't I?

"Is Lieutenant Rivera here?" I asked. I was using what Elaine called my nose voice.

The woman behind the desk gave me the once-over. "You want to see the lieutenant?" She had curly brown hair, a square face, and boxy conformation. I was all for women in law enforcement, but if someone ever had to hotfoot it to my rescue, I hoped it wasn't her, as she didn't look extremely fleet. But who was I to judge physical prowess? An undersized legal secretary had once come into the Warthog to accuse me of flirting with her man. Her man happened to weigh in at 327 pounds and walk like a platypus. Not being overly diplomatic in my younger years, I had informed her that I had not been flirting, and if I were about to, I would do so with someone with whom I shared the same number of chromosomes.

She'd hit me like a Mack truck. And she was pretty fair at kicking, too. It had taken two bouncers and a bevy of creative threats to drag her off me.

I gave the boxy policewoman a smile and wondered mildly if I could take her in arm wrestling. It's not like I'm competitive or anything, but every once in a while, I like to check if my juices are still flowing. "Yes," I said with all due politeness, "if he's in."

She looked me over again, gave kind of a tilted "This should be interesting" glance, and turned away.

I studied the room at large while trying to look nonchalant and maybe a little bit superior. I think I managed sane.

"You wanted to see me?"

I glanced up. Rivera stood there in all his officious glory. He was wearing a lightweight gray sweater tucked into black trousers. His belly, if one could call it that, looked as hard as rock candy. His expression was somewhat less appealing.

"Yes." I tried a smile, but true to form, it failed to bring him to his knees. He only looked peeved. Maybe a little suspicious. "If you have a minute."

He glanced at his watch. "Half a minute," he said, and turned away.

I stared. He turned back. "You coming?"

I reminded myself not to scurry after him. I was wearing Prada. No one should scurry in Prada. It cost more than I made in a month—at least for its original owner, and though I wasn't that auspicious individual, I forced my steps to remain cadenced and casual.

His expression, I noticed, had darkened further by the time I sauntered through his office door.

I glanced around. I'm not sure what I had expected. Prisoners, parched and pleading, handcuffed to his desk, maybe. But his space was notably absent of torture implements. There was a framed print above his file cabinet and a photo of his ex-wife hugging his ex-dog.

I felt immediately guilty and absolutely desperate to cover it. Casual, casual, casual.

"Is that your wife?" I asked and did my best to sound congenial.

His scowl deepened. "No."

Huh? "Your ex?"

He stared at me. "What makes you think I'm divorced?"

My mind froze. A thousand placating reasons sprang to mind, but I remembered our past encounters, and, not wanting to stoke his naturally suspicious nature, gave him my most jaded expression. "Please," I said. "I believe we've met before."

He stared at me for half a breathless lifetime, then snorted and sat down. "Came to charm the pants off me?" he asked.

My knees felt weak. Maybe it was because of my duplicity regarding his ex. But it might have had something to do with the thought of him sans pants. Yikes.

"Lieutenant." I launched immediately into the safety of my practiced spiel before my mind could delve too deeply into that well. "I've come to apologize."

He remained absolutely silent, but one brow had risen a single millimeter. I waited for him to speak. He didn't. Bastard. He could keep his pants on till he dropped dead for all I cared.

I cleared my throat. "Aren't you curious what I'm apologizing for?"

He shrugged. "I assume you're sorry you killed the Bomb."

"I did not kill the Bomb."

There was another long pause. "Okay. I give up. What are you apologizing for?"

"I feel I've been less respectful of your authority than I should have. I'm sure your job is very difficult. I am also certain that I seemed a likely suspect considering the circumstances of Mr. Bomstad's death. And though I can categorically assure you I had nothing whatsoever to do with his demise, I still—"

"What the hell do you want?" he asked, and leaned aggressively across his desk.

I refrained from leaning back. I also refrained from leaping over the furniture and throttling him. I hate to be interrupted. In a house with three hyper, driven boys, I had reached the sagacious age of seventeen before I'd been able to finish a single coherent thought. Still, I didn't spit at my antagonist as I had been wont to do in former years, but mustered up my best smile.

Somehow he managed to resist my charming congeniality once again. Maybe it was the fact that my teeth were gritted. "I want to offer my services, Mr. Rak—" I stopped myself. "Lieutenant."

His eyes suddenly gleamed, as if he wanted to laugh. I braced myself and held my wrath. I'd been laughed at by better men than he.

"And just exactly what services are you offering?" His gaze never dropped from my face, but it might as well have. The insult, and the compliment, were right there.

"My *professional* services," I said.

His lips actually curled up this time. "And what profession might that be?"

"Listen, Mr.—Lieutenant, I realize you harbor very little respect for mental health. I mean..." I smiled again and tried not to blink at him like Jessica Rabbit. "For mental health *services,* but I happen to be an intelligent, well-educated individual."

He stood up, looking restless. "I don't doubt it at all."

I watched him roam around the front of his desk and did my best to hide my surprise. "Then let me assist you with your investigation."

He settled his left cheek on the corner of his desk and crossed his arms against his chest. "What investigation would that be?"

I snapped my gaze to his face and remembered not to kill him. "Bomstad's case."

"Ahhh." He nodded, then, "No," he said and turned toward the door behind me. He had his hand on the knob before I realized I was being excused. He opened the door. I stared in disbelief. Lest you forget, I was wearing Prada. I rose to my feet with a snap.

"Just like that?" I said. My voice might have sounded a little raspy.

He canted his head as if thinking, then, "Yeah," he said, "just like that."

"What is it, Rivera?" I asked. "You scared?"

He stared at me, his eyes deadly flat. Whoops. He closed the door. We were standing close together, and the room felt strangely devoid of oxygen.

"Scared?" he asked and took a step toward me. "What would I be scared of, Ms. McMullen?"

I think I may have licked my lips. I think he may have watched the process. His eyes were gleaming like an alpha wolf's as he settled his gaze on mine. I couldn't think of a damned thing to say. Or maybe I couldn't speak.

He took another step toward me, though there wasn't more than a pair of inches between us. "You threatening me," he asked, "or seducing me?"

"Seducing! Ha!" I actually laughed. "Jesus, Rivera, you don't need a psychologist, you need a dream analyst."

"You think I'm dreaming?" he asked, and his gaze dipped to my mouth again. I swear it did. Three weeks ago I'd bought Raspberry Passion lipstick because it sounded like ice cream. I wondered if it was the raspberries or the passion he was attracted to. "About you?"

I was feeling shaky. I steadied my knees and refused to back away. I was a professional. I was above this. "I didn't come here for a piss—" I drew a deep breath and started again. "I didn't come here to trade insults," I said.

"No?"

"No."

"Then why are you here?"

"I told you—" I began, but calmed my voice and drew my back a little straighter. "I realize my evaluation of Mr. Bomstad was somewhat skewed. But—"

He snorted. I demonstrated remarkable restraint and refrained from knocking him against the wall with my purse.

"But," I continued, "I believe that amongst the lies, he did offer me a modicum of truth."

"And you believe that based on your own phenomenal ability to judge character?"

I ignored that. "And therefore," I continued evenly. "I am certain I am capable of helping you find his diary if given a chance."

"Ahh. The diary again. Great," he said. "Help away. Where do you think it might be?"

In his house. In his bedroom, I thought, but I had no desire to tell him that. Maybe it was because, as a professional, I had a deep-seated need to see my work fulfilled, to justify my belief that all people have a grain of goodness in them, and therefore Bomstad had told me some truth. Or maybe I was just being pissy and wanted to find the damn thing myself. Whatever the case, I kept my cool and stood my ground. I am woman. Hear me roar! "It would be helpful," I said, "if I could see his living quarters. Refine my perceptions. As his therapist, I might be able to decipher clues that police officers would find insignificant."

"Of course," he said, "us ham-fisted blue-collar workers might trample the Bomb's delicate treasures under our muddy heels."

"Tell me . . . Lieutenant." I was struggling to continue to call him by his title. Turns out mutilating his name had been the highlight of an otherwise shitty few weeks. "Are you trying to perpetuate the police department's barbaric persona?"

"Tell me, miss," he said, "isn't it hard to walk with that stick up your—"

A knock sounded at the door. Rivera kept glaring at me as he granted entrance.

It was the boxy girl, looking strangely thrilled, I thought, to see us faced off across a narrow scrap of industrial carpet. Her gleaming brown eyes skimmed from him to me and back. "Call for you on line two, Lieutenant."

He grunted something, and she delayed just a second before pulling her squat body back into the hall and closing the door regretfully behind her. She could just as well have said "aw, shucks" and scuffed the floor with her sneaker. But such was the maturity level of the LAPD.

And so our stare-down continued.

"Is there anything else, Miss McMullen?" I wasn't sure when he had switched to calling me miss, and although I've often thought women's rights were a lot of hooey—I mean, if a guy wants to open a door—I found that anti-quated form of address disturbingly disturbing.

"No, Mr. Riviter," I said, "I think I've learned just about everything I need to know about you."

"That about sums it up," he said and reached for the phone.

I couldn't help but stop him. "What does that mean?"

"Can't even get my name straight," he said, "and you think you know everything about me. Seems about right for someone in your line of work."

I opened my mouth to argue, but he was already answering the phone, and I was far too classy to either listen in or wrap the telephone wire around his neck until his eyes popped.

So there wasn't much point in sticking around.

17

Men are like dogs. Some are ... Well, men are just like dogs.

—*Chrissy McMullen*

I WAS IN a Friday afternoon session with a self-proclaimed sex addict when an idea came to me. There had once been a time when I thought there was no such thing as a sex addict. Or, maybe, more correctly, I used to think every man was a sex addict, but after meeting Raymond Eliot, I had changed my mind. It may have been the tale of his ongoing relationship with his Hoover that made me see the light.

Anyway, he was telling me about "the bazoombas" on someone he had seen at the bus station that morning. That's how he referred to women's breasts. Bazoombas.

Maybe he thought the term endearing. It wasn't, but that's when the truth dawned on me.

I had to break into Bomstad's house.

I'm not sure what the exact connection between the two thoughts was, but suddenly, it was all very clear. Nancy Drew wouldn't have sat around listening to some pervert talk about bazoombas while her life slid down the drain. She would have taken action, and her adventures always turned out swell. She was never raped or imprisoned, but then, as far as I knew, she was never accused of murder by a barbaric officer of the law, either. Still, like Nancy, I wasn't the kind to let my life just slide along unheeded. Generally, I felt a stirring need to sabotage it by whatever means necessary.

So it was, on the following afternoon, that I badgered Solberg into getting Bomstad's home address, got directions on MapQuest.com, and set off on my adventure.

I took the 405 south and exited onto Burbank Boulevard. Oakland Drive was lined with oleander and jacarandas. A hot September wind rustled their branches as I drove around the block, trying to act as if I owned a home in the area, though as things stood, I would have been lucky to afford a mailbox in that zip code. Even my dusty little Saturn seemed to feel outclassed. I gave it a cerebral pat on the dash and circled the block again, getting the lay of the land.

Bomstad's house was surrounded by a Gothic-looking wrought-iron fence with pointed tips and double gates that arched across the smooth sweep of black tar driveway. Most of his actual domicile was hidden behind

impressive-looking trees and the crest of a perfectly manicured lawn.

On the fifth circuit past his towering gates, I parked on
Bellflower Street and gave in to thought. My current plan
of action was crazy. Despite evidence to the contrary, I
knew that. I wasn't Nancy Drew, and going into the
Bomb's house uninvited might very well be misconstrued
as breaking and entering by certain members of the law
enforcement community. On the other hand, I had already
been accused of far worse.

The sun was beginning to set over the Santa Monicas,
but it was still hotter than hell in the valley of angels. I
pulled a half-melted Snickers out of my purse and ruminated. And sure enough, once the undiluted sugar started
amping up my system, I began to think more clearly.

Bomstad, I realized, was apt to have a first-flight security system, and there was little point in going through the
trouble of scaling his carnivorous-looking fence if I was
going to be hauled off in handcuffs before I reached his
front door.

I finished off the candy, licked my fingers, and chewed
on my lip. It wasn't as inspiring as the infusion of sugar,
but I knew what I had to do.

Turning the ignition, I shifted into gear and pulled up
beside the cherry trees near Bomstad's front gates. They
loomed over me like a demon's dark wings, but I forced
myself out of my car. The parched wind snatched at my
blouse, but I barely noticed the heat. I was sweating like a
zealot from nerves already.

Nevertheless, I donned my most casual expression and
sauntered up the sloping driveway, silently chanting my

mantra: I am innocent. I am unafraid. I am innocent. I am cool.

And if anyone asked, I was with the Jehovah's Witnesses. No one's cooler than that.

I felt strangely disembodied as I approached the closed gates, but once there, I glanced surreptitiously up and down the street and squeezed my face up to the bars.

A little red light gazed back at me from a narrow black box behind the wrought iron.

The fence was armed and dangerous. I couldn't get in without telling the world, or at least American Security, that I had breeched their defenses.

Something rustled behind me.

I spun toward the sound, certain Rivera had come to slap me in irons, but there was no one there. A cherry tree branch scraped against the Saturn's fender. Who would have thought it would sound like the lieutenant?

Heart still pounding, I goose-stepped back to my car, propped myself behind the wheel, and power-locked the doors.

I wouldn't be able to break into Bomstad's house, after all, and as I turned the ignition and sped toward home, I realized I had never felt more relieved in my life.

*D*uring the following week, I debated whether it was normal to doubt my clients' every innocuous word. I was trying to put the horrors of the past behind me, but it wasn't going well. And it wasn't just Bomstad's death that had put me on the skids. It was his lies. I couldn't help but wonder if Mr. and Mrs. Peters, who seemed painfully sincere about reconciling, were boinking every Tom, Dick, and Judy who crossed their paths. I wondered if Frances Rockwell really washed her hands five times before every meal, and if Nita Baldwin, who was as thin as Barbie on speed, actually ate Twinkies between meals, as she claimed.

And when I wasn't questioning such cosmos-shaking revelations, I wondered if I was a coward. I had never thought of myself in those terms. In fact, when graduating from Holy Angels some fifteen years before, I had been voted the girl most likely to spit in someone's eye. My classmates hadn't been very specific about whom that someone might be, or what they might do to deserve my ire, but I had still been impressed with the categories those little high-school geniuses came up with.

Now, however, I wondered if they had chosen the wrong girl. Maybe Evie Johnson deserved the title. Or even Katherine Townsend, since she had, on graduation day, convinced her second cousin to streak across the stage wearing nothing but a ski mask. A decade and a half later, I realized that if I had been allowed a ski mask in such a situation, I probably would have worn it on an entirely different body part. But there you go, different strokes.

Anyway, I didn't like the idea that I might be less than courageous. It was demoralizing. And I didn't appreciate the fact that I was now questioning every insignificant scrap of information my clients fed me. It wasn't right. It wasn't professional. It wasn't propagating my sanity.

The days crept by with lingering problems and unanswered questions. By Friday I found myself cruising down

Bellflower Drive again. Every yard was immaculate. Every shrub flowering. It looked like a fairyland.

I had always wanted to live in fairyland—someplace where even weeds dare not trespass, where the sun always shines, the grass is always green, and cellulite turns to muscle without lifting a finger.

There was only one problem. People like Andrew Bomstad tend to own fairyland, and though they could afford to poison the weeds and suck out the cellulite, it may very well be that both still existed.

I drove past Bomstad's estate one more time, then trundled home to my dehydrated yard and ramshackle little house. It didn't look half bad.

But by Sunday I felt certifiably insane. I had watered the thistle in my yard, washed every sock in the house, and thought about Bomstad until my brain was about to swell through my auditory canal.

I either had to take a look in Bomstad's house or have myself committed. I closed my eyes as I gripped the phone and waited for Solberg to answer.

"Chrissy." He sounded as happy as a songbird. I felt my shoulders droop.

"Hey, J.D."

"Howdy do. Say, I still haven't heard from your secretary yet."

"She's been pretty busy." And I hadn't told her anything about him. I knew it was wrong of me. But asking a friend to endure his company seemed significantly worse.

"I'm busy, too. Maybe we can get busy together," he said and brayed like a tickled burro into the receiver.

I winced. "Listen, Solberg, I have another favor to ask." Hell waits for no man.

The bray stopped in mid hee-haw. "No."

"Come on." I admit I hadn't expected him to turn me down flat. After all, he was still Solberg, and last time I looked I still had boobs. It defied all sorts of logic. "This is simply an insignificant little nothing. I'm sure you could do it in your sleep."

"You know what my IQ is?"

Now there was a question I hadn't anticipated. "No. I don't believe I have that information on file, J.D."

"It's off the charts."

"Uh-huh."

"I know what you're trying to do."

Stay out of jail?

"You're trying to flatter me, get me to do some stinkin' job."

"I don't know anyone else who can do it, Solberg."

I admit that I may have let a little bit of a girly whine enter my voice. But what was a little whine in the face of a life sentence?

"Yeah, well, the answer's still no."

I closed my eyes, said two Hail Marys, and jumped in. "That's too bad. Elaine's free next Saturday night."

There was dead silence from the other end of the line. It was punctuated with debilitating guilt which oozed from me like noxious fumes.

"What do you want?" he asked.

"It's not much." My heart was pumping like a thigh master. "Really."

"Is it illegal?"

"I'm a psychologist," I said, trying to sound aghast. "Trained—"

"Is it?"

I drew a deep breath and closed my eyes. "Maybe a little bit. But just—"

"Forget it."

He was right. Absolutely. I'd lost my mind. "You're right," I said. "It probably can't even be done."

The phone went quiet. "What can't be done?"

"Don't worry about it. I shouldn't have asked."

"That Eileen..." He paused, knowing he was wrong again and fighting his social ineptitude like a master swordsman. "Elise...E—"

"Elaine," I corrected.

"Yeah. Is she really free Saturday night?"

"She was supposed to go to a movie with a friend, but he got the flu."

"Yeah?"

I could hear him weakening. If I had a soul, I'm pretty sure it would have cranked up my conscience just about then. I did a quick, spiritual check. Nothing. "Listen, I'm sorry I bothered you," I said and drew the receiver slowly away from my ear.

"Wait!"

I'm ashamed to say that I may have smiled. But just a little. "What's that?" I asked.

"Is she as hot as she looks on the Net?"

"Laney?"

"Yeah."

"She takes yoga."

"No lie?" He sounded a little breathless.

"Can bend in half like a pretzel."

There was silence again, then, "God damn it, McMullen, if I get busted you're going down with me."

18

Fair play is all well and good. But knowing how to
kick 'em in the balls can get you out of a jam nine
times out of ten.

—Glen McMullen,
when Chrissy came home
from third grade in tears

THE SKY WAS as black as sin as I sped down the 405. I
turned onto Burbank and parked around the corner from
Bomstad's house. It was the perfect position, well away
from my ultimate destination, but with a view of the top
floor through the foliage. I had all of my espionage gear. A
flashlight and dark clothes. Espionage, it seemed, was
cheap to fund.

But I sat in my Saturn and waited for my heart to slow
down. A dark sedan cruised by. I refused to look at it, sure
the driver knew the exact nature of my plans and had
Rivera's number on speed dial.

But finally the car passed and I was left alone. It was

now or never. I stepped out of my Saturn and shut the door. The sound seemed loud enough to wake the dead, almost loud enough to drown the frantic beating of my heart. The climb up the slope toward Bomstad's front gate felt like I was ascending Everest. But finally I was there, panting furtively in front of the black wrought iron. Glancing about, I pressed my face to the bars once again and stared into the darkness, but try as I might, I could see no little red Cyclops staring back at me.

Who would have thought Solberg would be a man of his word? I gripped the bars in both hands and stared harder at the barely visible box.

"Can I help you?"

I almost screamed as I jerked toward the street. A silver BMW idled there as silent as a ghost. A guy in a white polo shirt peered at me from behind the steering wheel.

"Yes." My answer came out in a pathetic warble. I winced, then went with the flow. "I'm sort of lost." Even to my own ears I sounded as if I was about to cry. If I still had a modicum of pride, it surely would have made itself felt just about then, but fear had pretty much swallowed up any other sensible emotions. "I was looking for Julie's house."

"Julie?"

"Yes. Julie . . ." Crap. "Andrews." Crap! Crap! Crap! "You don't . . ." I forced a laugh. The sound was wobbly. I prepared to run. "You don't happen to know where she lives, do you?"

"Julie Andrews? The actress?" I realized now that he had a slight accent. With my luck he was probably her nephew.

"No. No. Of course not. She's an . . . accountant."

"An accountant? In this neighborhood?"

I glanced down the street, hoping for salvation. It didn't come. "She married into the mob."

He stared at me for a moment, then laughed. "No. 'Fraid I don't know any Julie. But tell you what, come have a sit, we'll take a look round."

Was he nuts? Okay, I realized he was good looking, obviously rich, and seductively foreign. But I had already crossed paths with good-looking, rich, and . . . Well, okay, Bomstad had been as American as fornication, but he had also had the bad manners to die in my office. A fact I wasn't soon to forget.

"Thanks anyway," I said and dug in my pocket for the pepper spray Rivera had given me.

"Well, okay then, suit yourself, luv," he said and gave me a smile that, under normal circumstances, would have melted my intestines. As it was I just felt like peeing in my pants.

He revved his engine and zoomed off into the night.

I closed my eyes and leaned back against the fence. Down on Burbank Boulevard another pair of headlights turned north. I swore to myself, relinquished the defense spray, and scurried back to the safety of my Saturn.

In my rearview mirror, I watched the car turn east and disappear. I concentrated on my breathing. It didn't help, so I turned on the AC and tried to stop sweating. Maybe I should have taken yoga with Elaine. Which reminded me, I had to talk to her about Solberg. It couldn't be put off this time. I owed him big. I glanced idly toward Bomber's house. Even if I didn't scrounge up enough nerve to play cat burglar, he had come through with his end of the bargain. Maybe ol' J.D. wasn't such a bad egg after all. True, he brayed like a jackass and wore his pubic hair too far north, but he didn't seem to have any weird attachments to his mother's vacuum cleaner and he hadn't once chased me around my desk like...But in that moment all thought processes teetered to a halt because there—in Bomstad's upper window—was a light.

I blinked, then looked again, but it was gone.

Holy crap! Frantically scanning the house, I tried to convince myself I wasn't insane. I stared until my eyes burned, then, just before they shut down, I saw it again—a flicker of light.

Someone was in Bomstad's house. And it wasn't me.

I glanced out my side window, maybe searching for some answers, maybe certain someone had set me up. But it seemed apparent that I had to try to determine who the intruder was.

Mind spinning, I reached up and clicked off my dome light so that it wouldn't flip on when I opened the door. My hand, I realized, seemed strangely unsteady, but I managed the gargantuan feat. Foresight. I was proud of myself. But when I opened the door, the Saturn blared as if it were being carjacked. I fumbled manically, trying to pull the keys out of the ignition. They tumbled to the floor. A dog barked, jerking my attention to the east, but he was farther away than my frantic mind suggested, so I gathered the keys in spastic fingers, stepped out of the car, and carefully pressed the door closed. I couldn't have made more noise if I had shot a cannon across Bomstad's front lawn.

I waited, hearing nothing but the dog and my own heart trying to hammer its way through my ribs.

Between the branches of nearby trees I thought I saw a flicker of light again, but I was pretty sure I was imagining things this time, because it was pink and rising to the tree-tops. I didn't think there was really an ogre breathing on my neck, either, but I turned woodenly to check, just the same. Sure enough, no ogre, which left me pretty much without excuses. I was going to have to investigate the house.

My legs felt as ungainly as stilts as I crept across the grass, and it was no simple task to shimmy over the wrought-iron fence. The spikes at the top poked me in the belly and caught at my sweater on the way down. Yeah, I'd worn a sweater. In September, in L.A. I'd needed something black with sleeves and didn't want to snag my Dior just to keep from going to jail. In retrospect, that might have been a bit shortsighted.

Before I was halfway across the yard, I was sweating like a pig—which is a strange analogy because my cousin, Kevin the pig farmer, had assured me the porcine species doesn't sweat. But he'd always seemed strangely defensive about his animals and may simply have been . . .

Holy crap! The light was back! I froze like a Popsicle, staring at the house. I was only fifty feet from it now, so I could hardly be mistaken. Although, an instant later it was as dark as Hades again. I couldn't think over the sound of my own breathing, but a light had been there. I was sure of it. Wasn't I? But what if I was right? What then?

Then I'd have to figure out who was in there. But how?

An excellent question. Maybe I should call Rivera. Tell him someone had broken into Bomstad's house. Someone besides me. I winced. A noise scraped, off to my left. I didn't pass out. Instead, after a moment of petrified immobility, I crept, breath held, off to the right, heart pounding like mad, knees weak.

If someone really had broken into Bomstad's house, they'd probably gone through the back door or a window. Which meant they must have either known the security system was disabled or had the code or . . .

Something shone on the grass in the moonlight. Was it glass?

I think it was curiosity that pushed me forward. I'm pretty sure it wasn't courage, and I have a bad feeling about good sense. Good sense, if I had any, was surely urging me to get my ass out of there as fast as my little wooden legs could carry me. But instead I continued to creep along like a demented monkey. I held my flashlight in one hand and my pepper spray in the other, but I was totally unaware of both. Nothing mattered but the light in the window.

Maybe this was a clue, a piece of evidence, a means of extricating myself from the position I found myself in. If I could learn who was in the house, I could surely use that information to—

"Don't move."

The voice was right behind me. I squawked like a pigeon and pivoted around, swinging with all my might.

I heard a grunt. Someone grabbed my arm, but I jerked free and swung again, terror clawing my throat. I felt my flashlight strike flesh. My attacker cursed and wrapped his arms tight around my chest. I couldn't move, couldn't breathe. So I did the only thing I possibly could. I bit him.

"Jesus Christ, McMullen!" Rivera growled. "What the hell's wrong with you?"

19

Sanity is highly overrated.

—Whack,
  proprietor of Tats "R" Us, just
  before tattoing a heart on
  Christina's left buttock

W HAT THE FUCK are you doing here?" Even through
the haze of terror and adrenaline, I noticed his tone didn't
sound very happy.

"Rivera?" My voice was as breathy as a porn star's. I
would like to say I was disappointed to see him. After all,
he was the bane of my existence. And yet, I was pretty
sure he wasn't going to bludgeon me with my flashlight
and dump my decaying body into the bay.

Which couldn't necessarily be said about whoever was
skulking about in Bomstad's darkened house.

On the other hand, Rivera *did* take my flashlight. He
gripped both my arms, and none too gently, I might add.

Maybe I'd sue for that police brutality thing after all. He had no right to—

"Any idea what the penalty is for breaking and entering?" he asked.

I jerked my attention in the direction his had gone. Sure enough, there was broken glass amongst the shrubbery.

"Hey!" I said, righteousness rife in my tone. So what if I had hoped to enter the house in a similar manner? "I didn't do that."

"Really?"

"Really!" I tried to pull away. Seems he was stronger. Who would have thought? "There's someone in there."

"Have you been drinking, McMullen?"

"There is someone in there!" I repeated, slower now, in consideration for his gender and his occupation.

He leaned closer. It took me a minute to realize he was smelling my breath. I gave him a shove. He teetered back a half a step but that was it. I'd been right about the percentage of his body fat. Nil. If I ever got tired of psychoanalysis I could go into psychic body fat testing.

"I'm telling you..." I was hissing now as I glanced toward Bomstad's house. "I saw a light."

"Here's a little pertinent information for you," he said, ushering me toward the walkway with a hand on my arm, "officers of the law are issued flashlights. It's standard equipment."

It took a moment for his words to sink in. "It was you? With the light? It was you?" Holy crap, I'd snuck up on Bomstad's house only to find Rivera. What were the chances?

He pressed me up against some shrubbery. Little barbs

pricked through my sweater. I'd learned shortly after arriving in L.A. that most of its vegetation is engineered to try to eradicate the human species.

"What are you doing here, McMullen?"

My heart rate slowed to a mere gallop and I realized we were standing really close. In fact, my hands had somehow landed on his waist. Maybe I was trying to fend him off. Anyway, even through his shirt I could feel the bunched muscles of his abdomen. It reminded me of my Batman dream, but I think I'd read somewhere that Batman wore Plexiglas armor during the movie. I was pretty sure Rivera's abs were the real deal.

How long had it been since I'd been so close to that kind of muscle? Years, for sure. Maybe decades. Maybe I never had been. Although my old beau, Luke Harken, had had muscle to spare. Unfortunately, most of it had been firmly packed inside his cranium and—

"Jesus, McMullen! Snap out of it!" Rivera ordered and shook me.

I realized then that I seemed to have slipped into some sort of hypnotic state of shock. I shook my head, disgusted with myself.

"Listen. I saw a light," I said. "I had no way of knowing you'd be skulking around in there."

"Police officers don't skulk."

I gave him the look I reserved for perverts and liars, which in my line of work included most everyone I met. "I assumed someone had broken into Bomstad's house," I said, using my nose voice. "Thus, I—" I realized somewhat belatedly that my explanation might not justify my current whereabouts. I'm not sure if I should blame that tardy logic on hormones or stress. Or both. Both are good.

"So you what?" he asked, his tone deceptively level.

I found his gaze and rethought the idea of him bludgeoning me with my flashlight. "I didn't know it was you," I repeated. A mynah bird would have sounded as intelligent. "And I didn't break the window."

"Maybe it spontaneously combusted."

I wasn't sure, but I thought he was being somewhat facetious. "Be a smart-ass if you like," I said. "But I didn't break the window."

"What the hell are you doing here?"

Back to that. It seemed to be a recurring theme. "Well..." I was thinking fast, or trying to, "you wouldn't let me help with the case."

He neither argued nor tried to justify his reasons. He merely stared. I hated that.

I drew my hands away, but he didn't do the same. It would have been nice to believe he just liked touching me, but it could be that he thought I'd zap him with his own defense spray if he let me go. And I have to admit, the thought had crossed my mind.

"So I thought I'd just..." I glanced away. It was difficult holding his gaze, even in the dark, although I had absolutely nothing to be ashamed of. I hadn't killed Bomstad, after all. And if Solberg wanted to disarm the man's security system... But wait a minute. Maybe Rivera had shut it off and Solberg hadn't come through at all. In which case I didn't owe him any favors and Elaine wouldn't hate me for the rest of my natural life. Which would be really nice, because the way things were heading

I was going to need friends to visit me in Sing Sing, or wherever third-degree murderers went.

"You thought what?" he asked and shook me a little. "You'd break into the Bomb's house for a little evening entertainment?"

"This is not—" I began, but at that moment I saw a flicker of light behind him. I tried to speak, to tell him, but my life had become strangely surreal.

"Is it the diary?" he asked. "Is that what you're looking for? What's in the damn thing, McMullen?"

The light! It had shone in a window. I was sure of it. But it was gone. No. There. No. Gone.

I tried to pull out of his grip, straining to see through the darkness.

"What the devil did you do to make—"

"There's a light!" I rasped.

"Will you shut up about the fucking—"

I yanked out of his grasp. "A light!" I hissed, my brain finally kicking in. "I didn't break the window. I assume you didn't." I waved somewhat frenetically. "Someone did."

He glanced at the house, then hissed low and shoved me into the bushes. "Stay there. Do you hear me? Don't move. Don't speak, and for God's sake, don't do anything stupid."

I was trying to conjure up a sufficiently insulted rejoinder when he slipped away. In a heartbeat he was invisible. I couldn't even hear him, at least not over the thumping of my own heart. But then I thought I heard a sound, something from inside the house. Someone was coming. Maybe they were searching for the very thing I wanted. Maybe they had it already.

Holding my breath, I sidled closer, skirting along the bushes with my knees rattling and my hand curled around my pepper spray. I missed my flashlight something fierce. It didn't put out much light, but it was nice to have something in my left hand besides sweat. When I was just about even with the window I stopped. Crouching there like a cowed kitten, I waited, and sure enough, someone appeared in the window—just a block of blackness beneath the jagged shards of broken glass. My throat ached with tension. Where was Rivera?

Then suddenly a beam of light cut a swath through the darkness and across the window. "LAPD! Stay where you are."

For one fragmented second I caught a glimpse of white skin and dark clothing, and then the figure leapt. I saw Rivera go down under the attack. The flashlight spun into the darkness. Someone grunted. Bone thumped against flesh. There was a rasped curse, and then, like a fleeing rabbit, the intruder lurched to his feet and bolted away.

Now, as I recall it, the encounter seemed as if it took place in slow motion. But in reality, everything happened in a heartbeat, in a breath of time. One moment there was someone perched in the window, and the next there were foot beats racing past me into the darkness.

Rivera coughed. I glanced frantically at him, then jerked my attention in the direction of the escapee. For one wild, inexplicable second I actually thought of racing after him. As I tell my clients, even the most lucid of us has bouts of insanity, but the lunacy quickly passed. Just as quickly, the black shape was gone, the racing footfalls disintegrating into silence.

Rivera cursed, making me wonder if I might be safer going after the window guy, but he coughed again and sat up and it didn't seem like there was much I could do but approach him.

"Are you okay?"

He turned toward me. He hadn't been Mr. Congeniality before. I doubted if he was going to qualify for the title at this late date. "Wanna tell me who that was?"

I was actually, physically, taken aback. "You think I know?"

He let loose a fluid string of obscenities that made me wonder where one quit and the next began. Impressive.

"You're not making this easy on yourself. I'll give you that," he said, and seizing the escaped flashlight, he struggled to his feet. The beam of light wobbled. I realized it wasn't my own. Apparently the LAPD really did spring for flashlights.

"Listen," I said. My adrenaline rush had started to subside, leaving fatigue and irritation in its wake. "You think I'm dumb enough to tell you someone's inside if I'm his damned accomplice?"

He looked at me as if thinking it over, but in a moment I realized he wasn't thinking at all; he was sliding down the brick exterior toward the ground. I caught him just before he hit the rhododendrons. He wasn't the featherweight Solberg was, and he wasn't making my efforts any easier. He hit the ground. I did the same a second later. In fact, I may have landed on top of him because I heard a little *ummph* of pain. Not that I'm heavy.

Silence echoed around us. Fear zapped in. Maybe he was dead!

I put my hand on his chest and squinted into his face.

"Jesus!" he said. I realized somewhat belatedly that his eyes were open and his face intimately close to mine. Was he talking to God or just being blasphemous again? "Why the hell don't you just cut my throat and get it over with?" Just as I suspected—he was too ornery to be dead.

"You're blaming this on me?" I was immediately irritated, which is unlike me. Must have been caused by an influx of estrogen. "I didn't ask you to—Oh, crap!" Even in the dark, I could see a dark streak creeping down his face. "You're bleeding."

"No shit, Sherlock," he said and wiped it away with the back of his hand. "Did you see which way he went?"

I watched the blood ooze onto his brow again "Who?"

He gave me a look I could have deciphered in a coal mine. "Our friend in the window. Which way did he go?"

"Oh. That way." I motioned with my head.

He struggled, but seemed to have difficulty getting his feet under him.

"What are you doing?" I asked and leaned automatically against his chest.

"Get the hell off of me," he growled, but I had dealt with illogical men since the day I was born. Granted, my brothers were generally drunk when they decided to do something obviously suicidal, but drunk and concussed seem to have the same effect on the male thinking apparatus. Actually, a lot of situations seem to have the same effect on the male thinking apparatus.

I leaned over him, applying weight to his chest. He struggled for a moment longer, then settled back into the rhododendrons. But I didn't trust his capitulation and stayed where I was.

He dropped his head back against the bricks and coughed weakly. I eased up a little, but not too much, in case it was a trick.

"How the hell much do you weigh, McMullen?" he asked.

"Not..." I began, then, "It's none of your damned business what I weigh."

I thought I saw a flash of teeth in the darkness. Was it a smile? Was he delirious? I applied more of my nearly insignificant weight, just in case he'd lost his mind and was going to make a dash for it. He didn't.

"Did you find what you were looking for?" he asked.

"Still proceeding on the asinine idea that I broke into the house?" I asked and tried not to look at the blood on his forehead or consider the idea that that was exactly what I had intended to do.

"Why else would you be here?"

"I was just curious... Bomstad turned my life upside down. You can't blame me for trying to set things in order." I shuffled my weight, settling a little more firmly against him. Rhododendrons may look just dandy in a hedgerow, but they'll never sell as daybeds. A branch was goosing me with constant regularity. Randy little pervert.

"Is that why you keep coming back here?" he asked. "To set things in order?"

I zapped my gaze to his. "You've been following me?"

He snorted, but he neither agreed or disagreed. "What do you want, McMullen?" he asked. Beneath my hand, his chest felt as hard as the long arm of the law. And for a moment I considered telling him the truth. I'd really like to see him naked, not necessarily in the rhododendrons, but . . .

"Tell me your part in this," he said. "I'd like to believe you're innocent, but—"

"I am innocent," I breathed, leaning closer.

"You're making it hard," he said.

"What?" I refused to glance down the length of his body, but my own tingled in anticipatory interaction.

"To believe," he said. "You're making it hard to believe."

I felt my face flush, but if he could see it in the darkness, he said nothing. Instead, he grasped my wrists and, while I was distracted, shimmied up the wall behind him. In a moment we were standing against the bricks, albeit a bit unsteadily. He pulled me close, hip to hip, I assumed for support. His head wobbled a little. I wrapped an arm around his back. It seemed like the right thing to do.

"Did he go over the fence or back to the street?"

"What?" I staggered a little, trying to keep him upright.

"The intruder," he said. "Which direction?"

"It's dark. I couldn't—"

"What did you hear? Think. Scrambling through bushes? Scraping over a fence?"

"I . . ." I shook my head. "You coughed," I said. "I thought you were dying."

He grunted. "You must have noticed something. You should have been able to see a silhouette from where I left you."

I said nothing.

"You did stay there, didn't you?"

"Of course." I shifted my eyes away. "But I couldn't see past the shrubs. Then it was just running feet."

"Okay," he said and wobbled as if to move away from the wall. I tightened my grip on his shirt.

"What do you think you're doing?"

"My job," he said and stepped forward.

I pressed into him. "Is it your job to drop dead in an ex-tight end's rhododendrons?"

He swayed.

"Because if it is," I said, forcing him back up against the wall and supporting him with my infinitesimal weight, "I'd rather you didn't do so with my flashlight in your pocket." I could feel it pressing against my hip, though it seemed to move slightly even as I spoke. I raised my eyes to his and blinked with all the faux innocence a thirty-something ex-cocktail waitress could muster. "That *is* my flashlight, isn't it?"

20

The theory of relativity don't amount to a hill of beans when there's a bonfire in your shorts.

—J.D. Solberg,
    upon first seeing Chrissy
    McMullen in her Warthog
    uniform

*H*IS TEETH GLIMMERED AGAIN, and he dropped his head back against the house. "Jesus," he said, "you are a one-woman catastrophe."

The "flashlight" moved again. Did that mean he liked one-woman catastrophes?

"I didn't do anything," I reminded him, but he shifted slightly so that my breast was pressed a little more firmly against his chest.

"Come on," he said, gripping my waist as he stepped forward. "I'll get you to your car."

I complied, guiding him through the shrubbery and around the corner of the house, but the meaning of his words dawned on me in a moment. "Where are you going?"

"Hard to say, since you didn't have the foresight to watch which way the suspect went."

I snorted. Ladylike as always. Was he pressed a little tighter than necessary against my left breast? "You need your head examined."

"Looking to drum up business?" he asked and stumbled a little.

I tightened my grip on his waist. Tight as a frickin' yardarm. "I meant medical attention. But now that you mention it, I could suggest a good therapist."

"You don't consider yourself qualified?"

"I don't like to waste my time on lost causes."

We'd reached the fence. I looked at it, wondering how the hell I was going to get him over. Maybe I could just kick him in the shins and roll him underneath. He stumbled to a halt and gazed up at it.

"Shit," he said. Eloquence was not his strong suit. Or diplomacy. But muscle tone . . .

"Yeah," I said, and winced. "You going to need help?"

I thought I saw one eyebrow rise. He shifted his weight slightly so that I found my back against the wrought-iron railing. It felt cool even through the cotton sweater. I was sweating like a Percheron, and suddenly Rivera had me pinned against the metal, one hand on the bar on each side of me. His body felt hard and suspiciously strong against mine. Maybe he'd been supporting *me*. "You offering to give me a lift, McMullen?"

Sometime during our unsteady journey across Bomstad's manicured lawn, he had slipped his flashlight into its holster at his side. Mine was still in his back pocket.

Which only left one option as to the identity of the hot weight that pressed against my belly. "Seems I already did that, Rivera," I said.

He leaned closer. "Well, that's a first," he murmured. His voice was deep and low and did funny things to my already jittering nerve endings.

My heart was beating like a racehorse's. "Been a while for you, has it?" I asked, trying to remember the exact phrase he'd used on me.

He grinned, actually grinned, full-blown. I felt a little light-headed. "That's the first time you got my name right," he explained. "You nervous, McMullen?"

"Nervous? I'm with an officer of the law. Why would I be nervous?"

"I don't know. You seem to be breathing kind of hard."

"I think I overdressed for the occasion."

"Want to remedy that?"

Hell, yeah, my hormones screamed. But by the time I was on my eighteenth loser boyfriend I'd learned to override any influx of screaming hormones. "I think I'll wait," I said.

He grunted something unintelligible, then, "Can you get your ass over the fence or do you need assistance?"

"Please!" I scoffed, trying to inject my tone with injured self-confidence. But mostly I was still arguing with my hormones, and my knees felt a little unsteady. Also, I really didn't want him to see my fence-climbing techniques. If I remembered correctly, they were less than noteworthy.

"You first," he said and eased away. I tried to adjust to the separation of our bodies and hardly staggered at all as I turned around to grip the bars.

Adrenaline was more powerful than I had expected, because I was halfway up the fence before I knew it. Of course, the fact that he splayed his fingers across my left butt cheek didn't hurt any. For a moment I considered shimmying down on top of him, but shame made me scramble faster, over the top and down the other side.

Even considering my prowess and his weakened state, his technique was somewhat superior. But once on the opposite side of the fence, his face looked pale in the darkness.

"You going to be able to get yourself to the hospital?" I asked.

"I'm an officer of the law."

"Of course. I forgot," I said, but I couldn't help noticing that he stumbled when he turned. Conscience kicked in. Something about my brother facedown in the peonies and my own stinging behind. "Where's your car?" I asked.

He bobbed his head toward the street, and we found his vehicle a minute later—a dark Jeep with a detachable roof. "Get in," he said. "I'll give you a lift."

I eyed him. He didn't look up to breathing, much less driving.

"How 'bout I drive, you sit?"

He canted his head at me. "You trying to seduce me, McMullen?"

I considered running him over, but I just told him he was an ass and took his keys. He relinquished them without much argument, then rounded the bumper and eased into the passenger seat. Even in the darkness, he looked limp and exhausted. Oh, crap.

"Which hospital?" I asked.

"Just take me home."

"Good idea. Then I can make an appointment right away to ID your dead body in the morning."

"I didn't think you cared, McMullen."

"So astute. Which hospital?"

He exhaled carefully and touched a hand to his head. "I just need some sleep."

"Glendale or Huntington Memorial?"

"Fourteen twenty-two Rosehaven. Want to carry me up to my bedroom? I hear you make house calls."

"Bite me."

"Not here," he said. "It's against the law. But anything goes in the privacy of my bedchamber."

I considered opening his door and kicking him into the street, but in order to do that I'd have to reach across his lap, and that seemed tantamount to sniffing cookie dough while dieting. "You scared of doctors, Reeves?" I asked.

"I don't like to undress in front of strangers."

"Really."

He nodded, but his head was listing against the Jeep's gray cushion. "Mother Superior taught me better than to show off."

I gave him a look, but it was wasted. His eyes had fallen closed.

"What part of Rosehaven?" I asked.

"Simi."

I lifted a brow at him. Simi was a posh part of town. "On the take, Lieutenant?"

"Ha," he said, and I wondered silently about his father, the affluent bastard senator.

"That what you're interested in, McMullen?" he asked. "Money?"

I started up the Jeep and eased into the street. There wasn't another moving vehicle as far as the eye could see. "Isn't everyone?"

"No," he said and left it like that.

I looked at him. "Just out to get your man?"

"Or woman."

"You're barking up the wrong tree."

He touched his head again. "Feels like I fell out of the damned tree. What the hell were you doing in Bomstad's yard?"

"I told you—"

"The diary's police property now."

My heart rate bumped up as I jerked toward him. "You found it?"

He opened his eyes to slits, but didn't bother to lift his head. "The Bomber led an interesting life."

My mind buzzed. "Then you know I had nothing to do with his death."

"Do I?"

"Yes."

"Because you were only interested in him professionally."

See, there was the sticky part. But my own private fantasies had no basis in reality. Never had, if truth be told.

"Seems he was more interested in the nonprofessional side of *you,* though," he said.

I stared at him. He was just baiting me. Wasn't he? I

mean, the Bomb had been found with a hard-on the size of the Getty Center. Any half-wit could deduce he wasn't much interested in my diploma.

"Ever heard of Stephanie Meyers, McMullen?"

My breath caught in my throat, but my mind was flipping out. Was he trying to trap me? Trying to tie the starlet's death to Bomstad and Bomstad's to me?

"Isn't she an actress?" I said, keeping my tone oh so casual.

I could feel his gaze strike me through the darkness. "Was. She died a few months ago."

I focused my serious expression on the street. "The entertainment field is fraught with emotional pitfalls."

For a moment the car was silent, and then he laughed. "Fraught with emotional pitfalls? Is that how you talk to your patients?"

"Forgive me if I prefer to maintain a professional image," I said.

The sound he made defied description. "Well, it worked for the Bomb, huh? Blasted his rocket."

I tried to think of something scalding to say, but he was already continuing. "He and Stephanie had a thing for a while."

"Stephanie Meyers?" I didn't even try to keep the surprise out of my tone. Rivera and I had something of a history and he had yet to call me by my first name. But his relationship with the late starlet seemed rather personal.

He had turned to gaze out the window. "She was just a kid."

"You knew her?"

"Our paths crossed from time to time."

Did those paths traipse through his bedroom? I could imagine them together—him, dark and protective; her, bright and dynamic.

"She was seeing a psychiatrist," he said.

I almost winced. "I didn't cause her death," I said. "Neither did her therapist."

"He didn't prevent it, either," he said, and there was something in his voice, a raw frustration that made me think he believed *he* should have prevented it.

"I'm sorry." It was a poor substitute for anything constructive, but it seemed to deflate his rigid anger.

"What'd you see in him?" he asked. "In Bomstad."

"As I told you before—"

"Fuck that," he said but there was no aggression in his voice now, just tired resignation. "What would she have seen in him?"

"Meyers?"

"Yeah."

Had Rivera been in love with her? Was he still? "I think you know the answer to that," I said.

"Humor me."

I passed the only car on the highway. L.A. felt strangely deserted at three in the morning.

"I'm considering the possibility that he was schizophrenic," I said.

"Split personality?"

"That's a bit simplistic. But yes. He seemed to be so gentle and . . . He was very convincing," I said.

"Convincing how?"

"He seemed genuinely kind, interested in others. Sensitive, even."

"And you didn't look into his background?"

"I had no reason to believe he was anything other than the image he chose to project."

He gazed into the night, a dark man with dark thoughts. "What image do I project?"

The image of a man who's been wounded by life, I thought, but shoved the idea behind me. It was not my place to try to fix him. It probably couldn't even be done. "When was the last time you slept?" I asked.

He turned wearily toward me, "You think I'm delirious, McMullen?"

"Fatigue has been known to change a person's personality."

"What's my personality now?"

Tired. And disturbingly vulnerable, like a battle-weary soldier, but I watched the road and refused to be drawn into his private war. I had gotten over my weakness for vulnerability a long time ago. Now I just wanted someone who used a single toothbrush each morning and didn't fantasize about the same guys I did. "I don't think now would be the proper time to analyze you, Rivera."

He snorted. "I am what you see."

"That's what I thought about Bomstad."

He nodded slowly. "Was he capable of murder?"

"What?"

"In your opinion," he said. "Did he have the temperament to take another person's life?"

"It's difficult to . . ." I began, but his meaning kicked in suddenly. "You think he killed Meyers?"

He looked at me, then scrubbed his hand over his face.

"I wish to hell I knew. I keep thinking about it. Thinking—" He paused.

"Maybe you need to quit thinking for a while," I said. "Get some sleep."

He nodded. "Sleep. Nice idea."

"You're an insomniac?"

"You shrinks have big words for everything?"

"It makes us feel superior. The one with the biggest word wins."

"Like guns in my line of work."

Our eyes met in the darkness. His looked tired and sad and honest, and there is nothing more dangerous than honesty to a woman who hasn't had sex in over a . . . while. "You got a big gun, Lieutenant?"

"Want to come in and find out?"

More than anything. "I'm not that interested in artillery."

"You never know, you might like it if you try it."

"I was speaking metaphorically."

"Me, too."

I couldn't help but smile. It was entirely possible that I'd never smiled at him before, but then he'd usually been accusing me of a capital offense. It tends to put a strain on a relationship. "I have one hard, fast stipulation, Rivera: I don't sleep with men who have accused me of murder."

"That rule out many guys?"

"You're the first."

"Bad luck for me. Would it help if I told you I have an M-fifty-seven?"

"Is that a gun or a disease?"

"I'm disease-free. It's documented."

"Girl can hardly ask for more than that."

"Well . . ." He shrugged. "And the—"

"M-fifty-seven," I finished for him.

"You always read people's minds?" he asked.

"I'm a trained professional," I said, "and men's minds are pretty one-track."

He didn't try to deny it. "But it's not a bad track."

No, I thought, and wondered a bit dizzily how big an M57 really was.

"Come in," he said. "Find out."

I shot a glance toward him, terrified I'd spoken out loud.

"I'm a trained professional," he said. "And a year is a long time."

"I didn't say it had been a year."

"How long, then?"

Fourteen months, five days, and about six hours. I hadn't been sleeping much lately, either. I'd had a lot of time to figure it out. "You need to have someone examine your head," I said.

"You could do that . . . after."

He was staring at me. If I weren't so grounded I would say his eyes were bottomless and enigmatic. Since I was grounded, I'd have to call them so fucking sexy it made my mouth go dry. "I'm not a doctor, Rivera."

"We could pretend," he said and reached across the car to touch my cheek.

I managed to keep the Jeep on the road and continue to breathe. What a woman.

"I'm not going to play doctor with you," I said.

He pressed my hair back. I suppressed a shiver like Xena, Warrior Princess.

"What if I pass out on the way up to my bedroom? Hit my head on the newel post. Never come to. That'd be the second death you'd be associated with."

"Are you trying to threaten me?"

"Actually, I'm trying to seduce you."

Hot damn!

"I hate it when women confuse the two," he added.

"Don't you have some kind of rules against fraternizing with suspects?"

"We could call it interrogation. Or therapy."

For him or me? "I don't think so."

He leaned closer. He smelled like jazz music and wood smoke. His lips were warm and firm when they touched my neck. I shivered down to my socks, and I may have moaned a little. I've got a lot of pride, but my hormones are sluts down to the core.

"Christ, you're making me crazy," he said, and slipped a hand under my sweater.

My nipples went stiff. I told myself it didn't mean anything, but suddenly the Jeep was bumping up against the nearest curb, and my fingers were wrapping themselves in his shirt. He growled like a pit bull when he kissed me, like an animal on the edge of control. Suddenly his buttons were gone. I'm pretty sure it wasn't my fault, but they sprayed around the car like fireworks gone mad.

His hands were on my skin, hot and handy and ready. I squirmed beneath him, my mind fuzzy, my hormones buzzing.

He was already on top of me. I was stretched out on the seat, trying not to pant.

Then someone rapped on the window.

Rivera's head jerked up, and with that motion, a ton of temporarily misplaced sanity came pounding back to me.

Mortified, I squirmed out of his grip. He sat up and blinked at the lights that beamed above Glendale Health Center.

He was already cursing as I slid out the door and onto the pavement. There was an ambulance driver standing only inches away. I grabbed his hand and pressed Rivera's keys into it.

"Concussion," I said, panting like a broken-down race-horse. "He needs immediate attention."

21

Generally, men are superior in the area of heavy lifting, where they're surpassed only by pachyderms and building cranes. Beyond that, I believe any right-thinking person will see that women have the indisputable advantage.

—Regina Stromburg, Ph.D.,
Coordinator of Women's
Studies

I TOOK A CAB HOME from the hospital, but the rest of the night was worthless. Couldn't sleep. Couldn't think. Even ice cream failed to work its usual magic. Lying down made me as jittery as butter on a skillet and pacing was nothing but a waste of hard-earned fat molecules.

I paced anyway. I'd done the right thing, I told myself. I hadn't dragged Rivera into the backseat of his Jeep and ripped off his clothes. Okay, I'd kind of ripped off his clothes, but I had refrained from sabotaging my life. I'd kept my head. I'd even delivered him to the hospital, just like a real adult. Not that he'd seemed very appreciative.

In fact, he'd acted mad enough to eat nails. Or me. I paced again, my mouth going dry at the thought.

I'd done the right thing, I reiterated. I was a professional now. A psychologist. I didn't make out in the parking lot with some guy who made me crazy. But damned if I hadn't wanted to. I couldn't forget how he had looked, how he had felt, how he had smelled—

My thoughts screeched to a halt as scents filled my memory. Rivera had smelled good, like musky midnight, but I had smelled something else when we'd been beneath Bomstad's window. It was . . . perfume. Holy crap! Reality burst in my mind like a ten-cent firecracker.

The man who'd jumped Rivera hadn't been a man at all. He was a woman!

I only had four appointments the next day. So I spent my lunch hour at the mall, testing scents and trying to recall every detail of the previous night. By two o'clock I was as horny as a teenage tuba player, remembering some parts of the evening better than others, but finally I narrowed the scent down to three finalists . . . maybe. It was impossible to be sure, of course, but since I had nothing else to go on, it seemed to be my best bet.

Although I had spent some time in discount stores, too, I was pretty sure the burglar's chosen aroma was either Bvlgari, Jivago, or Arpège. All upper-end products. But that would make sense. Bomstad hadn't exactly been destitute. It stood to reason that the women he knew would also be affluent. Although I had been at his house, too, and I wasn't exactly rolling in dough. Then there were the high school girls he'd been caught with, and Sheri Volkers, none of whom were likely to be raking it in.

I sat at my computer and considered knocking my head against the screen. According to the five million links I'd viewed, Bvlgari could be purchased from approximately forty different companies. Of course, each company could have as many as a hundred stores. And that wasn't even considering the possibility of buying on-line.

In other words, it would take me about eight lifetimes to investigate all the possibilities. Which might not be all that long in my case. I hadn't heard from Rivera since the hospital debacle, but I had a feeling he was the kind to hold a grudge.

Other memories crowded in—memories of hot gazes and warm skin—but I shoved them back and concentrated on more immediate problems. Like survival.

I had purchased samples of each of the three perfumes. Luckily, they came in bottles the size of my pinky toe, so I hadn't needed to take out a second mortgage on my house. With them in hand, I'd be able to check their scents against any possible suspects. Plus, there was the added bonus of smelling really great when Rivera threw me in the slammer.

I smelled all three options again, but my olfactory system was becoming overloaded, and it was then that the phone chimed. I picked it up on the second ring.

"Ms. McMullen." The voice was unfamiliar at first. Deep and lusciously male, it had my heart jumping with all kinds of unwanted emotions. "This is Miguel Rodriguez."

It took me a minute to place the name, but images came

flooding back—Latino, handsome, suave. He must have had the wrong number.

"Ms. McMullen?"

"Yes, hello," I said and wondered if I sounded as breathless as I felt. The night with Rivera had left me wound up like a Slinky. "Mr. Rodriguez, what can I do for you?"

"I was hoping I might do something for you." I had noticed in the past that a Spanish accent could make a death sentence sound sexy, and I had no reason to reevaluate my original assessment. If he had asked for a week of fornication in Barbados, his words couldn't have sounded more seductive. My glands hummed, drowning my nerves. My mind was a little slower to rev up, because I couldn't seem to think of a single reason he might have called, except for that week in Barbados, of course. "I have, I think, some information that may interest you."

"Information?" It wasn't until that moment that I finally remembered I'd asked him to call me. He was merely fulfilling his obligations and probably hadn't purchased plane tickets to some secluded island after all. Life sucks.

"Oh, that list of 'C' names," I said. "Did you think of someone?"

"*Sí*. But surely this is a topic best discussed in person. I was hoping we might meet later."

My glands slowed their leakage and something twisted in my stomach. Bad things had been happening when I left the sanctity of my home, and I didn't know much about this guy. Except that he had an accent like Julio Iglesias and eyes to match. Maybe that was enough. And maybe it would be rude to say I thought he intended to murder me over a cappuccino. I didn't want to be rude to Julio Iglesias. "What did you have in mind, Mr. Rodriguez?"

"Please, call me Miguel."

Miguel. Of course. He sounded as luscious as forbidden fruit to a tuba player from Schaumburg, Illinois.

"I had hoped we might meet for dinner. At Bella Vista, perhaps."

Dinner at Bella Vista? Not a hamburger at Micky D's or coffee at Denny's? It boggled my mind. He was like a real grown-up man or something. But I stomped down the glands that were starting to growl like starved pit bulls and fired up my professional tone. "I appreciate the offer, Mr. Rodriguez. But I'm extremely busy, and—"

"Yet surely, you must eat."

There was something about the way he accented his syllables that made the saliva pool in my mouth.

"Do you not?" he asked.

"Yes. I do eat."

"It is good then," he said. "I shall meet you tomorrow night at six o'clock."

I almost agreed before I remembered I'd spent more than a decade trying to extract myself from overbearing men. My brother, Michael, had once met my date at the door with a baseball bat. I'd weighed in at one hundred seventy pounds at the time. I could have squashed the poor little piccolo player with my left foot. I'd been mortified, and yet there was something about a forceful man that still made my mind go a little limp.

Shit, I thought, and shut the door on the estrogen machine. It had gotten me nothing but trouble since the day

I'd reached puberty. "I'm afraid I can't make it tomorrow night, Mr. Rodriguez," I said.

"But you do want this information, no?"

"Yes," I said and refused to acknowledge the relief I felt with that admission; I'd have to meet with him. "How about tomorrow for lunch? At Wellingtons?"

"But lunch is so..." There was a smile in his voice. "Plain."

"I'm a plain girl," I said, "and—"

"No," he interrupted me smoothly, "you are not. But lunch is acceptable."

We agreed on the time and place and hung up a few seconds later. I stared at the phone as if it were an alien and told myself I was not going to drag Mr. Rodriguez into the ladies' lounge and have my way with him, no matter how he accented his syllables.

*M*iguel rose from his seat the moment he spotted me. He wasn't a tall man, but he stood as straight as a soldier, and his gaze never left mine. There's nothing like a Latin man's eyes to make you feel like you've forgotten your underwear.

"Ms. McMullen," he said. I tried to be professional and brusque, but found my hand clasped between both of his. His eyes were dark and spaniel soft.

"Mr. Rodriguez," I said primly and retrieved my hand. He held it a moment longer, then released me and motioned toward the seat opposite his.

I slid into the booth, silk against leather. Apparently Wellington's didn't waste its time on vinyl. He studied me in silence for a moment, a little smile curling his lips. "I am surprised you have a single patient," he said. "They must, each of them, be cured after the first glance at you."

An accent and compliments. Down, girl! I hadn't gone there for a tête-à-tête, after all. I straightened my back and gave him my no-nonsense look. My blouse was canary yellow and wore like a second skin. It had cap sleeves and gray piping that crossed between my breasts. My skirt was ivory silk and slightly ruffled. The care with which I had chosen my ensemble had nothing to do with Mr. Rodriguez.

"I appreciate your researching those names for me," I said.

He smiled. "American women. So rushed. Would you not like a glass of wine before we begin with the business?"

I noticed that there was a shapely split on the table. His glass already sparkled with it, though it didn't look as though it had been touched.

"No, thank you," I said and settled my purse on the seat beside me. "I have appointments this afternoon."

"Of course," he said, and smiled again. "It must be interesting." He lifted his glass and swirled the wine. "Your job."

I thought of Mr. Lepinski's luncheon dilemmas. Poor guy. He had become the poster child for all things dull. "Yes," I said, "it is."

"And you have a chance to . . . how is it said . . . to make a difference."

"Sometimes," I agreed, and he sighed, then took a sip of his wine.

"There was little you could do for our Andrew, Christina. You do not mind if I call you Christina?"

His eyes had saddened at the memory of the Bomb, and I couldn't really think of a reason to insult him.

"Christina is fine."

"He was a disturbed young man."

No shit. "I'm afraid I wasn't fully aware of the extent of his troubles," I said, digging carefully. "I take it his womanizing was an ongoing problem?"

"Womanizing." He shook his head. "In my country, we appreciate a beautiful lady." His eyes gleamed and his lips curled again as he stared at me. "But Andrew...there were many times I thought he hated them."

"Hated women?"

"He was...attracted to them, of course. But strong women..." He made a fist and canted his head slightly. "Smart women...they angered him, I think."

I reached for my wine glass just for something to do. He filled it, maybe for the same reason.

"You are a strong woman, Christina," he said.

I took a sip of the wine and tried to keep my breathing regular, though the memory of Bomstad's hands on me made me feel like I needed a shower. "Do you know of anyone who would have wanted him dead, Mr. Rodriguez?" I asked.

He looked at me for a long time, then swirled his wine again. "My employers would prefer I lie to you, I think. But yes, Andrew was a man who made enemies."

258 ~ Lois Greiman

"Any that would be willing to kill him?"

"None of the people in my acquaintance."

And he'd been so honest up until then. "Forgive me," I said, "if I find that difficult to believe."

He shrugged. "We pay our players well," he said. "They have families, comfortable homes, good lives. They would be fools to risk that."

"I believe they might be fools."

He smiled. "Do you speak of professional athletes, Christina, or men in general?"

I thought it best to skirt that question, but there was no need because the waitress appeared. We placed our orders. Miguel ordered manicotti with extra marinara sauce. I settled on a salad.

He was smiling at me when the waitress left.

I raised a brow, hoping to look aloof and silently wondering if there was a Mrs. Rodriguez darning his socks at home.

"Tell me you are not concerned about your figure," he said.

"I, um . . ." I was a grown woman, for God's sake, but he had a way of making me feel like a teenybopper with my first crush. "I just like lettuce."

He laughed out loud. "It is good to know you are not worried about your weight," he said. "Because a woman cannot have too many curves."

That was a bunch of rubbish, and I knew it, but rubbish can't be all bad. "You said you had some names for me."

"So fast back to the business," he said. "But yes, I do. And I shall give them to you." His eyes sparkled. "If you promise me one thing."

Sex. Hot and fast. Right on the table. "What promise is that?"

He reached for my hand with both of his. "They make what is called a chocolate volcano here," he said. "You will share one with me, yes?"

22

You lose a couple pounds and get a guy good and drunk, you could have a hell of a good time even if you are smart.

MIGUEL GAVE ME two *C* names. One was the Bomb's father, Christian Bomstad. The other was his accountant. I followed up on both.

Bomstad's dad, it seemed, was a retired steel worker. He lived in a middle-income subdivision in Clinton, where one can still survive near Detroit, and was deeply grieving for his son. Or so it seemed. But I admitted at this point that one could never be sure. Still, it was unlikely he would send his son a bottle of wine with a cryptic inscription or spritz on a dose of Arpège to burgle his house like Catwoman.

Bomstad's accountant's name was Catherine Hansen.

She was fifty-two years old. She lived with a guy with a comb-over and a son called Rocko, possibly not his real name, who occupied the space above her garage.

When I met her at her office in Culver City I didn't think she smelled like either Bvlgari or Jivago. In fact, she smelled a little like cigarette smoke disguised with Scope.

By Wednesday evening I felt wilted and old. It hadn't rained for half a decade, and my air-conditioning seemed to be on hiatus. I lay spread-eagle, one leg thrown over the back of my couch, and lived for the moments the oscillating fan blew my way while I waited for inspiration to come knocking. It didn't, even though my mind was working considerably better than my body. Though, at that moment, it wasn't going to win me the Nobel Peace Prize.

Maybe I was a fool to rule out the *C*'s Miguel had ferreted out for me. As murderers went, they were certainly as likely as I was. And Rivera hadn't seen fit to cross *me* off the short list. But then he seemed to have something against psychologists. Which seemed strange because half the population of Los Angeles was in treatment of some sort. Little Tricia Vandercourt/Rivera, who seemed the most unlikely of clients, for one. Bomstad was another, though his reasons seemed a little suspect, now that I realized he had lied about everything from his hat size to his personality flaws. Stephanie Meyers, Rivera had said, was also someone's client. Which made me wonder if her death was somehow related to Bomstad's. I had the feeling Rivera thought so.

Dragging myself to a seated position, I gazed into my

shell-sized office. In a couple minutes I had managed to slither off my couch and turn on my PC.

It growled at me—something it did when the weather was unfavorable, or when I turned it on.

My search for information about Stephanie Meyers was more successful than most I'd tried. Despite her death, or maybe because of it, her photos were everywhere. I stared at the pictures on my screen. She was young, trim, and beautiful. One would think that would be enough. But there was more. It wasn't just that she was sexy, though she certainly was that. There was something about her expressions. She always looked as though she knew secrets you weren't privy to, but that she might be willing to share the fun if the spirit moved her. She oozed seduction.

Rivera had implied they knew each other socially. Had it been more than that? Had they shared a common bond? Had they shared a bed? Not that I cared on a personal level, but certainly it would have a bearing on how he treated the case. Wouldn't it?

I dug a little deeper and found a plethora of information regarding Ms. Meyers, most of which was completely useless. After an hour and a half I gave up and flopped onto my bed. I fell asleep before I came up with the cure for cancer, but by morning I had an idea. I chewed some coffee beans on the drive to work and fantasized about the chocolate volcano I had shared with Miguel Rodriguez. Actually, he hadn't eaten his share, bless his Latino soul. Spanish men, it is said, know the way to a woman's heart. I just hadn't realized they knew it involved large doses of chocolate and cream cheese.

Two clients and three cups of coffee later I got a chance to leave a message with Dr. David's secretary.

In some obscure piece of literature I had noticed that Stephanie Meyers had spent time in a rehabilitation center called Hope Everlasting. It was a facility I remembered David speaking of, and since I had nowhere else to go, I had contacted him for information.

It was good to hear his voice when he returned my call.

"I've been meaning to get in touch with you," he said. "How are things going?"

"Good." It was a knee-jerk response. I'd been trained from infancy to give a polite answer, and barring decapitation, would probably always do just that.

But it seemed like I failed to fool him, because he insisted we meet so that I could talk.

*C*hrissy." David must have seen me coming even before I entered the restaurant, because he hugged me as soon as I got through the door. "How are you holding up?" He stepped back to hold me at arm's length. There was something about his voice or his touch or his presence that made me want to curl up in his lap and confess everything. If I was his patient I would have brought a box of tissues and a pillow to every session. If I was his basset hound I would have died happy.

"I'm fine. Really," I said. "Thanks for meeting with me."

"Of course." He touched my back as we followed the host to a deep-seated booth. I had always liked the way men touch women's backs as they escort them along—a tender mix of possessiveness and consideration. For a moment I pretended we were together. Me and the classy guy with the great wardrobe and skyrocket IQ.

"How are things, really?" he asked.

I thought of lying again, but I was sure he would know the truth. David would always know. "Not great."

"Tell me."

I gave him the short version, adding that the board of psychology was at least temporarily off my back.

He was shaking his head when I finished. Again. "But this Lieutenant Rivera still suspects you?"

"I don't know." I felt more relaxed than I had in a long while. Maybe it was due to David's presence, but then again, maybe it was the booze. I'd ordered a Cosmopolitan because it seemed classier than a hot mint sundae with cashews and extra whipped cream. "I'm just..." I took a sip of the drink. It wasn't ice cream but it would do in a pinch. "Sometimes I think I'm going crazy."

He smiled at me and leaned across the table. "You're not."

"Are you sure?"

"Absolutely."

I sighed. "Then it must be the rest of the world."

"Now, that," he said with a nod, "is entirely possible."

I sipped again. He lifted his hand, motioning the waitress for another, one for himself and one for me. "Is there any point to it?" I asked. Alcohol tended to make me introspective... and prematurely drunk. Probably because of my minuscule weight. "Therapy, I mean."

He held my gaze. "I don't know."

I straightened, shocked to consider, for the first time, that Dr. David might be human, just like the rest of us?

"It seems like a giant scam sometimes, doesn't it?" he asked. "As if we're just taking their money for no earthly reason?"

I tried to formulate a response. Nothing came to mind.

He chuckled a little, but his eyes looked tired. "Forgive me. I have a client . . ." He paused and cleared his throat. "A young woman tried to commit suicide today."

"Oh, no. David, I'm so sorry," I said and felt like wrapping him in my arms. "I didn't know," I said, "or I wouldn't have called you. You probably want to be at home."

He shook his head and ran a finger around the edge of his glass. "Kathryn knows I need time with my colleagues."

So she was gorgeous *and* understanding. I hated her more with each passing moment. "She seems very nice," I said.

"She's a wonderful woman. Beautiful, intelligent, warm." He drank and then laughed at himself. "I'm sorry. We came here so you could talk."

"No. Please." Pour lemon juice on my paper cuts. "Go on."

"Suffice it to say, I'm a lucky man," he said and, reaching across the table, took my hand in his. "She's completely secure. No issues about my meeting an attractive associate for dinner. What did you want to talk about, Chrissy?"

Attractive? I thought dizzily. "I just . . ." Why had I come? My world felt a little crumbly under my feet. Dr. David thought I was attractive. Wow. "I read somewhere that Stephanie Meyers spent time at Hope Everlasting."

Our meals arrived. He turned his plate just so, thanked the waitress, and gave me a nod to continue.

"I know you sometimes recommend that particular facility, and I was just wondering if you had heard anything about her case."

He sat back, ignoring his steak for a minute. If I had ordered a steak it would have been gone before it had left the waiter's hand. And maybe the hand would be forfeit as well. But I had ordered the mandarin salad. The waiter was safe.

"Stephanie Meyers," he said. "The actress."

I explained things to him, how Rivera was investigating both deaths, how I thought he might believe they were somehow interconnected. How he seemed to blame me. . . .

"So I thought . . ." I took a sip of my drink, washing down a water chestnut. Yum. Those Asians really know how to eat. Maybe that's why they're the approximate width of my eyeteeth. "I thought you might know who had been counseling Ms. Meyers." I gave him a hopeful smile, mostly hoping there was no spinach in my teeth.

"I'm not sure if I can help you," he said. "Considering the necessary confidentiality."

"I understand the difficulties, of course," I said. "But she's been dead for nearly a year now." I played with a radish that had been cut to look like a rose. It didn't seem any more appetizing as a flower than it would have as a vegetable.

"Ten months," David corrected.

"What?" I abandoned the radish.

He sighed, letting his shoulders droop, and suddenly he looked entirely his age. "She was my client, Chrissy."

"Your . . . Really?"

He smiled, but the expression was faded. "For more than a year."

"I didn't . . . I'm sorry. I had no idea. I didn't mean to bring up more painful memories."

He shook his head and pushed his steak aside. "The media . . ." He sighed and picked up his Scotch. "They always portrayed her as a sex kitten. And God knows she was lovely. But . . ." He scowled at his drink, but didn't seem to see it. "She was so much more," he said, and I wondered suddenly if he had been a little in love with her, too. "Fragile. Insightful. Funny."

"Please forgive—"

He stopped me with a wave of his hand and sipped his drink. I followed suit. If there was ever a time to get drunk, this was at the top of the damned list.

"It was a difficult time, knowing I should have done more, thinking that if I had tried this or that things might have been different. But I'm glad now that I didn't give up my practice."

I stared at him, trying to keep my world from spinning out of control. "You were thinking of quitting?"

He smiled. I suppose I looked like a slack-jawed doofus, but it seemed as though a god had trembled. It was said he had counseled Alec Baldwin. I'd give my second virginity to meet Alec Baldwin.

"It was a low point in my career."

"You should have told me. I would have . . ." What? Sent ice cream and fed him in bed. ". . . liked to help."

"Thank you. But in the end, I think it was something I had to work out on my own. Still, it was...well, it was painful," he said. "The loss of someone so young and vivacious. But if I'm honest...if I'm really truthful..." He leaned across the table and his gaze, earnest and hurting, bored into mine. "You know what bothers me the most?"

I shook my head, stunned by a dozen revelations, not least of all the idea that he was sharing secrets with a girl who had once dared her cousin to pee on his electric fence. My excursions to my uncle's farm had always been a barrel of laughs—and some shock therapy.

"The fact that I don't know what hurt more—her death or my failure," he said and finished his drink.

"Failure. You can't believe you—" I began, but he interrupted me.

"I was in Seattle when she overdosed. Speaking at a convention with my peers." He closed his eyes for a moment. "Being important."

"You couldn't possibly have known she planned to kill herself."

He was silent for a moment, then, "She called my office that evening." He paused and drew a slow, steady breath. "But I didn't check my messages until late that night. I called her from my hotel room, just to make sure she was all right, but there was no answer."

"I'm so sorry."

"I assumed she'd just gone out. She had a thousand friends. Everyone wanted to know her—from busboys to billionaires. Some of them were a bit...unsavory maybe. But still, I didn't think..."

He shook his head. I couldn't come up with anything helpful to say. But "life sucks" came to mind.

"Well, that's just it, isn't it?" he said, his voice quiet. "I didn't think." He sipped his drink. "Not about anything but my own self importance."

I felt stunned and empty. The words "I'm sorry," seemed sadly inadequate, but I tried them again anyway.

He gave me a weary smile. "Well," he said, "I was expecting this to be a cathartic meeting. I just didn't expect me to be the one to purge." His smile lifted into a shadow of true amusement. "You're a hell of a therapist, Ms. McMullen."

It was nearly ten o'clock when he pulled his Mercedes up to the curb beside my house. I was grateful for the darkness. If he had seen my yard I would have had to fake an out-of-body experience and babble on about my life as an Abyssinian in Egypt.

As it was, my security light had burned out three days ago and I had failed to replace it. Good planning on my part.

He walked me to the door in utter darkness. Or, more correctly, he walked while I tottered. I'm afraid I may have overimbibed. Okay, truth is, I was drunk as an Irishman. But then, I'm part Irish.

I smiled at him from my stoop. I imagined myself as seductive yet classy. But my perceptions might have been a bit skewed, because on the following morning I found dried leaves stuck to my blouse, which meant either my wardrobe needed weeding or I had stumbled into my withered tea roses.

"You didn't have to drive me home, David," I said, finding my footing with graceful aplomb.

He grasped my elbow and steadied me. "I think I did," he said, and smiled as he stepped close for added support. "Besides, I appreciate you listening to me whine."

"You didn't whine," I said, but my words may have been a little breathless. He was standing pretty close, and even though I knew I was zonkered I didn't think I was misreading his signals.

"You're a kind woman, Chrissy, and a beautiful one."

Really? I felt wobbly and very near tears, but I kept my mouth shut. If there's one thing I had learned from my brothers, the cretin three, it was to keep quiet when inebriated. Almost anyone can seem intelligent if he's silent long enough.

"I'm sorry for the trouble you've been through," he said. "But it'll blow over."

"Will it?"

"Certainly. You're entirely innocent. The LAPD will figure that out eventually. And your life will return to normal." He pushed a tendril of hair behind my ear. I'd aimed for a sophisticated business look that evening. But sometimes my hair forgets its mission.

"Normal." I think I laughed, but I hope I didn't, because I tend to snort when I'm drunk and/or amused. "Is that a good thing?"

He took my hand in his. His fingers felt warm and gentle. "Isn't it?" he asked.

"I don't know." My eyes felt a little watery, and I'm afraid I may have forgotten the only worthwhile lesson my idiot brothers had ever taught me. I felt lonely suddenly, and hideously vulnerable. "This deal with Bomstad." I swallowed. "It's been tough. I mean, he's put me through hell, and yet, when I think of him I remember...Well, you know, he was so ..."

"Accomplished?" he finished. "Well spoken?"

"Hot," I said and he laughed.

"You can't blame yourself for being attracted to him," he said. "You're flesh and blood."

"But he turned out to be such a ... turd." I knew even then that I should have thought of a more sophisticated term, but hell, if Bomstad wasn't a turd, no one was. "I'm a trained professional. And I still can't judge men."

"I think you're a pretty good judge, Chrissy."

I shook my head and managed not to fall off my feet.

"You like me, don't you?"

I gazed up at him and resisted the urge to drool. He smiled and cupped my cheek. I tried not to lean in like a harp seal at feeding time.

And then a door slammed. I jerked. David turned. Someone was striding up my driveway. I squinted through the darkness.

"Rivera?" I asked, but when he spoke there was little room for doubt. His voice was as soothing as sandpaper.

"We need to talk," he said.

His tone set off a dozen warring emotions. I'm pretty sure the predominant one was anger. After all, he had no right invading my privacy at such unorthodox hours. But sometimes it's hard to tell mind-numbing fear from outrage.

"Lieutenant Rivera," David said. "I'm Dr.—"

"I remember you," Rivera said.

"You know each other?" I asked, trying to catch up.

"A little late for a consultation, isn't it, Doc?" Rivera said.

"I was about to say the same thing," David countered. "What do you want with Chrissy?"

Rivera turned his feral eyes on me. The corner of his mouth lifted. I could tell that much in the darkness. "That's between *Chrissy* and me."

David straightened. "I believe you've harassed her enough, Lieutenant."

"How do you know each other?" I asked.

"Really?" Rivera ignored me as he stepped onto the stoop. I considered saying something clever like "This stoop isn't big enough for the three of us." But in retrospect I'm pretty glad I didn't. "Because I don't think I've harassed her nearly enough."

"She doesn't need to speak to you," David said. "Not without legal representation."

Rivera barked a laugh. "Why the hell would she need legal representation? Unless she's guilty of something."

"If I were you, Lieutenant, I'd be careful about throwing around false accusations."

"False accusations," Rivera scoffed. "Cozy as you two look here, I guess she didn't tell you about her late-night excursion to the Bomb's—"

"How the hell do you two know each other?" I almost

shouted the words. They turned toward me in tandem, as if they'd only just noticed my existence.

"Didn't he tell you?" Rivera asked. "Your Dr. David here was Stephanie's psychiatrist."

"I didn't cause her death," David said. "Just as Chrissy had nothing to do with Mr. Bomstad's demise. If you were capable of doing your job, Lieutenant, you'd know that."

"And if you'd done your job, Stephanie would still be alive," Rivera said and stepped closer to David. They squared off like a pair of Cousin Kevin's roosters.

"Back off, both of you," I said, and stepped into the fray before it became unraveled beyond recognition. "David." I turned toward him, feeling hideously sober, but a little sick to my stomach. "Thank you for coming to my defense, but I'd best speak to Lieutenant..." I was tempted almost beyond control to screw up his name, but it seems my consuming desire to appear mature in David's eyes won out. "Rivera."

David calmed himself with no visible effort and took my hand gently in his. "I'll stay if you like."

"No." I gave his fingers a squeeze for the gallant gesture. "But thank you."

He turned toward Rivera. "Hurt Chrissy," he said, "and you'll be out sweeping streets for the city of Santa Monica. I don't care who your father is."

I stared after him wide-eyed as he strode down my tilted walkway, and I think in some inebriated corner of my mind, I actually thought the words "my hero." But a moment later his Mercedes purred to life, and I was left alone with Lieutenant Laugh-a-Lot.

23

There is no surer road to perdition than to let your glands dictate your direction.

—Father Pat,
upon finding Chrissy necking
with Marv Kobinski in Holy
Angels' chapel

RIVERA TURNED BACK toward me. I couldn't see very well in the darkness, but I was pretty sure he wasn't smiling. "Well, *Chrissy*, curious why I'm here?"

I swallowed, pulled my gaze away with an effort, and sifted through my purse for my keys. Nonchalant and dismissive. Go, me! "Not particularly."

"Really?" he asked. "And why is that?"

"Murphy's Law," I said, and pulled out my trophy, eleven keys and a big-ass can of pepper spray. I couldn't remember the purpose for half the keys, but knew what to do with the spray. And damn, if it wasn't tempting.

Rivera was watching me with the cozy warmth of a

glacier. "Are you saying you know why I'm here, or that you're too shit-faced to care?"

"For your information, I am not shit-faced," I said, and finding the proper key with startling aplomb, turned to slip it into its lock. Strangely though, it no longer fit. In fact, the doorknob seemed to be doing some sort of intricate fandango. I tried to follow its lead. Rivera waited, fuming silently behind me, then cursed with some vigor, pushed me aside, and grabbed my keys.

The door opened like magic.

I stepped regally inside. Magicians had never impressed me. They always have it up their sleeves.

Rivera followed me inside. I scowled, or tried to. "I don't remember inviting you."

"Sorry if I'm not as suave as Dr. Trueheart." He flipped on the hall light and turned toward me. We were standing awfully close. Seems I had forgotten to move away from the door.

I glared at him. "What do you want?"

"What exactly were you planning for the good doctor, Chrissy?" he asked. "Hoping for a deep psychological bond, or just a roll in the hay?"

"Excuse me for saying so," I said, proud of my sophisticated tone even though the floor was starting to undulate gently beneath me. "But I don't believe my private activities are any of your concern." I turned coolly away, but he grabbed my arm.

His teeth were gritted. "Where'd you get the hound?"

I was temporarily perplexed, until I remembered he was nuts. "And there it is," I said, giving him a dismissive glance. "Proof that you've gone mad. I've no idea what you're talking about."

Maybe he intended to smile, but his teeth were still clenched. "The greyhound," he said. "I believe its name was Sissy Walker."

"Oh, crap," I rasped. Reality came rushing in like a three-hundred-pound linebacker. I felt the blood drain to my knees and tried to stumble away, but he tightened his grip.

"How'd you find Tricia?"

I should have apologized right then. Should have fessed up, vowed to refrain from speaking to anyone ever again, and prayed he considered me unworthy of torture. Instead, I tilted my face up to his and gave him my best glare. "You're not the only one who can investigate, Reebler. In fact, David's right. It looks like you're doing a piss-poor job at it."

I think that for a moment he considered tossing me out the window. Luckily, the contractor who'd built my house was too cheap to put a window in the vestibule. "My wife is off limits, McMullen. You understand that?"

"Ex!" I said, which makes it pretty clear, I think, that I harbor some latent suicidal tendencies. "Ex-wife, Rivera. That means she left you. Why do you suppose that is?"

His face was red now, his jaw clenched. "Stay the hell away from my family."

"Or what?" I tried a sardonic chuckle. I might have snorted a little. "Or you'll beat me senseless?"

I was thumped up against the wall before I had time to cover the snort.

"You're already fucking senseless," he snarled. "What the hell did you want from her?"

His fingers dug into my upper arms, his body was flush against mine. I was breathing like a winded sprinter. But my dander was up and my adrenaline was rushing along at a heady pace, melding with the alcohol in my saturated system. In my experience, there's not a combination in the world more likely to scramble brains than the heady mix of adrenaline and liquor. "Let me go or you'll wish to God you had."

He chuckled at my threat. No snorting at all. "How so?" he asked. "I don't need Viagra, and I'm not partial to wine. What did you want from her?"

It took me a moment to remember who we were talking about, but he was leaning closer now, so close I could feel his thighs against mine. They were really hard. As was my breathing. "I didn't want anything from her."

"What was it, then? Take a Greyhound to the Park Day? They must have forgotten to send me the memo."

"Forgive me," I said. One of his thighs was propped between mine, pressed with insane intimacy against my crotch. "But I'm not accustomed to being accused of murder. It makes me do strange things; I might even try to exonerate myself—or figure out why you're such an ass."

He scowled and his grip loosened a little, but he didn't move away. "Maybe it's because of women like you."

"Did you know a lot of women like me when Daddy saved you from juvie?" I asked.

If he was surprised I knew about his past transgressions, he didn't show it.

Instead, he smiled. "What did you do to make Bomstad go off the deep end?" he asked.

"I didn't do anything." When I inhaled my breasts brushed his chest. I was pretty sure it wasn't making my nipples hard. I was probably just cold. "And you damn well know it."

"Christ!" he said and closing his eyes, leaned away the slightest degree. "I don't know anything."

I laughed. Probably because of that suicidal problem again. "And you think that's my fault?"

"Did he need the Viagra, Chrissy? Even around you?"

"How the hell would I know? I wasn't—" My breath stopped for a second. My heart may have, too. I bit my lip, trying to think. It didn't help. "What do you mean . . . even around me?" I asked.

"You know exactly what I mean," he said and leaned close again. And now I felt something hard and long against my belly. I was pretty sure it wasn't a flashlight this time. In fact, it felt more like a nightstick.

"Oh," I said. It might not have been my brightest quote. Then again . . . He was staring at my lips. I licked them. I'm not a tease or anything. My lips were just dry. "You don't even like me, Rivera."

"No." His gaze never left my mouth.

"And I detest you."

"It's a pickle, isn't it?"

A frickin' big pickle if I was any judge. And I was. "You accused me of murder."

"Did you do it?"

I growled. Really. Like a she-wolf or something. I

shoved at his chest. He swayed back a little, which just pressed his crotch more firmly against mine.

"Did you?" he asked.

"No!"

"Well, that makes it simpler, then," he said, and kissed me.

I'd like to say I tried to fight him off. That I was shocked and outraged. That he was too powerful for me, teeny as I am. That I thrashed wildly... or at least... called him a big meanie or something. But I think I might have been a little too busy tearing at his belt. One second I was up against the wall and the next he was flat on his back and I was atop him. Life's funny.

But my hands were shaking, and I was having trouble with his buckle.

"Jesus, woman!" he growled and pulled me up the length of his body. It's embarrassing to think about, but I'm afraid I might have whimpered. "No wonder it's been fourteen months." He pulled my head down to his and kissed me, hard and deep, making something curl up in my gut and go soft between my legs. But my brain was still functioning. Kind of.

"It hasn't been fourteen..." I paused, put a little space between us, and realized suddenly that my bra was undone and his hand was cupping my breast. I tried to stifle the groan. Maybe. "Months," I finished, but his fingers were doing some sort of forbidden voodoo and I think my tongue was hanging out.

"Closer to fifteen," he said, and unbuttoned my blouse with his left hand. Wow. An ambidextrous cop with a nightstick!

I was panting hard. "You don't know that," I said, and fumbled with his buttons.

"Unless you lied about your relationship with Bomber." He kissed my breast. I managed to refrain from passing out. "Or were doing it with your lawn boy."

His lips touched my nipple. When I opened my eyes next I found that his shirt had been ripped open. Maybe that should have given me pause, but his firm chest was as alluring as Swiss chocolate.

I mean, despite my rather checkered past with men, I'm a pretty fair judge of chests. His was beautiful.

"McMullen?" he said.

"You've got a really nice body," I said, and felt suddenly and inexplicably like I was going to cry.

He propped himself up on his elbows. His erection moved with him, under my skirt which had pooled up around my waist like vanilla pudding.

I leaned down and kissed him for all I was worth.

He kissed back, then growled and pushed me to arm's length. "How the hell drunk are you?"

I pressed up against him, my emotions a tangle of hormones and frazzled senses.

He puffed out a breath and eased his hand along my thigh. I was pretty much bare to the waist. His fingers skimmed under my skirt and he gritted his teeth. "Don't you wear underwear?"

"Yes," I said as his thumb snagged my thong. "But I don't have to."

"Holy Christ," he groaned. I felt his erection buck between my legs.

"I didn't kill Bomstad," I said and slipped out of my

blouse. My bra drooped below my breasts. I let it fall onto his chest, white lace against dark skin.

He exhaled carefully. "Okay."

"He was a client. Nothing more." Leaning down, I kissed him again. My hands were on his biceps, which bunched and quivered as my nipples brushed his chest.

I pushed back up. He gritted his teeth against the increased contact of our lower bodies.

"Did you want more?" he asked.

I let my gaze travel down his chest to his belly. There wasn't a molecule of fat. Just smooth, lovely muscles and a narrow band of dark hair that disappeared beneath his waistband. I put my hands on his belt buckle again, moving slower this time, lest I screwed up again and had to kill myself.

"He seemed like a nice man," I said. The belt opened beneath my quaking fingers. "You know?" I glanced at his face. A muscle jumped in his jaw as I released the buttons on his fly.

"Is that what you want?" he asked. "A nice guy?"

His erection eased out, bulging, thick and long, through his boxers. I swallowed. "Of course. I mean—" Thank you, Jesus. "—what else would I care about?"

That muscle jumped in his jaw again. He brushed his thumb over my nipple. I jerked like I'd been shot and let my head fall back, but I managed to remember his words and refocus.

"What'd you think?" I asked. I might have been panting. My hair had come loose and was falling down around my face like a waterfall gone mad.

Maybe it dawned on me that I was straddling him like a

mountain lion in heat, that I'd torn off his shirt and was now peeling off his pants. Maybe I realized the ridiculousness of my words, but maybe I was pretty much past that point of coherency.

"I don't usually do this," I said.

He brushed his knuckles between my breasts, then slipped his hand behind my neck. "Once every fifteen months?" he asked and pulled me down for a mind-bending kiss. I stretched against him, balanced on top.

"I'm really . . ." I began, but he slid his hand up my thigh and massaged my ass. "Sensible," I finished and sighed, because it felt so good, so ridiculously right. And at that moment I sniffled. I couldn't help myself.

I felt him tug at my panties, felt his erection shift between us, and wiped my hand across my nose, trying to hide the traitorous emotion.

I knew the minute he knew. He stiffened beneath me. All of him. Not just the good parts.

"McMullen?"

I hid my face against his shoulder.

He shifted slightly, trying to see me. "McMullen?" His voice was soft.

I sniffled again, then bit my lip and swore like a fat linebacker in the heat. But only in my head. "I've got a little bit of a cold," I said. "Sorry."

For a moment I could feel him trying to believe my lame-ass lie, then, "What'd you have to drink?"

"I told you, I'm not—"

He rolled me onto my side. I tried to stay where I was, but I'm so light . . .

We lay side by side, touching here and there. It was

hard to avoid eye contact, but I reached down and pulled up my skirt, baring all . . . or at least most.

His gaze lowered, darkened, held. "Jesus!" His voice was raspy with emotion. And in that moment I thought I loved him.

My eyes filled with tears.

"Oh, Christ!" he said, and before I could stop him, he was on his feet and dragging me with him. "You're drunker than . . ." His gaze dropped like lead to my breasts. His jaw flexed. "Shit!" he said and, turning on his heel, he marched out the door.

24

There is no greater hell than realizing you're in love
with the guy you hate.

—*Elaine Butterfield,*
when her nemesis bested her
in a high school debate

I SAT STRAIGHT UP in bed. I was certain my insomnia
wasn't due to sexual frustration. I hadn't really wanted to
do it with Rivera, anyway. He'd accused me of murder, for
crying out loud. No self-respecting woman would want to
do it with a guy who had accused her of murder, even if
he was as hard as a Greek statue and . . .

I yanked myself out of bed and tottered across the floor.
I was barefoot. I was also naked. And why not? It wasn't as
if some crazed officer of the law was going to barge in and
take advantage of me. Hell, David would have been a
more likely candidate. And far more desirable. He actually
had a brain.

My pacing brought me to the kitchen. The air from the freezer felt good against my face. The ice cream felt even better on my taste buds.

But the truth hurt. I had probably read David's intentions entirely wrong. He probably had no interest in me, either. Maybe Rivera was right. Maybe I had been a little bit drunk. And maybe that had colored my perception somewhat. David's fiancée, the fabulous Kathryn LaMere, probably had no reason to be jealous of me, as David had intimated. Okay, not intimated, said right out loud.

I sat down with the ice cream carton and felt sorry for myself. I mean, I wasn't chopped liver. I looked down at my boobs, examined them philosophically one at a time, and nodded. Not bad. I straightened in my chair, sucked in my gut. Okay. I scooped up another spoonful of ice cream and decided that I'd be jealous of me.

Bitch. If she had a lick of sense she would be, too. In fact, she must be. What kind of red-blooded American woman would let a guy like David fraternize with another woman and not worry? The answer came with disturbing speed: Kathryn LaMere, a woman who was young, gorgeous, classy, and smelled like . . .

I stopped masticating. She'd smelled like Jivago. I was sure of it. Or Shalimar. Okay, perhaps I wasn't quite so sure. But maybe she'd been the woman in Bomstad's house. Maybe she'd wanted . . . ummm . . . I hit brain freeze for a second. But then it all came storming in: She was insanely jealous—of course she was. That's why she felt such a need to pretend to David that she wasn't. I plowed up another load of ice cream and thought harder. Not only was she jealous, she was probably a murderer. She'd probably killed Stephanie Meyers because David had been interested in her. And then Bomstad. Well, okay, Bomstad didn't exactly tie in. But there was a lot about Bomstad that didn't make sense. Maybe they were having an affair and the Bomb had threatened to tell David. So Kathryn, knowing about his heart condition, had loaded him up on Viagra and sent him to me. Because, yes indeedy, she was jealous of me, too, and was hoping to implicate me in Bomstad's death.

The insanity of the entire idea was not lost on me in spite of the fact that I had just consumed my weight in alcohol and ice cream. Still . . . I closed the carton and took a seat in front of my PC. I typed in Kathryn LaMere and after a grinding hesitation, her engagement photo popped onto the screen. Yep, she was still gorgeous and classy and young. I continued to search. There was something about a Feed the Children banquet where there was a picture of her spooning up mashed potatoes to an underprivileged crowd in East L.A. Her hair was upswept and her expression demure. I had never quite managed demure. I'd tried it once for the senior prom. Dad had asked if I was constipated.

I continued the search and came up all but empty.

Hmmph. I sat back in my chair and ruminated. All the info I had found on Ms. LaMere had taken place in the past two years. Where had she been before that?

Maybe in the back of my mind I hoped she was playing a shell game, conning the innocent elderly out of their pensions in Trenton, but then I remembered her accent and did a search of the LaMeres in Europe. There were several hits. None of which turned out to be her.

Curiouser and curiouser. Not that I was a techno genius or anything. But David's fabulous fiancée looked like she came from wealth. One would think I would be able to find a few tidbits about her sailing with the Kennedys or having high tea with the queen.

I shut down the computer and stretched. Still naked. Still looked pretty good, I thought, and wobbled back to bed.

Sleep finally took pity on me. Alcohol is a sedative for some people. For me it's copious calories.

By morning, I had a splitting headache and had come to the realization that I was an idiot. David's high-priced fiancée was about as likely to commit a murder as she was to dance on the moon.

Still, I couldn't get the idea out of my head, even after my final appointment, when the retiring Mrs. Feinstein confessed she had been a bunny in a former life. I'd always suspected it anyway, I thought, and turned off my office light before wandering into the reception area. It was Elaine's night to work late. I glanced at her, remembering my promise to Solberg and feeling guilty down to my salmon-colored Aldos.

She looked up as I fiddled with some papers in the file cabinet.

"So . . ." I kept my tone casual, because that's what I do when guilt is gnawing at my guts like a piranha, or when I need a favor I can never repay in this lifetime. "How was your date the other night?"

She leaned back in her chair. "What's up?" she asked.

"Nothing." I have no idea why I felt the need to lie, but I think it has something to do with being raised Catholic;

everything's a sin, therefore it's best to lie about it. "I was just wondering about your date."

"Uh-huh."

"Did you have fun?"

There was a pause, then, "Have you seen any more of the dark lieutenant?"

"This has nothing to do with Rivera," I said, but my face felt as if it might be melting.

"Did you sleep with him?"

"Laney!" I gasped, and she laughed.

"All right. I'll play along. My date's name was Brad. He drives a '96 Corvette, has an on-again, off-again spot on *Days of Our Lives,* and can do twenty-five one-handed push-ups in as many seconds."

"Wow. You know all that?"

"I knew all that in the first fifty seconds." She crossed her arms over her chest. It was a nearly impossible feat. In elementary school, she'd been hopelessly skinny, wore glasses as thick as my wrist, and sported braces reminiscent of the Union Pacific. I missed that ugly little girl. "What do you need?" she asked.

"Can't I just take an interest in your—"

"Mac . . ."

"Okay!" I snapped. "I need a favor. All right?"

She stared at me, brows raised. Mine tend to shadow my eyes like hungry vultures. When she raises hers, she looks like a startled Garbo. "You all right?" she asked.

"Oh, crap," I said, and collapsed into a chair. "I'm sorry."

"What do you need?" she asked, and scooted her chair

around the corner of the desk and up to mine. "Come on, spill it. It can't be that bad."

I knew for a fact she was wrong, but I told her anyway. "I've got this . . . friend. His name is J.D. He's—"

"Sure."

"What?"

"I'll go out with him."

"He's five foot seven."

She shrugged.

"And obnoxious."

She smiled.

"Brays like a jackass," I said and she laughed out loud.

I don't care if Laney's got boobs that would make Pamela Anderson bitch-slap her surgeon; I love her madly.

Solberg?" I said, speaking into the mouthpiece. "I—"

"No." His tone was petulant and not very pleasant, but I hadn't expected him to be ecstatic when I called. I could hear him bombing a space station in the background.

"I haven't even asked you anything yet."

"And you might as well save the oxygen." Another target exploded. It was often said that men who didn't get laid were fabulous at electronic games. He could probably join the international circuit. " 'Cuz I ain't gotten a call from E—" He stumbled over the name. I rolled my eyes.

"Elaine?" I supplied.

"Yeah. She ain't called me yet. So there's no way in hell I'm going to do another favor for you. Not after you kidnapped my Porsche and—"

"She said yes."

" 'Bout got me—What?" he rasped.

"Laney said she'd go out with you."

"God's truth?" I heard something plastic clatter to the floor. "You ain't lyin'?"

"She agreed," I repeated. "On two conditions."

"Yeah?" His tone suggested there wasn't a lot he'd refuse to do, short of self-mutilation.

"First you have to check out another person for me."

"Done."

"Don't you want to know who it is?"

"Is it the mob or something?"

"No! Why would it be—"

"All right then, what's the second condition?"

I scowled and switched gears. "You don't lay a finger on Laney."

He was silent.

"You hear me, Solberg?" I asked. "If she gets home with a hair out of place, I swear, I'll staple your balls to your joystick."

*H*e brought me an entire file the very next evening. I looked through it as he shuffled from foot to foot on my tilted stoop. His findings consisted of a half dozen Internet pics and nine pages of information. I skimmed them, then glanced up. He'd left his Armani at home. His blue jeans hung askew on his skinny hips, and his button-up shirt looked like it'd seen better days.

"This is all about the last twenty-eight months of her life," I said.

"Listen . . ." He bobbed to his opposite foot, pushed his

glasses firmly back up the oversized bow of his nose, and gazed up at me like a nearsighted flamingo. "That's everything I could find."

"How hard did you look?"

"Didn't sleep last night," he said.

I glanced up, ready to scoff, but then I noticed the dark circles etched beneath his horn-rims. "Something wrong?" I asked.

He grimaced and shuffled again. "She's hot."

I knew he meant Elaine, but I wasn't sure what that had to do with his insomnia. Then, "Oh," I said. "You spent the whole night searching?"

He shrugged, shuffled again. It made him look kind of young, and almost, *almost* likable. "I wasn't tired anyway," he said.

"You spent what . . . nine hours on this search and . . ."

"Fourteen," he corrected. "Started soon as I got home from work."

I stared at him. I'd seen desperation before, but it was usually in my bathroom mirror. "You spent fourteen hours on this and didn't find anything about LaMere's early years?"

He shook his head.

"Childhood . . . adolescence?"

"It wasn't there," he said. He sounded panicky. I hoped he wasn't going to cry. "I swear. If it had been I'd have found it."

"No Social Security number or—"

"No," he said. "Nothing. It's like she didn't exist before 2003." He scowled, shuffled, scowled. "Do I still get to go out with . . ."

292 — Lois Greiman

I heaved a sigh. "Elaine, Solberg. Her name is Elaine. Why can't you remember that?"

I sifted through the papers again, and when I looked up, he was blushing, red as a radish.

"Solberg?"

"I call her Angel," he said and scuffed his sneaker against my crumbling concrete. "You know. To myself."

25

Just when you think you got life by the tail, it's likely
to whip around and take a hunk outta your balls.

> —Glen McMullen,
> *upon learning about Chrissy's*
> *impending birth*

$\mathcal{E}$LAINE WENT OUT with Solberg that Saturday.

I spent the majority of the evening staring at Kathryn
LaMere's photos. They didn't give me much more than a
roaring headache and an aching sense of inadequacy.
There was one of her at a charity function with David and
one of her at the beach in the summer of 2002. She was
wearing a netting cover-up over her two-piece, but her
lack of cellulite was still obvious, even when I pulled out a
magnifying glass.

But sometime during my quest for imperfection I noticed an ultrafaint circle above her left breast. Or at least, it
looked like a circle, though upon closer inspection, I was

pretty sure the circle was a tattoo. And that was baffling, because the Kathryn LaMere I had met just didn't seem to be the tattoo type. Besides, I had seen her in a bone-colored silk blouse and hadn't noticed even a trace through the sheer fabric.

I looked at the photo again. It was a grainy newspaper shot, and though the story hadn't actually been about her, she was listed as one of many who had enjoyed a hot day seaside.

I sat back, ate another carrot stick, and refused to fanta-size about German chocolate cake. Why would a woman like Kathryn LaMere get a tattoo? And why would she have it removed?

I looked again. Okay, maybe I was wrong. Maybe it wasn't a tattoo at all, but what if it was? What if she was a raging lunatic who had met David, realized he was loaded, good-looking, and sophisticated, and decided she wanted some of that action? What would she do? She'd adopt a classy persona and get rid of the competition, i.e., Stephanie Meyers. But wait a moment, what about David's first wife?

How had she died and when?

It was then that the phone rang.

"Mac?"

"Laney!" Guilt swamped me immediately; my best friend had taken a bullet for me, and I had been so wrapped up in my own problems I'd forgotten to even light a candle or something in her defense. Granted, I'd been accused of murder. But still . . . "What happened? Are you all right?"

"I'm fine, Mac. Relax."

She sounded funny. Almost . . . *happy*. I glanced out the window into the black abyss of my yard. By the looks of things, hell hadn't frozen over. "Where's Solberg?"

"He just dropped me off a little bit ago."

"No, Laney. You didn't give him your home address."

"Sure. Why not?"

"'Cuz he's Solberg."

She chuckled. "Actually, he was kind of sweet."

Holy crap. Things were worse than I realized. "He's still there, isn't he?" I asked and lowered my voice a little. "Does he have a gun?"

"All right," she said. "He's a little nerdy, maybe . . ."

"Maybe!"

"But he's smart."

"Should I call the cops or come over myself? Yes, for the cops. No for me alone."

"I'm serious. He was nice."

I let that sink in for a while. "Did you leave your drink unattended for any length of time?"

"I'm not drugged."

"Okay. Let's assume that's true. How many times did he call himself the Geekster of Love?"

"You're kidding," she said, and laughed as if it was the most hilarious thing she'd ever heard, which was pretty clear evidence that she was either drunk off her ass or hadn't heard it before.

I scowled, thinking back. "How bout babe? How many derivatives did he think of for babe?"

"He called me Elaine and nothing else."

"Well, that solves the mystery, then," I said. "It wasn't Solberg at all. It was an imposter."

"Uh-huh," she said. I could hear the refrigerator open as she waited for me to go on. She was probably searching for her imitation soy nuts.

"'Cuz Solberg can't remember names," I said.

I could hear her gasp and sat up straight, wired for trouble.

"What's wrong?" I asked.

"You don't suppose that's why he had 'Lane' written on his arm, do you? So he could remember my name?"

I closed my eyes and rubbed my forehead. The thought made me tired. "Why yes, Dr. Holmes," I said. "I do believe that might be the case."

"Ohh, that's sweet."

I opened my eyes and scowled at the receiver. "Seriously, Laney, are you feeling okay?"

"Everything's fine. I just thought I'd check in with you. You doing all right?"

"Sure," I said, discounting my latest flights of fancy about LaMere being a murderer. I could hear Elaine munching. Apparently imitation soy nuts are crunchy.

"You need to get out more," she said.

"Yeah, maybe we could double-date." I checked my own fridge. There were no soy nuts. Imitation or otherwise. But I had a tidy leftover box from Chin Yung's, the best Chinese restaurant in the universe. My stomach rumbled hopefully, but I have a strict rule: no lo mein between one and six in the morning. "I think Charles Manson is available—for about another ten to life."

She laughed. "If you dated more you'd remember what's out there."

"You think I've forgotten?"

"Yeah," she said, "I do."

But when I hung up the phone, memories of Bomstad's breath against my neck bobbed to the surface. I checked my locks, pulled the drapes, and went to bed.

No, I hadn't forgotten.

O fficer Crane?" I asked. I was standing on the sidelines of a soccer field where a bevy of gangly girls were chasing a ball around a dehydrated court. It reminded me of the time Cousin Kevin's chickens had spied a grasshopper, but I set aside that odd analogy.

I'd driven halfway across the city to talk to Crane, though I'd tried to sound casual on the phone. After all, my theory of LaMere murdering Mrs. Hawkins seemed a little far-fetched even to my far-fetched way of thinking. Still, he was the officer on scene when her car had been found at the bottom of a canyon off Mulholland Highway.

"Yeah." He had a big smile and a big voice. Unfortunately he had a gut to match. That's the problem with family men, I thought, as his eyes strayed to the soccer field again. They tend to let themselves go. Oh, yeah—and they're married.

"That-a-way, Chelsea!" he yelled and beamed.

I almost sighed. Because regardless of the size of their guts, big-hearted men who yelled encouragement to their spindly-legged daughters always looked good.

He'd been reluctant to meet with me, saying he was busy, and probably thinking I was a whack job. But I'd promised to keep it short and meet him anywhere he liked. And that was where we were.

"Sorry," he said and offered me a hand and a smile. "That's my Chelsea. Best forward in Maplewood Middle School."

I didn't know what to say about that because I didn't know what a forward was, and "Yeah, she's gonna be a heartbreaker" didn't seem appropriate for the situation. Even from halfway across the field I could tell Chelsea had teeth like an overzealous beaver. But then, so had Laney, and look what happened there.

"You wanted to know something about a car accident?"

"Yes. Victoria Hawkins. She died a couple years ago."

"Fall back. Fall back!" he yelled. I was startled, but then realized with my usual stellar genius that he wasn't talking to me. "Sorry about that. Two years is a long time."

"I know, and I regret springing this on you, but it's extremely important."

"Can you refresh my memory a little?"

What did that mean? Was I supposed to pay him or something? My mind was pumping madly, remembering the mortgage and my cantankerous septic system. How much info would a fiver get me?

"The circumstances," he said, frowning a little, as though I might have lost my mind. "Where it happened. That sort of thing."

"Oh, yes. Of course." It looked like my lonely five bucks were safe. "She was heading north on Mulholland Highway. The date was July seventeen, 2003."

He shook his head and hugged his clipboard to his belly. "Summer 2003," he said. "Christ, there are so many car wrecks."

"This was a Mercedes."

"Yeah." He chuckled a little. "And this is Hollywood."

"She was the wife of a rather prominent therapist."

He opened his mouth as if to yell again, then closed it and turned toward me. "That psychiatrist fellow? The one who wrote the book?"

My heart beat a little faster. "Yes. That's the one."

"Oh, sure—"

Hang in there, Chels! Hang in there!

"It was late when I seen it," he said, switching gears like an old Corvette. "Near two in the morning. I remember that: I saw skid marks on the road and went to take a look. Sure enough, there was a car at the bottom. Looked like she'd almost made the curve then wham . . . lost control."

"Was there . . ." I felt silly saying it, like a wannabe Matlock, but I had driven a long way to meet with him. "Was there any evidence of . . ." I wanted to say "foul play" but I'd forgotten my Sherlock Holmes hat in my armoire. "Do you have any idea why it happened?"

He shook his head. "Road curves like a son of a bitch in the hills down there. And I think . . . I might be wrong," he added, squinting slightly. "But I think I heard she'd been drinking."

I have to admit I felt a little disappointed when I started up my Saturn. I'm not sure what I'd expected. Maybe I'd hoped for some fresh-faced officer of the law to tell me that yes, indeed, there had been a car bomb planted in Victoria Hawkins's glove compartment, and uh-huh, they'd been able to lift Kathryn LaMere's prints from it, but the press had neglected to report it.

It was getting dark when I pulled onto Mulholland Highway. As long as I was there, I might as well take a look at where Victoria had died, I thought. But by the time I passed Yerba Buena Road it was all but impossible to see into the craggy wasteland beside the winding road. Besides, I realized, as I cruised up a long grade, it was all craziness anyway. I was crazy. Rivera was for sure crazy. And Bomstad *had* been crazy. He'd taken an overdose of Viagra, knowing he had a heart condition, and Rivera, looking for a culprit, had accused me. But he didn't really believe I was guilty. If he did, I'd 'a' been pleading my case to a jury of my peers a long time ago.

Feeling somewhat relieved by my thoughts, I checked my rearview mirror, did a U-turn, and headed back from whence I'd come.

It was then that my brakes failed.

I pumped them twice, or possibly a hundred times, but things were happening faster and faster. The Saturn was picking up speed. The scenery was spinning by my window. I heard my tires squeal on the road, felt a bump beneath me. I'm sure I was terrified, but that memory is vague, swallowed by a million blurring thoughts. Maybe I had an impression of trees skimming past my left ear. Maybe I thought I was going to die. But suddenly there was nothing. Just blackness and the distant sound of a honking horn.

26

Maybe life does suck, Pork Chop, but it beats the hell out of the alternative.

—Glen McMullen,
    imparting wisdom to his only
    daughter

I WOKE UP STARING into a broad bank of snowy clouds. Hmmm. Apparently, I'd made it to heaven. So Father Pat's prediction had been entirely wrong, despite the fact that he'd found me necking with . . . What was that kid's name? I could remember his face perfectly. It had been as red as his hair and . . . Marv Kobinski. He'd had ears the size of cantaloupes and . . .

"Mac?"

I turned my head and was mildly surprised to find Elaine sitting beside me. Her eyes looked shadowed and her face gaunt.

"Laney?" It seemed unlikely we'd wind up in heaven at the same time. Or at all, maybe. "Umm..."

"Mac!" She was holding my hand. "You scared me to death. I thought... But you're okay. Right? Just bruised?"

I stared at her in a haze for a moment, then shifted my gaze around the room. Turns out the ceiling wasn't made of clouds but of bumpy white plaster. The room's linoleum was beige and the other bed was narrow and perfectly made. Nothing looked familiar, and I was pretty sure my bed had never been perfectly made. "You were scared?"

"I called your mother."

She *was* scared. No one called my mother unless absolutely necessary. Dad's Chevy had once broken down on I-294. So he'd hitched a ride north in a cattle truck, then hoofed it home for the last four and a half miles. Mom had been telling him for weeks to get his car in the shop. Anyone with half a brain would rather take their chances afoot on the interstate than be I-told-you-so'd by my mother. "Why would you do that?"

"I thought you were dead."

Huh, I thought, but didn't voice my cleverness out loud.

"They brought you in last night." Her perfect face creased. Did I actually fraternize with someone that pretty on purpose? How masochistic was I? And did I use the word fraternize in everyday conversation? "Don't you remember anything?"

"No," I ventured, then, "Yes." A few details were drifting back to me. "The food's really great at Chin Yung's. I had chicken fried rice, and then..." It all rushed at me like high tide. "Oh, crap! There were flashing lights...and people." My head hurt. I raised a hand to probe my cranium. "They were holding up fingers and asking me to count them." I scowled, but my skull seemed to be in relatively good repair. "If they didn't know how many fingers they had, couldn't they ask someone else?"

Elaine laughed and stroked my hand, and I noticed that there were tears in her eyes. Holy cow! She must have been worried. She didn't even cry at *Gone With the Wind*. "I told you to get more sleep."

I tried to follow this new line of logic. "I fell asleep?"

"Don't you remember? You were on Mulholland Highway. And—" Her attention shifted away. "Oh, Lieutenant," she said and straightened. "Hello."

My gaze skipped past the bumps my feet made in the white coverlet. Lieutenant Rivera stood directly between them, looking dark and lean and carrying a good-sized parcel.

"What are you doing here?" Maybe it wasn't the most polite salutation, but I was still struggling to separate the memory of chicken fried rice from screeching tires and didn't want to have to worry about the condition of my coiffure. I stifled a weakling urge to run my hand over my hair. For all I knew someone might have shaved the Lions logo into the back of my scalp but there wasn't much I could do about it at that precise moment.

"What happened?" he asked.

Elaine was staring at him, but he kept his eyes on me, which made me wonder in a dim sort of otherworldly way if I was hallucinating. Everyone looks at Elaine.

"I think I might have had a car accident," I said.

"Don't be a smart-ass. What happened?"

I scowled. I was tired and hungry and didn't really need the fifth degree from a guy who wouldn't have sex with me just because I was drunk off my feet. Okay, I'd been a little weepy, too . . . and in his eyes there was probably still the possibility that I was a murderer, but still . . . "You tell me," I said. I was trying for tough, but I might have just sounded cranky.

"I know you think my position on the force gives me omnipotent powers," he said and took another couple steps into the room. His tone was still rough-edged, but there was something almost gooshy in his eyes. Maybe he'd called my mother, too. The thought made me feel a little sick to my stomach. "But I'm a cop, not God."

"I'll try to remember," I said and noticed that the box he carried said Frank's Garden Store and had a green plastic bag protruding from the top. "Did you bring me flowers?"

"I heard they'd brought you here."

I think I blinked at him dumbly. "And you came anyway?"

His lips jumped a little and maybe his eyes laughed as he relaxed. "Yeah. I came," he said. His gaze was steady on me as he stepped closer. It made me feel fidgety and a little breathless. "What the hell were you doing in the mountains?"

"I was just . . ." I fiddled with the coverlet. It had a pale blue diamond pattern. Maybe the powers that be thought bright colors would get their patients overly excited and send them spinning into cardiac arrest. "Visiting a friend."

"What friend?"

I gripped the stiff coverlet in my fingers. It was about as cozy as concrete. "I don't think I owe you an explanation,

Roper." Maybe it was unfair, but the memory of his rejection made me pretty pissed off. "In fact, I don't owe you anything."

"True," he said and, putting the package on the floor, sat on the edge of my mattress. "Except for a new shirt. That's the second one you've ruined."

It took me a moment to realize he was talking about the buttons that kept inexplicably exploding from his clothing. It was probably just poor workmanship. I wanted to tell him to buy American next time. It would have made my Dad proud. But I could feel a blush starting at my ears. I cleared my throat, then turned and stared pointedly at Elaine.

She stared back, her eyes wide with feigned innocence. "Oh," she said, with no inflection at all, "look at the time." She didn't. "I have to get back to the office. Mrs. Garner's due in fifteen minutes."

She kissed my cheek, whispered good luck in my feverish ear, and departed.

"You've got strange friends," Rivera said.

I brought my attention back to him. "I do not."

He raised a brow. "Eddie Friar?"

I felt immediately defensive. Eddie had enough problems without being investigated by a feral lieutenant. Being gay was probably even harder than being hetero. And being hetero very often sucked the big out. No pun intended. "How do you know about Eddie?"

"You used his dog as a shill to scope out my wife, remember?" he said. "Makes him fair game."

I thought about that for a prolonged moment but

couldn't think of any snappy comebacks. The old noodle didn't seem to be working at warp speed.

"Did you know he feeds his dog breakfast in bed?" he asked.

"Lots of people—"

"*His* bed."

I tried not to wince. "Maybe he's a little eccentric. That's not the same as weird."

He considered that for a moment, then, "How 'bout Bomstad?"

"He was not my—"

"Solberg?"

I paused, mouth open, then shut it carefully. "Now you're just being mean."

He grinned. It didn't do anything for my cerebral stability. Turns out he had a smile that'd make Tom Cruise look like a ghoul.

"What happened, McMullen?" he asked. Maybe I imagined it, but it seemed as if his voice got kind of soft and mooshy.

I shrugged, trying not to remember how his chest had looked as he lay spread out on my fake Persian rug. "I was just coming back from visiting friends—like I said. I guess I fell asleep."

He watched me in silence for a moment. "Do you have a lot of friends on the police force?"

It took a moment for my synapses to snap in the correct succession.

"I really hate it when you ask questions you already know the answers to," I said.

"Why were you asking about Mrs. Hawkins's death?"

"You accused me of murder." Damn him. His chest wasn't that great anyway. "Excuse me for trying to clear my name."

He was staring at me. "I like it when you get all uppity. It's sexy."

I rejected the idea of dragging him under the covers. "I should slap you upside the head," I said instead.

He laughed. My stomach coiled. "You're not a suspect anymore."

"What?"

He shrugged. "There's no substantiation. You can quit playing Nancy Drew."

"So who sent Bomstad the wine?"

The shrug again, slow and languid, but not exactly casual. "Could have been anyone. Turns out the unidentified substance was just a natural sediment of the aging process."

"What!" I sat up straight, wanting to kill him. "There was nothing in the wine, and you made me think it had been poisoned?"

"I had to wait for the tox report in order to—"

"How long have you known?"

"I guess the Viagra on top of a heart condition was enough to—"

"How long"—I took a deep breath—"have you known?"

It almost looked as if he was trying not to grin as he retrieved the bulky package from the floor and thrust it toward me. "Why don't you open your gift?"

"How long?"

"Just got word last night."

"You're lying."

"Why would I lie about something like that?"

I just stared at him.

He did grin now, just the slightest twist of his lips. "I'm pretty sure I can outrun you," he said. "At least in your hospital gown. It's slit up the back, you know. Open your gift."

I did so in something of a snit, but the roses I'd anticipated didn't materialize. Instead, I found myself staring into two prickly branches.

"It's a saguaro," he said.

I stared.

"A cactus," he added.

"Uh-huh," I said, because, what the hell, I wasn't going to win the Miss Congeniality contest, anyway. Not without ice cream. "I'm wondering why."

"I think it might be able to survive the hell of your yard," he said. "And it suits your personality."

27

Today's problems are yesterday's mistakes come back to bite you in the ass.

—*Michael McMullen,*
during the philosophical
stage of a hangover

*E*LAINE DROVE ME home from the hospital that afternoon. I now had a big-ass prescription for amped-up ibuprofen and an order to rest. I had called my mother before I left and simultaneously convinced her that she needn't fly down and that I was paying an exorbitant amount for the phone call, so I couldn't talk long. It had been a good day's work.

Once home I sat on my couch and wondered what to do with my time. I flipped through the television stations, then shut off the tube and glanced out the window. My yard glared back at me in dusty shades of gray and brown. The green fairy had failed to appear yet again. So I wandered outside and planted the saguaro in the south-west corner of my lot, where it stood prickly and staunch between me and the rest of the world.

After that, I tried to rest, but I was wide awake. I'd been worried about my continued survival for so long that I no longer knew what to do with my spare time if it weren't spent ferreting out information.

Still, I did my best, finally ending up in the kitchen.

I took a cab to work the following day. Everything still seemed a little surreal, but by Thursday, the universe was starting to settle back into a relatively normal routine. Elaine turned down three proposals from men she'd never met, and Mr. Lepinski expressed concern about his ham on rye.

On Friday, I felt whole enough to call the shop and ask about my car.

"Oh, yeah, the '96 Saturn."

"That's right," I said. "Can you tell me how much damage there was?"

"Well..." I could hear the guy expel his breath and imagined him scratching his head under his well-worn baseball cap—a man's man. "The body ain't too bad, considering you took a header into a canyon, but it'll take a while to fix the brakes."

The world slowed to a crawl. My mind crept along at the same lethargic pace. "What's wrong with the brakes?"

"They're wore out."

I waited three beats, sure the earth would soon continue rotating at its normal speed. "But I just had them checked."

"Yeah? Well, you shoulda come to us, 'cuz whoever's been takin' care of you screwed up big-time. Didn't no one tell you 'bout the brakes?"

"No," I said. "No one did."

"Huh, that's funny, 'cuz that lieutenant fella said he would pass on the info."

*A*ngela Grapier was my last client on Friday. She looked small and tired as she sat curled up against the armrest of my couch. I asked her about school, which was going okay, and Kelly the animal, whom she hadn't seen for a while. She looked a little sad about that. Apparently, she was fond of animals, even ones that were rabid. But upon further discussion, she admitted that she'd met someone new in Algebra. His name was Ethan. He was freaky smart, and he was kind of a nerd, but...and then she grinned. The expression was shy and guileless and glowing, exactly like a sixteen-year-old's smile should be. "Maybe," she said, "nerds aren't so bad."

It was then that I decided to let her continue to live with her father instead of begging her to move in with me. It'd just get messy if she were around when the LAPD killed me in my sleep.

As I closed the door behind her, my mind zinged like a sling shot pellet back to my own looming problems. I'd been clinging to my clients' concerns in an effort to hold them at bay. But I realized as I drove my rent-a-wreck home that my mind was jittery and my hands damp.

What the hell was going on? What had happened to my

brakes? Why hadn't Rivera told me about them? And had the blue Mazda I'd seen three cars behind on my way to work really been following me?

At home at last, I sat in the dark on the edge of my bed, having locked every lock and checked every window. Still, I jumped at each inconsequential sound.

I was entirely alone. I had nowhere to go. Not even to the police. Especially not to the police. I closed my eyes and stuck my hands under my thighs, trying to keep them from shaking as I spun facts through my overtaxed brain.

Had Meyers's death really been an accident? And what about Bomstad's? It seemed terrifyingly likely that they were tied together somehow. After all, they had known each other. But then, Rivera had known them both.

The idea made my mouth go dry. Had he been in love with Stephanie? Had he been jealous of her relationship with Bomstad? Had he killed them both and made their deaths look accidental?

I didn't sleep that night. Instead, I smoked the entire pack of Virginia Slims I'd fished out of the toilet, then considered the third death. Or the first, really—Victoria Hawkins. David's wife.

Had Rivera known her, too? Most likely, since he obviously knew David.

Mrs. Hawkins had died on a curving road just south of where my brakes had failed. But that had been years ago. Still, what were the chances that all those deaths, and my own near death, were unrelated? In my current sleepless state, they seemed astronomical.

But how would I learn anything about the circumstances of Victoria's death? I'd be better off sticking my head in the oven than going to the police.

She'd died in her Mercedes. That much I knew. But Mercedeses were as common as perverts in L.A. Still, maybe someone would remember her car and be able to tell me if there had been any unexplained brake damage.

I spent the rest of the night and half of the next morning learning all I could about Victoria's death. The info didn't amount to a pile of bunny turds. Nevertheless, I gathered my paltry notes and sat stiff and jumpy at my kitchen table, listening to every insignificant noise with one ear while my other was stuck to the phone receiver. I hit pay dirt with the twenty-seventh towing station I called.

I sat up straight, hardly able to believe my ears. "A Mercedes? On July seventeen, 2005? You're sure?"

"Yep. That's what I got down here."

I sat like a block of salt in my spindle-backed chair and gripped the telephone cord for support. "Do you remember the condition of the car?"

"Ahh, let's see. Looks like Billy did the report. Says here the vehicle was broke up pretty bad."

"Yes, I know, but I was wondering if they had determined a cause for the accident."

"Huh?" he said, then covered the mouthpiece and shouted to someone in the background. "Yeah, you too. See ya Monday.

"Sorry, what was that?"

"The cause," I said, breathless and terrified, "of the accident."

"That ain't our department. We just tow 'em and impound 'em."

"Do you think someone else might know more about it?"

"Listen, it's time to close up shop. Reeves will be in on Monday. You could stop by then, maybe."

Which was a fabulous idea. Only I might not be alive on Monday. "Isn't there someone I could talk to today?"

"I'm the last one here and I gotta get home. Wife's making ribs."

He hung up. I sat staring at the phone, but nerves and indigestion wouldn't let me rest. I made a circuit around my living room and glanced out the window at my saguaro. Maybe there was a camera in it. Maybe they were watching my house every minute. Maybe, I thought—and then I saw the car parked a half a block down on the opposite side of Opus. It was a blue Mazda. And there was someone slouched behind the wheel.

I felt immediately sick to my stomach. Holy crap! I'd been right. I had been followed. But why? I needed answers and I needed them fast, preferably while I was still breathing.

My mind whirled over the conversation I'd just had, desperately searching.

Thirty seconds later I was skimming the *R*'s in the phone book. I found a William Reeves with shocking ease. He was listed at 24371 Wilbur Drive in Fontana.

*L*aney." My heart was beating like an African war drum.

"Mac. What's wrong?"

"Nothing. Everything." I resisted the urge to look out

the window again. I'd done that a dozen times already. The Mazda was still there. "Laney," I said. "I need help."

*I*t took me a few minutes to find a skirt I thought might look similar to something Mrs. Al-Sadr might wear. I knew a modicum about Muslim garb from a woman with whom I had once worked. She'd kept every inch of skin covered and spent most nights in lusty fornication.

Tying a dishtowel over my forehead for a *hijab,* I used a bedsheet for the *khimar.* It draped to my hips and looked ridiculous. The veil I cut from an old scarf looked just as idiotic, but I hoped to hell that anyone who saw me would assume I was my Allah-fearing neighbor.

When I stepped out the back door, not a soul was in sight. My house stood between me and the blue Mazda. Still, my heart was beating against my ribs like a ball-peen hammer as I crawled over Al-Sadr's fence and into their backyard. Elaine was waiting at the end of their walkway in her Mustang. I bisected my neighbors' perfectly manicured lawn without looking back, opened their wire gate and did my best to keep from scurrying into Elaine's car like an overdressed rat.

Laney's hair was tucked under a baseball cap. She wore baggy jeans and a zip-up sweatshirt. "Where to?" she said, and did a U-turn in the middle of Opus Street.

I was sweating bullets when we passed the Mazda, but I managed not to stare. Instead, I watched it in the side-view mirror until we were out of sight. It never left its parking spot.

Finding William Reeves's house was relatively simple.

Convincing him I wasn't a mass murderer was more difficult. Luckily, Laney had worn a tube top under her sweatshirt. We were inside Billy's living room not thirty seconds
after she unzipped it.

"Yeah, says I got the car in on the seventeenth like Gilly
told you." He was bent over his PC.

I felt light-headed and breathless. "Do you remember
anything about its condition?"

He shook his head. "Naw. We don't worry 'bout that
kind of thing. Say, listen, I promised to meet some buddies in a half an hour and—"

"This is extremely important," I said. "Life or death."

"Sorry."

I glanced at Elaine. She leaned forward, nearly brushing
his shoulder with her breast as she pointed to the monitor.
"Mack Brady," she said. "Is that who took the car?"

He would have answered, but his mouth had fallen
open and his eyeballs had become adhered to her chest.

It didn't take us long to arrive at Brady's house. He was
sitting in a porch swing sharing a Bud Lite with his
Labrador retriever. Preliminaries were brief, but his memory was phenomenal. "Don't need to look it up," he said.
"I remember the car. Damned shame. Had upholstery
like butter, but them brakes was shot to hell. You've
gotta downshift on them steep grades. You'd think folks
would know that if they're gonna spend seventy grand on
a vehicle."

In less than ten minutes we were heading west on
the 10. My mind was spinning. Someone had disabled
Victoria's brakes. I was sure of it. But who? It couldn't be
Rivera. He was a cop. That sort of thing only happened in

mystery novels. And I had almost done the horizontal mambo with him on the floor in my vestibule. Not that I was all that attracted to him or anything, but if I were, and he was a murderer, what kind of person would that make me?

"You have to call the police." Elaine's voice was tight. I felt sick to my stomach.

"I can't," I said. I'd given her all the information I had. It had sounded just as garbled out loud as it did in my head.

She watched the road and nodded finally. "You can't go back home."

I wanted to be brave, to assure her that I'd be fine, but I had no reason for such suicidal optimism.

"You can stay with me," she added.

It was tempting, but I shook my head. She'd already gone out with Solberg. No one should sacrifice too much. "I'll check into a hotel."

"All right." I could tell she didn't like it, but she agreed. "Which one?"

My mind was too overloaded to deal with such a mundane decision. "I'll have to pick up a few things. Toothbrush. You know." My head felt as if it were being crushed.

"The Mazda's gone," Elaine said, glancing down Opus.

I wondered if she thought I was losing my mind. I wondered if she was right. I looked down Vine Avenue. There were seven cars parked along the street. I couldn't tell if any of them were occupied.

"Drop me off at Al-Sadr's," I said. "I'll go in the way I came out."

She gave me a worried look.

"I'm sorry to drag you into this, Laney."

"You kidding?" she asked and lowered her voice like someone I was maybe supposed to recognize. "I live for this shit."

I had no idea who she was impersonating, so the world hadn't gone completely insane.

"Do you want me to wait in the car or come in?" Her face was pale, but her voice was steady. A friend to the bone.

"Pick me up," I said. "Same place in fifteen minutes."

It was difficult to force myself out of her car. I felt exposed and vulnerable, even behind the veil. But if my neighbors wondered why I was climbing over their fence in a bedsheet and granny skirt, no one made mention. Down the block, a screen door slammed and someone yelled. My breath hitched but I kept walking, straight to my back door. Once there, I pressed up close to the wall and glanced right and left. I don't know what I expected to see or what I intended to do about it, but I had my pepper spray and my keys and enough heart palpations to kill an ox.

The lock stuck for a moment, but finally I was inside. The phone was already ringing. I dropped my stuff beside the door and fought with my makeshift veil as I hurried toward the phone.

I wasn't going to become a Muslim any time soon, no matter how much sex they got.

Snatching off the bedsheet and dish towel, I answered in my sports bra and woolen skirt.

"Chrissy, where were you? I was just about to call the police."

"Mom. Hi. I just got—"

"You're supposed to be resting. The doctor said."

"You talked to the doctor?"

"He seemed smart. Is he single?"

I slipped out of my shoes. My head was beginning to throb. I doubt it had any connection to the concussion, and probably wasn't directly related to the fact that someone was trying to kill me.

"I don't know. Listen, I—"

"I think I should fly out there and take care of you," she said, and suddenly the idea of being murdered didn't seem so bad.

"That's not necessary. Really. I'm fine."

"You've always tried to be too brave."

I wondered vaguely if I could possibly twist that into some kind of compliment.

"Remember the time you jumped off the roof with your brothers? Remember how that worked out?"

"I didn't jump off the roof." I covered my eyes with my hand, trying to hide from the world. "Pete pushed me." Which wasn't exactly true. He was threatening to push me. I'd panicked and fallen. But the results had been the same. A broken thumb and a fear of heights. "Anyway, I don't have much time, Mom. I promised Elaine I'd—"

"How is she? She sounded worried sick when she called."

"She's fine."

"When are you two coming home?"

The question sent me into panic mode, because despite everything I'd learned during the first three decades of my life, the idea was almost appealing.

"I've got to go, Mom. I'm sorry, I'm on the other line."

"They can wait. I've—"

"It might be my doctor," I said, and hung up in raw panic. Leaning my butt against the counter, I covered my face and tried not to cry.

"Chrissy."

I spun like a top at the sound of my name.

Dr. David smiled as he rose from my La-Z-Boy. "That was indefensibly rude."

28

Some men are warriors and some men are weenies.
The trick is figuring out which is which.

—*Elaine Butterfield,*
on dating

*D*AVID!" I'm not sure what I was thinking in those first few moments. Maybe that he had come to save me. And although I've been told I'm overly suspicious, usually by boyfriends who are screwing my hairdresser, it took a second for me to realize the oddness of the situation. "What are you doing here?"

I skimmed my gaze past him, half expecting Elaine to pop up and say she'd let him in.

"I have to tell you . . ." he began, advancing a couple steps. "I'm quite impressed."

"I don't . . ." My mind was reeling now, and I think I said something clever like, "How did you get in?"

He shrugged. "You don't have a security system. But they're costly, aren't they? And . . ." He glanced about my pea-sized kitchen. "Times are hard. Still, you have a fine mind. It's rather a shame."

"A shame?" There was something in his tone that finally made my mind kick in and my stomach clench.

"You know, Chrissy, I'm going to miss you," he said, advancing another couple inches.

"Am I going somewhere?" I asked, and backed away.

He laughed. "You see, it's repartee like this that makes you so intriguing."

"Uh-huh." My mind was spinning out of control. Logic insisted this wasn't what it seemed. No one had ever tried to murder me before. Therefore, it couldn't happen this time, either. But instinct suggested otherwise. "Why are you here, David?"

He shook his head, his expression disappointed. "You've been digging too deeply."

And then I knew. "Kathryn!" I gasped. "You're protecting her."

He stopped in his tracks, waiting, brows raised.

"She killed Bomstad, didn't she?"

He smiled blandly.

"She killed Bomstad," I continued, breathless and crazed. "But you can't protect her."

"You think not?"

My mind screamed that I should find an avenue of escape, but it seems that when intellect is most needed, it is also most lacking. "No," I said, cautious now. All I had to do was keep him talking for a while. Keep him interested. "She had an affair with Bomstad," I lied. "Did you know?"

"As a matter of fact, I did," he said.

"What?" I rasped, and he laughed.

"What else do you know, Chrissy?"

My mind kicked back into gear. "I think..." I inched toward the phone. In the movies, the protagonist always keeps the murderer talking until she can brain him with the blender. I didn't have a blender. But the phone was antiquated and oversized. It would have to do. "I have reason to believe she killed Stephanie Meyers, too."

"And my wife?" he asked.

"Her, too." I felt strangely disembodied, as though I were watching the scene from above. "Her brakes were tampered with. As were mine."

He raised his brows, looking genuinely surprised. "She disabled your brakes?"

It was the first sign of hope. "Yes," I said. "She's not well, David. I'm sorry."

He scowled, his expression introspective. "But she is beautiful."

"Yes. Yes, she is. But you can't save her."

He stopped and sighed. I held my breath. He shrugged. "You're right, I suppose," he said. "Or would be, if I were trying to save her. But I fear..." He shrugged. "I'm only trying to save myself."

"I know you love her, but..." It was then that the truth piled in on me. "Holy mother of God." I could feel the blood drain from my face. "You did it. You killed them."

"I realize now that my arrival here was a bit premature," he said. "But see, you were bound to come around to the proper conclusion eventually."

"You killed them." For a moment I couldn't think of

anything else to say. I couldn't think of anything at all, then, "Why?"

"Oh, come now, Chrissy . . . *Why?* Bomstad was a worthless waste of flesh. The human equivalent of a cockroach."

I tried to formulate some sort of question. Nothing came.

"He was blackmailing me." He shook his head as if mildly surprised by a piece of gossip heard over a late-night latte. "After he found out about Stephanie, he tried to blackmail me."

"About Stephanie?" My tone was breathless, my mind reeling. "You . . . you killed her, too?"

"I did," he said, "but Andrew didn't know that. And he was far too slow to figure it out. But he did know about my affair with her. And you know how the board would feel about that." He faked a shudder. "God forbid we should socialize with our clients. Well, true . . ." He smiled, looking absolutely normal, in perfect mental health. "I admit I did a bit more than socialize."

"And . . . your wife?"

"She was just . . ." He sighed. "She was so very tiresome."

"So you killed her?"

He lifted his hands, palms up.

"Why not divorce? Why not—"

"No prenup," he said. "But you're failing to see the bright side here, Chrissy."

"There's a bright side." I was thrilled to hear it.

"There's always a bright side. You should know that, in our profession."

"What is it?"

He smiled. "Their deaths were perfect for them."

I stared at him. "I have to admit, I was hoping for more."

He laughed. "My wife was a grasping bitch. Clothes, clubs, cars. You know, she had forty-two handbags. Not forty. Not forty-one, but forty-two. She died on her way home from a weekend shopping spree."

"You killed her because of a . . . purse?"

"Come now, Chrissy, surely you know murder has been committed over far more trivial things."

"And Stephanie?"

"She was unstable. I couldn't trust her to keep our little affair private. So moody. So dramatic."

"But you were in Washington when she died." I blinked like a moron. "You said so."

"Seattle." He laughed. "Yes, I was. So nice to know you were listening. I even gave a speech there. But later that night, while my little prerecorded message was calling her answering machine, I was making sure she took her prescription. It was quite ingenious, actually. An overdose was her perfect demise."

"And Bomstad's was Viagra."

"Obviously. He first saw you when you came by my office. Did you know that? He was threatening to expose me even then. Thought you were"—he made quotation marks in the air with his fingers—"hot. Hence he came up with the harebrained idea of pretending impotency." He shook his head and chuckled a little. "God knows the Bomb was no genius, but he was entertaining."

"So you killed him," I said, still numb.

"Without remorse," he admitted. "But if it makes you feel any better, I will regret your passing."

"It doesn't really."

He was advancing. I was retreating.

"What of the fact that it is your own intellect that has caused your demise?"

I shook my head. "Doesn't really do anything for me."

"But it will be the perfect death."

"Which is?"

"A burglary gone awry."

I shook my head, confused.

"Look around you, Chrissy. Despite your above-average reasoning ability, you're really nothing more than white trash. A run-down little house, no security system. And your yard . . ." He gave a delicate shudder. "Put a washing machine and a couple of beer cans out there and you're in Alabama."

"You're doing this because you don't like my yard?"

He was smiling at his own wit. "I'm doing this because you can't leave well enough alone," he said. "I'm doing it with this"—he pulled a knife from somewhere behind him—"because you don't have a stereo."

I felt sick to my stomach. Sick and faint. "You're insane."

He laughed. "Insanity, as you well know, is highly subjective," he said, and raised the knife.

I was frozen in terror. "Please," I said, but I saw in his eyes that I was wasting my breath. He was going to kill me . . . without remorse.

I leapt for the doorway, but he was already after me. I

felt something skim my back and screamed. He laughed. The sound echoed in my brain. I dashed around the La-Z-Boy, panting and trembling.

He halted on the far side, blade held toward me.

I was only a few feet from the door, and I had the advantage of youth. He was only slightly farther away and had the advantage of insanity.

"I know what you're thinking, Chrissy," he said. "Indeed, I know every thought that goes through your head. You're weighing your chances. But you can't win. You know that. I must win. For if I fail, I will lose everything, and I've worked too hard to let that happen. I'm sorry. Truly," he said and sprang around the chair.

I jerked away, but he was already changing direction. I tried to adjust, to spurt toward the door, but my skirt tangled around my legs and I fell. He was on me in a second. I rolled onto my back, but he was atop me. The knife slashed toward me. I kicked out of pure instinct, striking out in wild terror. He stumbled to the side. I scrambled to my hands and feet, but he was right behind me. I could feel him there, breathing on me, grasping for me. I grappled forward. My fingers brushed something. Pain slashed across my arm. I screamed, closed my fingers, and twisted toward him. The fan struck his head. The noise echoed sickeningly in the room. He staggered backward. Blood was dripping down his forehead. He touched it with his free hand, then stumbled toward me.

"Chrissy," he managed through gritted teeth, and I hit him again.

He dropped to his knees just as two doors burst open.

"LAPD!" Rivera shouted.

"Stop it! Just stop it!" Elaine was crying, and I thought, though I wasn't quite sure, that she was threatening David with a nailfile. But I was never quite sure because just about then I passed out.

29

Maybe there's no such thing as happily ever after.
Maybe okay for now's the best you get.

—Mr. Howard Lepinski,
after three months of therapy

I RESTED THE NEXT couple of days. Elaine called my mother. Told her everything was peachy and that she definitely didn't have to come down even though I'd had a bit of a mishap. Meanwhile, she stayed with me every minute of the day, fetching ice cream, cleaning my toilet, and making me realize I'd enjoy having a full-time slave. But all good things must come to an end and when Solberg dropped by to pick her up, I knew the fairy tale was over.

I stood on my little stoop as she gave me a careful hug, but even before she'd driven off, Rivera arrived. He parked illegally across the street and got out, all lean lines and terse movements.

He was carrying a bag that said Chin Yung and a six-pack of Pabst, but I refused to get excited, since my last gift had been short on roses and long on spines.

"Guess what I brought you," he said when he was close enough. His eyes were all dark and solemn and made me wonder if he'd been worried about me, if he fantasized about the night we almost did it in the vestibule and if he regretted caring that I'd been drunker than sin.

"A porcupine?" I guessed.

He gave me a look.

I nodded a little nervously toward my front yard where the cactus was looking staunch and formidable behind a trio of rocks I'd given it for company.

He surveyed the wreckage of my yard. "No way roses were going to survive here."

"I could grow roses if I wanted to."

He grunted. "I light candles for the cactus every night."

"Sentimentality," I said. "The multifaceted Lieutenant Reebler."

We stared at each other. There was a colorful swelling on my forehead and a scrape on my jaw, but he didn't seem to be looking at that. My hormones cranked up another notch.

"You going to ask me?" he asked.

I stared at him a couple more seconds and sighed. "Okay. Why were you watching my house?"

His eyes were dark and brooding. And damned if dark and brooding isn't sexy. He glanced across the street as though he could see into my neighbors' living rooms, could detect crimes through the airways.

"Invite me to come in," he said, "I'll tell you."

"Tell me here." I guess I was still mad at him about the rejection, despite the fact that I knew it was for the best . . . and that he'd possibly saved my life.

"I'll share the porcupine," he said, lifting the bag, and then I caught the whiff of egg foo young. I'm not cheap but I can be bought.

I shoved the door open and followed him inside.

He was wearing jeans. The snug kind. I steadied my breathing and went to fetch dinnerware. Had he not been there, the boxes might never have exited the bag before the contents were consumed, but I'm a classy broad when I have company, multicolored bruises et al.

Either he had secretly gone through my cupboards or he was good at guessing where to find glasses. He set the beer on the table, but memories of my last encounter with alcohol convinced me to pour myself a glass of milk. A minute later, the tantalizing aroma of Chinese cuisine was teasing my olfactory system.

I refrained from inhaling the box, took a few ladylike bites, and said, "Well?"

"Originally I thought you were banging Bomstad and had probably killed him. God knows everyone else wanted him dead."

I thought about that for a moment as I masticated. "Originally?"

"Yeah."

"How long is originally?"

He shrugged, still eating.

"How long—"

"Till I saw you in your pajamas."

Had he been attracted to me even then? I wondered,

heart palpitating. Had he found me so irresistible he re-fused to believe I could possibly be guilty?

"I figured anyone with so little pride in her appearance couldn't have been screwing the Bomb."

I might have kicked him out then, had I not been afraid he'd be vengeful enough to take the entrées. "I have pride in my appearance," I said instead.

"You wore a donkey shirt."

"That was not a donkey shirt. That was Eeyore."

He stared at me blankly for several seconds. "Uh-huh. Anyway, once I learned you were connected with Hawkins I needed to keep you around."

"Why?"

"I'd been looking at the good doctor for a long time."

I stared at him, but couldn't quite stop myself from eat-ing. It was going to take a while to get over hospital food. "Shall I assume you thought he might be guilty and neg-lected to warn me, or that your sexual fantasies run con-trary to the norm?"

"He was a link," he said. "Between Stephanie Meyers and Bomstad. But I couldn't clinch it."

"So you used me as bait."

He snorted. "Bait!" He was scooping up fried rice as he glared at me. "I all but handcuffed you to your kitchen sink to keep you out of the way."

Was I wrong to find that image erotic?

"You wouldn't back the hell off," he added.

"You could have told me David was a suspect."

"And let you botch my whole mission?" he asked, and poured himself a beer. "You were dangerous enough the way things were."

"I was not dangerous."

"You just about got yourself killed." He lifted his gaze to mine. Darker than hell. A muscle twitched in his jaw. "Twice."

"You could have told me someone had tampered with my brakes. At least then I wouldn't have thought you were trying to kill me."

His eyes almost smiled. "You couldn't have really believed that."

"What was I supposed to think? You obviously had feelings for Meyers. You hated Bomstad. They had a thing." I shrugged.

His lips twitched. "What about Hawkins's wife? How'd you tie her in?"

Was he laughing at me? I don't like to be laughed at. "You hated David, too."

"So you deduced that I killed his wife? No wonder you jumped me in your hallway, seeing's how highly you thought of me."

I fiddled with my noodles. "I did not jump you," I muttered. The following silence was painful. "Exactly."

He laughed.

"Well forgive me for not guessing that L.A.'s most respected psychologist was a murderer."

He gave me a somber nod in concession, though I suspected he still felt like laughing. Damn him. "As it turns out, Hawkins wasn't the one who messed with your brakes."

"What?"

"It was his fiancée."

"I knew it!" I couldn't have been happier. Not even if he'd brought dessert.

"Her name's Mary Ellen Ensign. From Elkhorn, Alabama."

"You're shittin' me!"

His lips quirked up a half-inch. "Sometimes I wonder who *you* really are."

I ignored that. Obviously I was the classy Christina McMullen, Ph.D. "So what are you saying? She was a nobody from nowhere, met David, and decided to make herself into his dream girl?"

"It was a little more complex than that. She was boinking Bomstad...and a half a dozen other guys by the sound of it. The Bomb told her about David. She says she was immediately attracted to him and didn't suspect anything out of character. Personally, I think she found out about his escapades and decided she could blackmail him for all he was worth. But once she met him her plan expanded. I don't think she expected him to off Bomstad, but she sure didn't want you messing up her plans. Thus, the brakes. And the attack at the bar."

"She sent that goon to . . . to . . ."

"She swears she just wanted to scare you. Warn you to mind your own business."

I chewed, ruminating. "So she was the one in Bomstad's house."

He took another bite and nodded. "Seems the Bomb had some video of her and him together."

"He filmed them in bed?"

"Unthinkable, isn't it?"

"And others?"

"Uh-huh."

He waited, watching me, and the truth dawned like fireworks in my head.

"That's his diary! The videotapes."

"It was recorded into the middle of an Oscar-winning little flick called *Cum and Get It*. Took two days to find it even after talking to Ensign. I never thought I'd get tired of porn." He ate some more noodles and glanced at me. "Maybe I should have let you in his house after all. Could have saved me some time."

I gave him a look, pushed my plate aside, and chose a fortune cookie. "Your loss."

His eyes were all sultry again. "Almost," he said, and suddenly my fingers weren't working very well.

"Well . . ." I focused on breathing for a minute. "I'm glad it's all over." I managed to break open the cookie and read the little message. Generally, I think they should be called "random nonsense cookies," but this one made sense.

"What's it say?"

I cleared my throat. "Says I'll embark on an intriguing new adventure."

He raised a brow. "Really?"

I could feel my insides heat up. "I think it means my career," I said. "I'm considering a change."

"Yeah?"

"Forensics," I said.

"Intriguing," he said. "But career changes can be tricky, and I think you have enough problems already."

"Problems? Like what?"

"Celibacy," he said and caught my fingers in his. "I think

we should take care of that little celibacy problem before you worry about anything else."

"It's not a problem," I said, but my tongue felt swollen. "It's a choice."

"Really? I thought it was more like a sentence."

"Maybe for you." I considered bolting, but he still held my hand, and I remembered how his chest had looked. "For me it's..." He skimmed his fingertips over my knuckles. I swallowed hard. He raised his gaze to mine. "An intelligent decision."

"So the other night when you tore the buttons off my shirt—"

I cleared my throat. "I may have been a bit tipsy."

"Yeah?" He skimmed his fingernails up my forearm. I shivered down to my bone marrow. "Is that the reason for the milk?"

"Osteoporosis," I said. "It's a serious problem."

He leaned in. My toes curled. "Not as big as celibacy."

"I told you," I breathed, "it's not a problem, it's—"

But in that instant he kissed me, and for a while there were no problems at all. And maybe that's as good as it gets.

About the Author

Lois Greiman is the award-winning author of over fifteen novels, including romantic comedy, historical romance, and mystery. She lives in Minnesota with her family and an ever-increasing number of horses.

You may write to her at Lois Greiman, PO Box 16, Rogers, MN 55374 or visit her online at www.loisgreiman.com.

Don't miss Lois Greiman's
next sassy mystery starring
cocktail-waitress-turned-shrink
Christina McMullen.

Unplugged

BY

Lois Greiman

**Available in March 2006
from Dell Books**

**Read on for an exclusive sneak peek—
and look for your copy at your
favorite bookseller.**

Unplugged

by Lois Greiman

On sale March 2006

"Matrimony and fire fighting. They ain't for cowards."

—*Pete McMullen,*
shortly after his first marriage

You MARRIED?"

I hadn't known Larry Hunt thirty-five minutes before he popped the question. But the fact that he was scowling at me as if I were the devil's handmaiden suggested our relationship would never work out. The fact that he was sitting beside his wife also posed a problem for our connubial bliss. Weighing all the signs, I guessed they'd been married for about twenty-four years.

But I'm not a psychic. I'm a psychologist.

Mrs. Hunt had called my clinic, L.A. Counseling, two weeks prior for therapy. As a result, Mr. Hunt now seemed to be wondering what the hell he was doing in some shrink's office, and had decided to fill his fifty minutes by probing into my personal life.

According to the forms they'd completed, he worked for Mann's Rent 'n' Go. Judging by his slightly rumpled dress shirt and loosened tie, he had left his place of employment just minutes before for this inauspicious introduction to couple's therapy. Judging by his attitude, I suspected what he really wanted to know was what made me think I was qualified to counsel him and his heretofore silent wife.

"No, Mr. Hunt, I'm not married," I said.

"How come?"

If he hadn't been a client, I would have told him it was none of his damned business whether I was married, ever had been married, or ever planned to be married. Ergo, it was probably best that he was a client, since that particular answer might have seemed somewhat immature and just a tad defensive. Not that I secretly long to be married or anything, but if someone wanted to lug salt downstairs to the water softener for me now and again, I wouldn't turn down the offer. Even my thirty-seventh ex-boyfriend, Victor Dickenson, sometimes called "Vic the Dick" by those who knew him well, had been able to manage that much.

"Larry!" Mrs. Hunt chided. She was a smallish woman with sandpaper blonde hair and a lilac pantsuit. Her stacked platform sandals were of a different generation than her clothing and made me wonder if she had a disapproving teenage daughter who had taken it upon herself to update her mother's footwear. Her eyes were sort of bubblelike, reminding me of the guppies I'd had as a kid, and when she turned her orbicular gaze in my direction it was pretty obvious she'd been wondering about me herself.

It's not uncommon for clients to think a therapist has to be half a couple in order to know anything about marriage. I soundly disagree. I've never been a lobster, but I still know they taste best with a half gallon of butter and a spritz of lemon.

According to the data forms the Hunts had filled out before entering my cashew-sized office, Kathy was forty-three, four years younger than her husband of rumpled dress shirt fame. They both sat on my comfy, cream-colored couch, but to say that they sat together would have been a wild flight of romantic fancy. Between Mrs. Hunt's polyester pantsuit and Mr. Hunt's stiff-backed personage, there was ample space to park a Mack truck hauling a butt load of toxic waste.

I gave them both my professional smile, the one that suggests I am above being insulted by forays into my personal life and that I would not murder them in their sleep for doing so.

"You're an okay looking woman," Mr. Hunt continued. "Got a good job. How come you're still single?"

I considered telling him that, despite the availability of men like himself, I had managed to retain a few functioning brain cells. But that would have been unprofessional. It would also have been untrue. Then again, it was five o'clock on a Friday evening, and I hadn't had a cigarette for five days and nineteen hours. I'd counted on my way to work that morning.

"How long have you two been married?" I asked, deflecting his question with the stunning ingenuity only a licensed psychoanalyst could manage.

"Twenty-two years," said Mrs. Hunt. She didn't sound thrilled with the number. Maybe she'd been doing a little math on her way to work, too. "This May."

"Twenty-two years," I repeated, imbuing my tone with a suggestive whistle of admiration while chiding myself for over-guessing. It was her pastel ensemble that threw me. What woman under sixty wears lilac pants? "You must be doing something right, then. And you've never had any sort of therapy before today?"

"No," they answered in unison. By their expressions, I guessed it was one of the few things they still did in tandem.

"Is that because you didn't feel you needed help or be-cause—" I began, but Mr. Hunt interrupted.

"I don't believe in this crap."

I turned toward him, wondrously even-tempered, which shows how mature I've become. Five years ago I would have taken offense to that kind of remark. Twenty years ago I would have called him a moron and given him a wedgie. "Whyever are you here then, Mr. Hunt?" I asked, my tone a dulcet meld of curiosity and caring.

"Kathy says she won't . . ." He paused. "She wanted me to come."

So ol' Kat was withholding sex. Uh-huh.

"Well," I said, "as I'm sure you're aware, you don't have to tell me anything you're uncomfortable with."

I glanced from one to the other. Mr. Hunt beetled his brows. Mrs. Hunt pursed her lips. They didn't really look like they'd be comfortable with much. Maybe a noncom-mittal, how-was-your-day kind of exchange—if no pro-longed eye contact was required.

"And of course," I continued, "everything hinges on your own specific goals."

"Goals?" asked Mr. Hunt, and rather suspiciously, I thought. As if I were trying to trick him into mental health and conjugal happiness.

"Yes." I swiveled my chair a little and crossed my legs. I was wearing a ginger-hued sleeveless sheath and matching jacket by Chanel. By purchasing it second-hand, I had still been able to afford my flax colored sling-back sandals for twelve dollars and ninety-five cents without taking out a second mortgage on my soul. The shoes matched the ensemble's piping and did good things to the muscles in my lower legs. I looked fantastic. Who needs a husband when you're wearing Chanel and look fantastic? "What are you hoping to accomplish with these sessions?" I asked.

Mr. Hunt stared at me with a mixture of irritation and absolute stupefaction. I turned toward Kathy, hoping for a bit more acumen.

"What is *your* main purpose for coming here, Mrs. Hunt?"

"I just . . ." She scowled and shrugged. I got the feeling she might have had quite a bit of practice at both. "I thought it couldn't hurt."

A ringing endorsement. Some day I'd have to have that embroidered and framed above my desk.

"So you're not entirely content with your current relationship?" I guessed.

"Well . . ." She throttled the strap of her beige handbag. It was the approximate size of my front door. "No one's completely happy, I suppose."

I gave her an encouraging smile and turned to her husband. "And what about you, Mr. Hunt? Is there anything you'd like to see changed in your marriage?"

"Things are okay," he said, but he was still glaring at me.

I gave him my "aha" smile, as if I knew things he didn't. Maybe I did, but chances were he didn't care where my house key was hidden or how to wax his bikini line without screaming out four-letter expletives.

"So you're here just to make your wife happy," I said. It was a charitable way of saying I knew she'd dragged him in kicking and screaming. Nine times out of ten, that's how it works. Men tend to think everything's hunky-dory so long as the little woman hasn't put a slug between his eyes within the past seventy-two hours. So apparently, Mrs. Hunt's Glock was still in the gun cabinet. But judging by her tight-lipped expression, Larry might want to sleep with one eye open. "It was very considerate of you to agree to come. Is he always so considerate, Kathy?" I asked and turned toward the little woman.

Her lips pursed into an almost indiscernible line and her eyes narrowed. For a second I wondered if she'd brought her Glock with her. God knows, her purse was big enough to house a cannon and the man o' war that carried it.

"He leaves used Kleenexes in the living room," she snarled. Her tone was suddenly terse—as if she'd caught Larry sans pants with the woman in charge of weed whacker rentals.

I realize that for the uninitiated her statement might seem like a strange opening gambit, but I'd been in the game long enough to realize it's not the sordid affairs that most often end a marriage. It's the toothpaste left in the sink. *Psychology Today* says the human psyche is a complex and fragile thing. Personally, I think people are just funky as hell.

"I have a sinus problem," he said, by way of defense.

"So you can't put your Kleenex in the waste basket?" Her tone was becoming more shrill by the moment.

"You leave your wet towel on my side of the sink every morning. You don't see me making a federal case of it."

"That's because you don't care."

"I don't know what the hell you're talking about," he said, his voice rising. "I bring home a paycheck every other week to buy the groceries you don't even bother to cook. You think I'd do that if I didn't care? You think I give a damn how many floor grinders Mann's rents out per week?"

"Yeah, I do," she said, her cheeks red and her eyes popping. "I think you care more about floor grinders than you do about me."

The room went abruptly silent. I refrained from grinning like a euphoric monkey.

The first half hour had been the conversational equivalent of pabulum. But this . . . this was something I could sink my teeth into.

Twenty minutes later I was ushering the Hunts out the front door. They still looked less than ecstatic, so apparently I had failed to work my usual therapeutic magic, but they had agreed to try a couple of my suggestions. He would pick up after himself and she would make him breakfast on Tuesday and Thursday.

I waved congenially, then turned with a sigh and slumped into one of the two chairs that faced the receptionist desk. My receptionist was behind it. Her name is

Elaine Butterfield. We'd bonded in fifth grade, agreeing that boys were stupid and stinky. In general terms, I still think they're stupid. But sometimes they smell pretty good.

"Want to pick up some Chinese?" I asked.

Elaine stuffed a file in the cabinet and didn't turn toward me. "Can't," she said. "I have an audition tomorrow morning."

Elaine is an actress. Unfortunately, she can't act.

"So you're not going to eat?"

"Chinese makes my face puffy."

Elaine's face has never been puffy in her life. At ten she'd been gangly and buck-toothed; at thirty-two she was gorgeous enough to make me hate my parents and every fat-thighed antecedent who had ever peed in my gene pool.

"What are you auditioning for?" I hadn't heard a single hideous line in several days, which wasn't like my Laney. Usually she spewed them about the office like pot smoke at a Mick Jagger concert.

"It's just a little part in a soap."

"A soap opera?" I asked, managing to shuffle straighter in my chair. "You love soap operas. They're steady work."

"Yeah, well . . ." She shrugged and stuffed another file. "I probably won't get the part."

"Laney?" I tried to see her face, but she kept it turned away. "Is something wrong?"

"No." She was fiddling through the V's. The only file left out was Angela Grapier's. Elaine had an IQ that would make Einstein look like a shaken infant victim. I was pretty sure she knew Angie's name came before Vigoren.

I stood up. "What's wrong?"

"Nothing. I'm just tired."

"You don't get tired."

"Do, too."

"Laney," I said, and rounding her desk, touched her shoulder. She turned toward me like a scolded puppy.

"It's Jeen."

I blinked, unable to believe my eyes. Her face *was* puffy. And her nose, flawlessly shaped and perfectly pored, was red. "What?" I said.

"It's . . ." She shook her head. "Nothing. Don't worry about it. I just—"

"Jeen?" I repeated dumbly, but then the truth dawned. For nearly two months now, she'd been dating a myopic little geek to whom I'd had the bad manners of introducing her. It had been patently cruel on my part, but I'd been in a bit of a bind. In fact, I'd been accused of murder and he had helped me out by doing a little "creative investigating" on the Internet. His name was J.D. Solberg. I could only assume his real name was Jeen, since Elaine wasn't vindictive enough to think of such a nomenclature on her own. Unfortunately, the same obviously couldn't be said of his parents. "What'd he do?" I asked, imagining the worst. "He didn't touch you, did he?"

She didn't answer.

Anger flared up like fireworks. Some people think I have a little bit of a temper. "Damn that nerdy little troll! I warned him not to—"

"No." She glanced at the floor and cleared her throat. "That's not the problem."

Oh dear God, did that mean he had touched her? Did that mean she'd liked it? Did that mean the world was crumbling beneath my very . . . but then another thought struck me. "Dammit, Laney, he didn't hit you, did he?"

"Of course not." Her gaze rose to mine. Her gigantic eyes were filled with puppy dog dejection. If I wasn't a raging heterosexual I would have begged her to marry me on the spot.

I relaxed a little. "Then what's the problem?"

"He just . . . he hasn't called me, that's all."

I waited for the bad news. She wasn't forthcoming. "And?"

She gave me a disapproving glance as she shoved Grapier's file somewhere in the XYZ group. I refrained from comment. "I haven't heard from him since he left for Las Vegas."

"Oh, yeah," I said. I remembered her telling me about NeoTech's esteemed presence at some big-ass technology convention. J.D. was supposed to be some kind geek master there. I probably should have been paying attention when she first told me about it, but I'd been trying to deal with a few issues of my own. My septic system, for instance. It had been installed sometime before the Miocene Epoch and kept threatening to spill its venom down the hall and into my antiquated kitchen.

Then there was my love life. Well, actually, there wasn't.

"He's probably just busy," I said.

"He left almost three weeks ago."

"Well . . ." I began, then, "Three weeks?" It hadn't seemed like nearly that long since I'd seen the little Woody Allen look-alike. "Really?"

"Seventeen and a half days," she said.

I winced. She'd been counting the days. A girl has to be pretty loopy to count the days. I tried not to gag. Solberg had rubbed me the wrong way since the first time I'd met him—more than ten years ago at the Warthog where I used to serve drinks. His come-on line had had something to do with his hard drive getting it on with my mother board. The man was lucky he wasn't singing soprano and drinking his meals through a straw after that little witticism.

"You said it was a really big deal," I reminded her. "He's probably just tying up loose ends. That sort of thing."

"He said he'd call me every day."

"And you haven't heard from him?"

"I did at first. He phoned all the time. And e-mailed. Sometimes he'd fax me." She gave me a watery smile. "Left text messages with little hearts."

Yuck. "Uh-huh," I said.

"And then . . . nothing." She shrugged, then glanced at the desk and shuffled a few papers around. "I think he met someone else."

I blinked. "Solberg?"

"He was in Las Vegas," she said, as if that were explanation enough. It wasn't. She continued as if she were lecturing a retarded Dachshund. "There are more beautiful women per capita in Vegas than in any other city in the world."

"Uh-huh."

She scowled a little. Somehow it didn't manage to create a single wrinkle in her rice-paper complexion. I would hate her if I didn't love her to distraction. "It's tough to compete with a hundred topless girls juggling armadillos and breathing fire."

"Armadillos?" I asked, impressed.

"He's got a lot going for him, Mac," she said.

I kept my face perfectly expressionless, waiting for the punch line. It didn't come. "Have you heard him laugh?" I asked.

She grinned a little, but the expression was pale. "He sounds like a donkey on speed."

"Whew," I said. "We are talking about the same guy."

"I've dated a lot since moving out here."

I couldn't argue with that. Laney got marriage proposals from guys who hadn't yet exited the womb.

"But Jeen . . ." She paused. I didn't like the dreamy look in her eye. "He never once bragged about how many push-ups he could do or how fast he can run the mile."

"Well, that's probably because he can't do—"

She stopped me with a glance. "I don't even know his astronomical sign."

"He's a Scorpio."

"You know?"

Sadly, yes. He'd told me when he was drunk off his ass, just minutes after the mother board come on, in fact.

"Laney," I said, taking her hand and trying to think of a nice way to inform her that her boyfriend was a doofus. "I know you like him and everything. But really . . ."

"He's never tried to get me into bed."

My mouth opened. Solberg had propositioned me approximately two and a half seconds after I'd served him his first drink. I would like to think that's because I'm sexier than Elaine, but apparently I wasn't brain-dead yet, no matter how long it had been since my last cigarette.

"You're kidding," I said.

"No."

"Does he call you babe-a-buns?"

"No."

"Stare at your chest till his eyes water?"

"No."

"Pretend he stumbled and grab your boobs."

"No!"

"Wow."

She nodded. "I thought he really cared about me. But . . ." She laughed a little, seemingly at her own foolishness. "I guess he just wasn't interested. You know . . . that way."

I raised a brow. Just one. I reserved two for purple extraterrestrials with wildly groping appendages. "We're still talking about Solberg, right?"

She scowled.

"Geeky little guy? Has a nose like an albatross?"

Now she just looked sad, which made me kind of ashamed of myself, but really, the whole situation was ridiculous. Solberg would sell his soul for a quick glimpse of an anemic flasher. He'd probably auction off his personal computer to hold hands with a woman of Elaine's caliber. And she actually liked him. What were the odds?

"Listen, Laney, I'm sorry. But really, you don't have to worry. Just call him up. Tell him you . . ." I took a deep breath and tried to be brave. "Tell him you miss him."

"I did call him."

It was my turn to scowl. Laney generally doesn't call guys. All she has to do is sing the eeney meany miny mo song and snatch a suitor off her roof. Sometimes literally. "No answer?" I asked.

"No."

"You leave a message?"

"On his cell and his home phone." She glanced at the desktop again. "A couple of times."

"I'm sorry," I said. "But I'm afraid the answer is obvious." She raised her gaze to mine. "Our dear little geek friend is dead."

"Mac!"

I couldn't help but laugh. "Listen, Laney," I said, squeezing her hand. "You're being ridiculous. Solberg is wild about you. He probably just got delayed in Vegas."

"He probably got laid in Vegas."

I stared. Elaine Butterfield didn't usually use such trashy language.

"Maybe I should have . . ." She paused. "Do you think I should have slept with him before he left?"

I refrained from telling her that would be a sin of Biblical proportions. There's a little thing called bestiality. I was sure it would make even Jerry Falwell agree it made homosexuality look like petty theft by comparison.

"Elaine. Relax. I'm sure he'll be back in a couple days. He'll bring you tulips and call you snuggle bumpkins and sugar socks and all those other disgusting names he comes up with."

"Angel eyes," she said.

"What?"

"He calls me 'Angel Eyes.' Because I saved him."

"From what?" I hated to ask.

"From being a jerk."

Holy crap. If I had never met this guy I might actually like him. "He'll be back, Laney."

She drew a careful breath. "I don't think so, Mac. I really don't."

I laughed. "You're Brainy Laney Butterfield."

"I'm trying to be practical about this."

She gave me a look.

"Butterfeel?" I suggested. "Nutterbutter?"

"I hated the last one most," she said.

"Yeah." Middle school had been a challenge. "Simons was a creep of major proportions."

She nodded distractedly. "He *could* rhyme though. Which is about all you can ask of—"

"A WASP whose brain is bigger than his balls," I finished for her. It was a direct quote from my brother, Michael. I've always been afraid he meant it as an insult.

Elaine only managed a weak smile.

"Listen, Laney." I sighed. Twelve years at Holy Name Catholic School had taught me a lot of things. Mostly how to sneak boys into the rectory for a little uninterrupted heavy breathing. But I hadn't known until that moment that I'd learned to be a martyr. "I'm going to find Solberg for you."

She shook her head, but I hurried on.

"Because I know . . . I'm *positive* he's just been delayed."

"Mac, I appreciate your faith in my appeal. Really." She squeezed my hand. "But not every man thinks I'm God's answer—"

"Don't say it," I warned and backed away. "I don't want to hear any self-effacing crap coming out of your mouth."

"I'm not—"

"Quit it," I warned. "If you say one negative thing about yourself, I'm going to blame it on Solberg. And then . . ." I dipped into my office, grabbed my purse from out of the big bottom drawer and headed for the door. "When I find him, I'm going to kick his skinny little ass into the next solar system."

"Mac, you can't blame him just because he doesn't find me attractive."

"You shut your dirty little mouth," I warned her.

"He dumped me."

I turned toward her with a snap. "He did not dump you."

"What are you talking about?"

"Listen." I pulled open the front door. "He might be a stunted little wart, but there's no reason to think he's gone totally insane. Well . . ." I corrected myself. "There's no conclusive evidence that he's gone totally insane."

"Chrissy—"

"I'm going to go find him," I said.

And when I did, I was either going to give him a good sound whack upside the head . . . or a nice Irish wake.

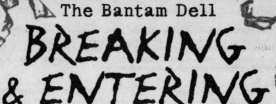